IDLE

BOOK FOUR OF THE SEVEN DEADLY SERIES
FISHER AMELIE

IDLE

LILY HAHN IS
IDLE

To mom & dad,
Thank you for showing me what it is to love and be loved. What a gift God gave me in you.

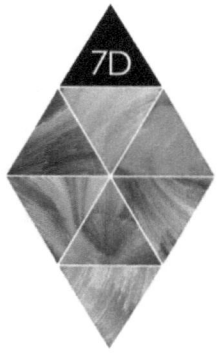

PROLOGUE

Apathy. It's a wonderful feeling because it releases you of all responsibility, and the best part? No one can blame you for inaction because you were just doing your own thing. You were keeping your head down. You were worrying about yourself and only yourself. You were minding your own business.

But there's a difference between minding your own business and letting someone drown, isn't there? Who cares, though? They shouldn't have gotten in the water in the first place, right? It's not your problem. You have other, no, *better* things you want to do instead and can't be held accountable for another's stupidity.

It's a powerful drug, apathy. It allows you to hide

behind computers, carelessly slinging unfounded opinions, too lazy to put yourselves in others' shoes. It allows us to pass by the homeless man, clearly cold and starving. He should just get a job already, right? It allows you to turn your head when you hear your upstairs neighbor beat his girlfriend. She chooses to stay. It's not your problem.

Apathy allows you to slake real responsibility toward those you share the human race with. It's a cure-all. It's the perfect alibi.

And when you're drowning, cast aside in a ditch, count the shoes that walk by. Count their steps. Let them echo in your brain. You are living proof of bad decisions, and you are not their problem.

IDLE

CHAPTER ONE

My phone rang and I opened one eye, rolled on my side, and checked the name that flashed on the screen.

"What's up?" I asked my friend Ansen.

"Are you asleep?"

I stretched my body, my bones cracking. "I was, but not now, thanks to you."

"Lily, it's fucking two o'clock. Wake the fuck up already. Get ready. We're going to get something to eat."

I rolled onto my back, my free hand splayed across my pillow. I cleared my throat of sleep. "I need my cash for weed. See you tonight, though?"

"Yeah, Ashleigh's house tonight."

"Fine."

He hung up and I dropped my phone on the bed

next to me. I needed to smoke. I sat up, gathered then tossed my hair over one shoulder, pulled on my jean cutoffs, and grabbed the joint on my desk. I stuck my phone in my pocket and made my way through my mom and stepdad's house to their back deck. It was barely hanging by a thread, and I was the only one willing to risk it, but it was a great place to get high without having to listen to my mom's complaints about the smoke.

I stuck the joint between my lips and reached into my pocket for my lighter. It wasn't there, so I rummaged the deck to see if I'd dropped one.

"Need a light?" my neighbor yelled over the fence.

I smiled at him. "Yeah," I answered. "Got one?"

He sauntered down his own deck, across the too tall grass, and approached the chain link separating our yards. "Can't go any further," he said, his forearms draped across the top of the fence, holding up a lighter in one hand.

I jumped off the back of the deck and hit hard, stood tall, and met him. "What's up, Trace?"

Trace and I had gone to high school together. He had a kid when he was seventeen but left the baby's mom, like, six months after the kid was born. I let my eyes roam up and down his body.

"Get a good look?" he asked with a smile.

"Not as good as I'd like," I countered.

He held out the lighter toward me. "You hitting up Ashleigh's later?" he asked.

"I might. You?"

"Maybe I'll see you there?"

"Maybe you will," I told him.

I lit my joint and took a drag. I offered it to him and he did the same. I handed the lighter back, but he refused it.

"Bring it to Ashleigh's," he said.

I stuck it in my pocket and nodded. "See you around, Trace," I said, turning around and heading up the stairs of my deck.

When I reached the top and faced the backyard again, he had just reached the top of his own stairs. He nodded his head my way and I watched him go back inside. I finished my joint, pinched the roach, and stuck it in my pocket. I slid the glass door open and stepped inside.

"I wish you would stop that, Lily," my mom pleaded for the thousandth time.

"Stop asking, Mom. It's just who I am."

She shook her head. "It's not," she whispered, feeling around in her barren pantry for food that didn't exist. "I need to go to the store," she said like she had money. She looked at me. "Any luck finding work?" she asked.

"Not really," I said, tossing myself on our creaky sofa. I picked up my controller and took my game from the night before off pause. She came through the narrow kitchen and studied me, but I ignored her. She shook her head then took the short trip down our small hallway to her and Sterling's bedroom.

I could hear them arguing when Callie and Eloise came bursting from their own shared room, laughing and carrying on, worn-out-looking Barbies in their hands. They jumped on the love seat perpendicular to the sofa I was on.

"You guys are so damn loud," I told them.

Eloise, the older of the two, scolded me. "Don't curse, Lily. That's gross."

I ignored her and sat up a little, trying to scale through a particularly hard level. I played until eight or so then decided to take a shower. I tossed my roach in the glass tray on my desk with all my others. When I had enough saved, I'd combine all the weed leftover and make one whole joint again.

After my shower, I brushed my teeth, put on a clean pair of cutoffs and a tank top, stuck my keys in my pocket, and headed toward the door.

"Where do you think you're going?" Sterling asked me when I reached the end of the hall.

"Headed out," I answered him.

Just ignore me. Just ignore me.

"Just where the hell is out?" he asked.

"Don't worry about it."

"Watch the way you talk to me!" he yelled, the veins in his throat popping. He rushed me, wrapped his hand around my throat, and threw me against the wall. "Lazy piece of shit. Do you have a job yet?"

I swallowed before pushing him off me. "Not yet. *Do you?*" I countered.

His eyes narrowed. "You're worthless, Lily. You're trash."

"I know this already, asshole," I said, pushing him away.

He didn't budge, though. He was a foot taller and had a hundred pounds on me. I tried to ignore him most of the time, but occasionally something he'd say would get through. He was a peach of a stepdad, let me tell you.

I slammed the creaky front door behind me and practically sprinted to my faded orange Scout International.

"Asshole," I said under my breath.

Something angry blared through my speakers, so I turned it up and headed toward Ashleigh's. When I pulled down her street, I could see Ansen and about ten others hanging out in her driveway smoking cigarettes. I came to a stop and idled next to them.

"What the fuck? It's fucking Lily!" Ashleigh screamed, stumbling forward and opening my passenger-side door. She was drunk as shit.

"Hey, Ash," I greeted with a smile.

"Hey, darlin', how are you?" she asked.

"Good, want a ride?"

"Where we goin'?" she asked.

"Come with me," I told her and she climbed in. I pulled forward, finding a vacant spot along her street.

I stuck my tongue at her and threw my car in park. "Not far, dummy," I said, helping her out. I stuck my keys in my back pocket and put an arm around her shoulder, guiding her floundering body back to her house.

"Damn, Ashleigh, how much have you had to drink?"

"Lots," she giggled.

We walked toward Ansen and the group he'd stood with when I'd pulled up. I bumped fists with Ansen and nodded at everyone else. Ashleigh's house was dark, but the music was loud.

I leaned on the bumper of the car at the end of the drive.

"Where's Paul?" I asked Ansen.

"Inside. You need something?" he asked.

"Yeah, I'm running low."

He nodded. I looked around the group. "What's new?" I asked everyone.

Justin's girlfriend, Amy, was leaning on him, and she smiled. "Not much, Lilypad. What have you been up to?" she asked.

"Absolutely nothing."

"Cool." Justin nodded, flicking his cigarette in Ashleigh's green grass.

"Trace was looking for you," Ansen said, taking a swig from his beer bottle. "Said you owed him a lighter or something."

I laughed. "He let me borrow his."

He gave me a funny look but shrugged. He emptied his bottle then chucked it in the forest area across the street from Ashleigh's house.

Just then two guys drove by. We all leaned down to see who it was, but I didn't recognize them.

They parked ahead of my car, and we watched them walk toward the house in the pale light of the weathered country streetlights. I stood and my heart started to race when I saw one of the boys.

He was taller than average, had pale skin, black hair that sat below his ears, but it was his eyes that arrested me. They were a translucent hazel, thin, and had a haunted, almost sad quality to them. His jaw was square, his lips full.

"Who's that?" I asked Ansen.

He knew exactly who I was talking about. "That's Salinger," he bitterly spit. "Don't bother, though," he added.

I swallowed. "What do you mean?"

"He won't go anywhere near you. Straight as an arrow and shit. Too good for us."

He was right. Salinger wasn't just "hot," he was beautiful, and not in a way I'd ever seen. He exuded something so stunning stars seemed to trail behind him. I saw them bounce around his feet and sizzle on the cold street they landed on, unable to survive without him. He just *looked*, carried himself, really, like he didn't belong anywhere near us.

I cleared my throat when they got closer. Ashleigh threw her arms around Salinger's friend.

"Noah!" she screamed. "I'm so glad you came!"

Noah wrapped his arms around her and they almost toppled into the street.

"Careful," I said, steadying my stupid friend. My gaze found Salinger's, though, and my heart beat wildly in my chest.

They stood upright and laughed at each other.

"You want something to drink?" Ashleigh asked both boys.

Noah nodded his head, but Salinger shook his.

Ashleigh playfully pushed Salinger's shoulder. "Come on," she laughed. "You're such a prude."

Salinger sarcastically bit, "Why do I feel this inexplicable urge to down shot after shot now?"

"Really?" Ashleigh asked, missing his meaning entirely.

I was embarrassed for her and rolled my eyes, shook my head.

"No!" Salinger laughed then smiled at Ashleigh. "I'm fine, thanks."

The boy Ashleigh called Noah went arm in arm with her into the house, in search, I assumed, of something to drink.

Salinger stood awkwardly to the side and examined the house with intensity.

I leaned forward. "I love a good roofline."

He looked at me and laughed. "What?"

"The 1950s ranch house is an underestimated design," I dumbly droned on.

He narrowed his eyes, trying to figure me out, I thought. "I guess."

I pointed toward the house. "I'm into short ceilings. Makes me feel like a giant." He nodded his head in mock agreement. "And don't get me started on the hundred-square-foot bedrooms."

"Perfect for a pair of twin beds," he countered.

"Exactly. Sleep is important. No room for *anything* else," I teased. His face turned a bright red and I fought a smile. "I've made you uncomfortable."

"No," he lied. "It's okay."

"I'm Lily," I said, holding out my hand.

"Salinger," he confirmed for me.

When his hand slid into mine, when our palms met, I felt it all the way down to the heels of my feet. His eyes widened briefly. "Nice to meet you," I whispered.

I hated to do it, but I let his hand go. "You from around here?" I asked.

"No, I'm new to the area."

"Why?" I asked.

He laughed. "Why not?"

"*Nobody comes* to Bottle County, that's why. Most of us who are born here are always looking for a way to get out. Only reason we stay is when we get stuck."

"Is that so? Are you stuck, Lily?"

I looked at my feet then back up at him, our eyes caught. "Yes," I told him.

The smile on his face fell. "Oh."

I fixed a smile on my own and hoped it was convincing. He swallowed but smiled back.

Just then Trace came bounding out of the house and my stomach dropped. *Don't come over here. Don't come over here.*

"Hey, Lily," he oozed, making me cringe.

I cleared my throat. "Hey, Trace."

He got closer and threaded his arms around my waist. "You got something for me?" he flirted.

One brow on Salinger's face rose and he fought a smile.

"What?" I asked, flustered. I pried his hands from around my waist.

"My lighter?" Trace said.

"Oh, uh, yeah," I said, fishing for it in my pocket. I found it and brought it out in front of me.

"Thanks," he said, pushing it into the pocket of his jeans. "You just let me know when you need it again," he seeped out with a wink.

I thought Salinger may have snorted, but he hid it well. Both Trace and I looked at him and he cooled his expression.

"Trace, this is Salinger," I introduced. "Salinger, Trace."

"Nice to meet you," Salinger said, holding out his hand.

Trace took it begrudgingly then dropped it quickly. "Nice to meet you," he lied, then turned toward me.

"Let's go somewhere private," Trace said, making me wince.

"Well, uh, I," I began.

"Salinger!" we heard come from down the street. We stared the direction of the voice.

It was a girl, about our age, tall, five times prettier than I was. I sank a little into myself.

"Lyric!" Salinger exclaimed, smiling from ear to ear. "I'm over here!" he exaggerated, waving his hands up and down wildly. "Can you see me? I'm right here!" The girl laughed, shaking her head. "Come here and meet some people," Salinger said, his arms dropping at his sides.

She jogged forward, a dopey grin on her face. "Hey," she said.

"Lyric, this is Trace and," his brow furrowed, "uh, I'm sorry, uh, I can't remember your name."

"Lily," I said, my confidence at an all-time low. I held out my hand for her and she shook it firmly then smiled.

"Lyric," she said.

"Nice to meet you."

Lyric didn't react.

It got quiet for a second.

"Well, uh, where's Noah?" Lyric asked.

"Inside," Salinger answered. "Let's go find him."

"Yeah, cool," she said.

"Nice to meet you guys," she threw over her shoulder.

"Yeah," Salinger added, "see you around."

I watched them as they climbed the front porch and disappeared into Ashleigh's house.

"I don't trust that dude," Trace said.

I looked at him like he was crazy.

"Why?" I asked, my curiosity piqued.

"I just don't like him."

"Why, though?"

"I don't know. I just know that I don't like him."

I laughed. "Well, I do."

"I'm *sure* you do."

I ignored him, but he followed me into the house.

"Everyone's got a type, and that guy is mine," I admitted when we were inside.

"What about me?"

"Are you kidding?" I sidestepped.

He smiled at me and edged me against the front door. "I can make you forget all about him," he said.

I yawned. Trace was hot as hell, but he was boring.

"Let's go to one of the bedrooms," he prodded.

I searched the sea of heads, landing at Salinger's.

"Uh, I'm cool, actually. Catch you around, though?" I tried for casual.

"Whatever, Lily! You fucking tease," he started yelling.

I rolled my eyes as he screamed obscenities, turning toward the part of the room Salinger was in. No one paid attention to Trace because they were used to him. Salinger talked to a few people in the corner of the living room, including that Lyric girl and their friend Noah, his back to me. I sat at the corner of Ashleigh's sofa next to my friend Courtney. She held her fist out for me and I bumped mine with hers.

"What's up, Court?"

"What's up, chump? You feelin' good?" she asked.

"Not yet. You got some stuff?"

"Always." She smiled.

She laid on the sofa, her body relaxed. Courtney was always relaxed, though, even if she wasn't on anything. It was her nature to be chill.

"You still looking for a job, fool?" she asked.

"Not really," I laughed, "but both Sterling and my mom are on my ass, so I don't think I've got a choice."

"You're a scalawag."

I laughed. "You're a nerd."

"I know this already, you rapscallion."

I laughed harder. "Shut up."

Her chest shook with silent laughter in answer.

"I'm gonna find my man," she said, standing up, "see if I can get him to dance with his girl."

We bumped fists again.

"Later."

I slid into her old place and laid my head back, trying to hear Salinger's conversation.

"I started last Monday," Salinger told the group.

"Where are you working?" my friend Craig asked. "Bottle Co. Market?"

Bottle County Market was the only grocery store in our very tiny town.

Craig laughed. "Yeah, everyone's worked there." *Not me*, I thought. "It's like a rite of passage or something," he continued.

"Well, it's the only place hiring, so," Salinger said, letting it hang.

"Not much around here," Lyric said. "Not that you have to worry," she added, then laughed a little.

"I don't know," Salinger answered her.

The group got quiet, waiting for more of the story.

Lyric put Craig and, to be honest, myself out of our misery when she said, "Salinger's in chess tournaments. The pots can be pretty big. It's how he pays for school and stuff."

I sat up a little.

"Dude, seriously?" Craig asked. "That's fresh as shit."

I took the liberty of glancing back at Lyric. She looked pleased with herself, like it was her accomplishment or something, and I snorted.

All four of them looked my direction. "What?" I asked.

"You've got something to say?" Noah asked.

I shook my head. "No, nothing to say."

Salinger turned toward me, making my heart race. "No, really. What was that about?"

I sighed. "Chess *competition*? Come on, man," I needled.

"Chess is an intelligent game," Salinger said, defending himself.

"I know that."

"Whatever," he said, rolling his eyes, and their group turned back to themselves.

"I could mop the floor with you. No offense," I told him.

It was Salinger's turn to disregard me, and that pissed me off.

"Let's go," I said.

He laughed. "What? Here? I'm not doing that."

"You scared?" I asked like a five-year-old. I was starting to embarrass myself, but I couldn't stop.

"He's on some national-level shit, dude. You don't scare him," Lyric spit out.

I stood, my heart racing. "Then let's go." I looked around me, found Ashleigh. "Ash! You gotta chessboard around here?"

She laughed and everyone around me looked at me like I'd grown five heads. My neck felt hot. *Commit.*

"My dad's got an old set in his office closet, I think. Why? Does my party suck that bad?" she asked, and everyone around us laughed, including me.

"Bring it to me," I told her.

She left down her hall to her dad's office and returned with a wooden folding chess set. "Have at it, playa."

"Shut up," I laughed.

I laid out the set on her coffee table and started placing the pieces. When I was done, I sat back on the sofa and stared up at them. Lyric looked at Salinger, who shrugged his shoulders. He brought up a small stool on the other side of the coffee table and sat down.

"Oooh!" Craig bellowed. "Give them some room! It's about to go down in this motherfucka!" Everyone laughed and I rolled my eyes. "Get Lily one of your dad's cigars and a glass of whiskey, Ash!"

"Sit down, Craig!" I yelled, and he playfully nudged my shoulder.

"I'm black," I told Salinger.

"To match your charcoal heart," Court chimed in.

I pointed at her and she laughed.

Salinger moved a pawn and I followed suit. He moved a second pawn and, again, I followed up swiftly. Knight, knight. Queen, pawn. Queen, bishop.

Knight, knight. We were switching moves quickly, and as the game progressed, Salinger's cocky smile started to dissipate.

What he didn't know, what many didn't know, actually, was I was only good at one thing in this world and for some reason, *it was chess*. Translucent lines seemed to appear on the board for me, moves came naturally, tactics seemed to emerge out of nowhere. I didn't know how or why, but I enjoyed the game, so I never questioned it. I'd never played a person, though, as strange as that seemed. I played online all the time and got better and better until the computer games started to prove a non-challenge. It was fun, but not as thrilling as the adrenaline I felt knowing this guy I didn't know was giving me his attention and I was going to beat him. My blood pumped harder with every single move.

To be fair, he was incredible.

On the forty-eighth move, though, Salinger made a fatal mistake, and I knew I'd have him in exactly twelve additional moves, if my calculations had been correct from play seven.

Eleven. Ten. Nine. Eight. Seven. He was playing *exactly* as I'd anticipated. Six. Five. Four. His face fell slack when he realized what he'd done. His king, my knight. My king, his pawn. His knight, my king. My king, his knight.

It was done.

He fell his queen and my senses became aware of the room again, having fallen into my own thoughts during the game. Much to my own shock, the room had turned quiet. Salinger's queen rocked back and forth on the board, the only sound in the room. His hand came into view and I looked up, straight into his face. Everyone's faces spelled disbelief.

"Holy shit," Courtney whispered. "Lily's like a savant or some shit."

"Maybe you're not that dumb after all," Ansen threw out.

I laughed, could feel it vibrate in my chest.

Everyone went back to the party and left me alone with Salinger and my racing heart.

"You're good," he said, his eyes narrowed.

I swallowed. "I like the game."

He shook his head. "No, Lily, you are, like, *incredible*."

"Thanks." I swallowed.

Lyric moved closer, sitting on the sofa's arm. Her stare burned into my skin.

"Ever thought of competing?" Salinger asked.

"No," I said, leaning back, "that's a little too stale for me."

"I guess," he said and placed his hands on his knees. His eyes narrowed even further. "How'd you learn the game?"

My fingers found strands of my light lilac hair near my waist and twirled it absently around my index finger. "Played online."

"Bullshit," he whispered.

I laughed again. "Why is that bull?"

"You're lying. No one can play like that unless they've been trained by a master."

I shook my head slowly. He studied me. "Apparently not," I whispered.

Lyric stood up. "Come on, Salinger."

His eyes locked with mine, but he stood anyway. He held his hand out toward me again, and I slid my palm over his. That tingling, drugging sensation flooded my fingers and arm. It sent a thrill down my spine. We stood, our hands resting on top of one another's. We stared down at them.

Lyric cleared her throat and we both startled. He pulled his hand away, his cheeks red.

I watched as he meandered through the crowd behind Lyric. Just as he reached the door, he turned, and we held eyes for countless seconds until Lyric yanked on the sleeve of his T-shirt. Then he was gone.

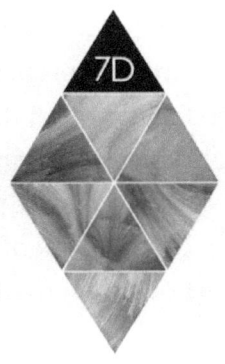

CHAPTER TWO

I got wasted that night and fell asleep on the same sofa I'd beaten Salinger. The morning light filtered through the living room, shedding an awareness of what had gone down the night before. Several people were strewn about, sleeping where they'd last fallen, so I stood, my head pounding, my stomach on the verge of retching. I stumbled across the room toward the door, throwing it open. I knew I didn't have time to make it to a toilet. All the contents of my stomach spilled in the grass just off the porch then I gulped air at a violent rate.

The sun beat down on my head, in my eyes, and I groaned, fishing my keys from my pocket and trying to remember where I'd parked my car. I found it and fell into the driver's seat. I pulled over twice on my way home to vomit into the street. I parked outside my dilapidated house, tried as best I could to avoid the creakiest boards on the porch, and headed for the door, but before I could open it, it swung open. Sterling stood tall and menacing on the other side.

One of his boots landed on the porch, his meaty hand landed heavily on the back of my neck as he dragged me into the house. I fought the urge to vomit once more.

"Time for you to learn a lesson, girl," he gritted near my ear before pushing me toward the floor.

My head swam, but I managed to roll onto my back. His fingers found my top, so I let him use most of his energy to pick me up. This was calculated on my part. He was only good for a few swings, at most. He was an alcoholic and, although he was tall, he'd deteriorated into barely anything. I knew to ride it out.

I watched as he cocked his arm back and swung a fist into my left eye. It stung so bad, but I fought the urge to cry. Instead of reaching for my face, like I wanted to, I smiled at him. This only incensed him more, and he brought his arm back once more, this time a little slower, indicating how much he'd had to drink the night before, but it didn't matter. The sharp bones of his knuckles met my cheekbone again. Ignoring the queasy feeling in my stomach, I fought to keep upright.

"What's the matter, old man?" I quieted.

"Watch your fucking mouth, you piece of shit," he spit in my face.

I gritted my teeth as my other hand found his chest and attempted to push him off me. He was drunk enough that I was able to throw him off-kilter, shoving him into the wall near the front door. The whole house shook, and I heard the girls scream in their room. He threw out an elbow, aiming for my temple, but I pulled back. He caught the corner of my mouth instead, though, and I felt my lip split. I could hear Callie and Eloise whimpering, and that sobered me. He pounced, shoving his forearm into my throat, and pinned me against the wall again.

The girls began crying and he let me go, his eyes seethed at me, promising a furious revenge, but I didn't care as long as he didn't scare the girls anymore that morning; that's all I cared about.

"Let's discuss this later," I offered. "Away from the girls."

He started to laugh. "Oh, we'll discuss it later, all right, when I put a bullet in your head."

"Promises, promises," I countered like a fool.

"You don't think I will?" he asked, a smile plastered on his face.

"You've promised to kill me thousands of times, yet you've never followed through."

"One day," he promised.

"And when that day comes, I won't stop you," I told him.

He laughed. "You're so worthless, even you know it," he told my back when I turned to head toward the girls' room.

Ignoring him, I headed down the hall and opened their door. They were huddled together on Eloise's bed, the blankets pulled over their heads. When they heard me, they pulled them down to see who it was.

I swallowed, hoping the blood wasn't too obvious, but from the looks on their faces, it was noticeable.

"You guys okay?" I asked softly.

They nodded their heads.

"Go back to sleep, all right? I'll keep you safe."

Both of their shoulders relaxed and they burrowed under their threadbare covers. I closed their door and went into my room, right next to theirs. I stood still, listening for movement from Sterling. He rummaged around in the kitchen, opening and slamming cabinet doors.

"That woman is fucking worthless," I heard him mumble.

I heard him stumble across the house to the front door, opening and closing it behind him. I listened for the engine of his car and heard it barrel past my window. I leaned against the jamb of my door and lightly brought a hand to my face. It came back bloody, so I ditched my clothes and took a shower, only to dress once more to try and get some sleep before he came back.

I never went to bed without being fully clothed, just in case I had to leave in a hurry, for obvious reasons, including shoes. I learned the hard way that running barefoot down our gravel road hurt like you wouldn't believe. I sat down, my back to the wall, one foot on the floor and one on the bed. It was the best position to feel any vibration from any approaching person.

I brought my tray out and rolled a quick blunt, taking a few hits to calm myself down. I winced at the pain in my lip as I took a puff. When I was done, I put my tray under my bed and laid back.

I fell asleep quickly, escaping into a rather nice dream, where Sterling was dead and the girls and my mom and I were happy and healthy.

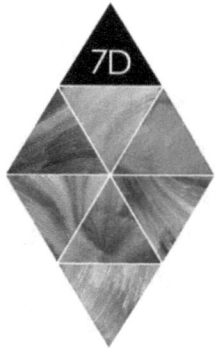

CHAPTER THREE

I felt movement in my leg and shot up straight, still slightly groggy. It was my mom.

"Where's Sterling?" I asked.

"He's not here," she said, sitting at the corner of my bed near my foot.

The back of my hand found my eyes, trying to rub the sleep away. "What time is it?"

"Two in the afternoon."

I yawned, then looked at her. "Where are the girls?"

"Next door at sweet Alta Mae's house."

I took a deep breath. "Good. How was work?" I asked her.

She shrugged. "It was work." She cleared her throat. "They've got a position open—"

I laughed at her. "No, thanks."

"I need you to find a job, Lily."

I leaned back against the wall. "Stop bugging me about it. I'll do it when I'm ready."

She shook her head. "You sound just like your father."

I bolted upright again. "That man is *not* my father, and I am *nothing* like him."

"He wouldn't be so bad right now, if you were working," she defended, ignoring me.

I laughed. "*He* could get a job, you know, if he was so stressed about cash."

"Lily," she said, sounding exasperated.

"How about this? I'll get a job when he does."

She didn't answer me. Instead, her eyes narrowed. "Why is your eye black? Your lip split?"

I looked down at my lap. "We got into it."

She sighed as she reached for my face, but I gently batted away her hands. "Don't worry about it."

"What did you do to him?" she asked.

I laughed bitterly. "Nothing."

"You shouldn't provoke him."

"Whatever, Mom. I seem to provoke him just by existing."

"That's not true. He only gets worked up like that when you do something to him."

I shook my head at her. "My God, you're delusional."

"What's that supposed to mean?"

"You're making excuses for him when you know deep down he's wrong. You know he's a violent drunk."

She averted her eyes. "He's just not himself right now."

I laughed so loud she jumped a little. "He hasn't *been himself* for as long as we've ever known him, Mom." I swallowed. "When are you going to realize this *is* who he is?"

My phone went off. It was a text from Ansen, asking if I wanted to go into town with him and his girlfriend, Katie. I stood up and my mom left, closing the door behind her without saying another word. I changed, smoked a quick blunt, brushed my teeth, and curled my hair, trying to hide the bruises on my neck and face with foundation I didn't normally wear, so it was a bit yellow. It didn't work very well, but I was hoping people would see it and know I didn't want to talk about it. I put on a deep red lipstick to cover up the split in my lip.

I traveled down the little country road we lived on, heading toward Ansen's. I picked up him and Katie and hit Main to get a burger at Chuck's.

"What've you been up to, Katie?" I asked.

"Nothing much. What's new with you?"

"Same," I said.

She leaned forward. "Doesn't look like it," she said, gesturing to my badly covered black eye.

"Yeah, Sterling and I got into it."

"That sucks," she said, leaning back in her seat.

That's when I noticed a tall boy walking on the side of the road about 200 yards ahead.

"What is this guy doing?" Ansen asked.

Katie leaned forward, squinting her eyes. "Looks like that Salinger guy from Ashleigh's party," she said absently.

I looked at him closer. I slowed down and as we passed him; his hair swept up slightly in the wind. He turned to look at us, and my heart started to beat hard in my chest.

"Holy shit, it *is* Salinger," Ansen said.

I pulled over and he kind of jogged up. I leaned over, closer to the passenger-side window. "What are you doing out here?" I asked him.

"My Jeep's in the shop and I needed some stuff in town."

"I can give you a ride," I said.

Salinger opened the passenger-side door and Katie hopped in the back with Ansen, who tucked her into his side, making her giggle.

"Thanks," Salinger said, jumping into the

passenger seat and closing the door.

I pulled back onto the road; gravel spit out behind us. Salinger put one hand on the dash and the other held his hair out of his face since I had the Scout's hardtop off. "Crazy running into you," he said with a smile, which made my stomach plummet at my feet.

"Yeah," Ansen agreed, "what? Your girlfriend doesn't have a car or something?"

Salinger laughed.

"What?" Ansen asked.

"I don't have a girlfriend."

My heart beat even harder.

"You're not dating that Lyric girl?" Katie chimed in.

"Nah, she's just a friend," he explained.

Ansen laughed. "Friendzoned."

Salinger shook his head but laughed. "I've been very honest with Lyric."

Now it was my turn to laugh. "So she's into you, you know it, and she sticks around thinking you'll change your mind."

He shook his head.

"I bet she thinks you're leading her on," I said.

His mouth gaped open, ready to defend himself, I thought, but narrowed his eyes instead. "What happened to your *face*?" he asked. He lifted a hand, like he was going to touch my skin, but let it drop.

I shook my head. "Got plastered and ran into a door," I lied.

I glanced in my rearview, Katie and Ansen were too entrenched in each other to notice I'd lied or didn't want to call me out on it, I wasn't sure.

"Oh," he said, looking disappointed. I hated how that made me feel inside, but I wasn't about to tell him what actually happened.

"What did you need in town?" I asked him.

"I need a few things for work. I work the night shift and don't have a lot of time, so you're really saving me here. Thanks."

"You hungry? Want to come eat with us?" I asked.

He narrowed his eyes and smiled. "Where are you going?"

"Here," I answered.

I found a parking spot at Chuck's.

"Stay there," he said, as I threw my Scout in park. "I'll get your door."

If I looked surprised by this, he pretended not to notice. He rounded the front of my car and reached my door, opening it for me and helping me out.

Katie squeezed through and he helped her out as well. "How come you never do this for me, Ansen?" she asked him.

"What would I do that for? Then you'll expect it every time," he said.

Salinger's mouth dropped open a little in shock. Ansen and Katie started to argue, so I left them there. He sped ahead of me and opened the door to Chuck's and we walked through. It was packed. It was always packed, actually. There was no other food joint in my entire county. Not even a McDonald's would put a restaurant in our sleepy town. It worked out anyway, because Chuck's had pretty decent food. Well, it was always hot, anyway.

"Going to school?" he asked me.

I swallowed, hoping my neck wasn't turning red. "Nah," I answered, hoping he'd drop it. He did, but you could tell he wanted to ask me more. "Are you?" I asked.

"I take online courses right now."

"Why online?"

"Just because," he said vaguely.

We reached the counter and I watched as he studied the menu.

"What'll it be?" Chuck asked.

"I'll take the usual," I told him.

Chuck looked over at Salinger. "What about you, sir?"

"I'll take your chicken sandwich."

"That'll be seven dollars even," Chuck said.

I swung my hobo bag onto one hip and reached for my wallet.

"It's on me," he said.

I put my wallet away. "Thank you," I said as Chuck handed him his change.

I mentally calculated what I had left over from money I'd gotten from graduation. *Definitely need to figure out a way to make some cash.*

"No problem," he said.

Suddenly a hand bolted toward me and I instinctively ducked, raising my hands. Chuck tsked under his breath, gently reaching for my chin, and examined my face.

"Sterling still hittin' on you?" Chuck asked.

Sterling's abuse wasn't new to anyone in town, but his asking in front of Salinger after I blatantly lied was utterly humiliating. I know my throat turned red for certain; I felt it. Chuck noticed, shook his head, turned, and yelled out our orders to the cook. I pivoted, searched for a table, and noticed there was one in the back corner along the windows nearest my car. We sat down and I looked out. Ansen and Katie were yelling at each other.

"Classy," I told him.

He ignored my comment, my attempt to distract him. "Who is Sterling?" he asked me.

I brought the backs of my hands up to my heated

cheeks. "He's a mean drunk. My stepdad," I offered.

"You live with him?" he asked.

"Yes," I answered shortly.

"Why don't you get out of there?" he asked point-blank.

I thought of my little sisters, even my mom. "Can't."

"Yeah, you can."

I studied him. "Trust me."

He nodded his head. "Listen, I don't really know you, but if you ever need a place to crash, I've got a couch."

"Thanks," I said and genuinely smiled.

He smiled back, reached into his pocket, and took out his phone.

"What's your number?" he asked.

I rattled off my digits as, I assumed, he programmed them in.

Ten seconds later, I got a text.

Hey, Lily, it's Salinger

"Thanks," I repeated once more.

"Any time," he said.

We both looked out the window again to see that Ansen and Katie were now making out against my car.

"Idiots," we both said at the same time.

Chuck came over and set our sandwiches down. I

smiled up at him and Chuck brushed my hair out of my eyes before he rushed back to the kitchen.

Salinger watched me intently, setting my stomach on edge.

"What?" I asked.

"Nothing," he said.

"What are you studying?" I asked him.

"Psychology."

I laughed.

"What's so funny?" he asked.

"It's just ironic that you happened upon the town's biggest nut case."

He took a bite of his food and swallowed, wiping his incredible mouth with a napkin. "Who?"

Me, I thought. "Ansen," I told him, and he laughed.

"What are you going to do with your degree?" I asked.

"Um, go into counseling."

"That's cool."

I'm a loser, I thought. *Ansen was right. This guy is actually going places. I'm just a worthless girl who smokes weed all day and is going nowhere.*

"You working anywhere?" he asked, sealing the nail in my coffin.

"Uh, no, I'm in between jobs right now," I lied.

"You should come work with me," he offered.

"They're pretty desperate for night crew. We just stock stuff all night and go home in the morning. The pay's all right."

I cleared my throat. *Holy shit, the prospect of working next to him actually appeals to me.* "Yeah, uh, maybe I'll do that."

I opened my mouth to ask him a question, but he distracted me.

"Where are your friends?"

I glanced outside. They weren't there. I looked around Chuck's, thinking they might have come inside without our noticing, but they weren't inside either.

I shrugged. "They're an enigma."

"What a bunch of nutters," he joked.

"You should open up a practice here when you're through with school. Business would be booming."

He laughed but shook his head. "I don't stay in any place longer than a year."

"What? Weird. Why?"

He shook his head. "I just like a change of scenery, you know?"

"I guess," I answered him. I shook my head. "It's still a mystery to me why you chose Bottle County, though."

"Wanted to see what living in a small town was like and my friend Noah lives near here, so," he left hanging.

"You won't find any smaller than here."

"Then it looks like I found the right place."

I took a bite of my sandwich, but it hurt to chew, so I set it back down and tried to pretend I wasn't in agony. It didn't work.

"Jesus, Lily, why didn't you call the police?"

I felt my face heat up. "I don't think I can talk to you about this. I don't know you."

"Fair enough," he said, but he didn't look like he wanted to let it go.

"Just trust me," I tried to appease.

"But I don't know you," he said. *Thief.*

I swallowed. "I can't call the police," I said.

"Why?" he asked.

"Because they already know, Salinger, that's why. They already know but this is a good ol' boy town, if you haven't noticed, and Sterling, my stepdad drinks while playing poker with the chief of police. Satisfied? My job is to keep quiet and not die from his injuries. That's my only job."

He sat back in his booth. "That's the most horrifying thing I've ever heard come from someone's mouth. I feel sick to my stomach."

"Let's drop this."

"You need to get out of there."

I laughed. "And go where? No money. No job. No

purpose," I let slip, making my face heat up even hotter.

"Get a job then."

"Nah," I said, sitting back a little. I shoved the basket with my sandwich away from me.

"You don't look like you eat much," he whispered.

"I'm fine, dude, promise."

"Lily," he said with pity in his voice, making me feel worse.

"I'm not a project, Salinger."

"Lily—" he began, but I'd reached my limit and stood. "Wait," he offered softly, "wait. I'll stop. I promise."

I sat back down and settled in as much my sore body would allow me to. We sat in silence for a good solid minute before he spoke up again.

"Where'd you learn to play chess like that?"

"I told you."

"You're telling me that you played a bit of computer chess and that's how you learned?"

"Yes. The game came naturally and every time I'd beat the computer, I'd try to find the next one, an unbeatable one."

"What program? Fritz?"

I snorted. "Child's play."

"Shredder?"

"Shredded it. Several times."

"Komodo?"

"Yes, of course. I've beat them all."

"Even Houdini and Stockfish?"

"Yes, Salinger, like I told you, I beat them all."

He stared at me, his mouth agape. "If that's true, you could be one of the best in the world."

"Shut up," I said, laughing.

"Lily," he said with weight, "it's true. You were moving in ways I hadn't even thought of, didn't think was possible. You knew every move I was going to make."

"I knew nine moves in every move you were going to make. I knew I was going to win nine moves in."

"I believe you."

I smiled to myself. "At least I'm good at something," I whispered.

"You're not good, Lily, you're a phenom."

"Shut up," I laughed. "You've only played me one time."

"Fine," he said, "let's go."

"Where?"

"To the park. Let's play a little before I have to work."

"What about your errands?"

"Screw the errands."

"Okay," I said, grabbing my hobo bag and making my way toward the doors.

Salinger and I played until it was dark and he had to go. I dropped him off, which felt weird. I asked him if he wanted me to come get him in the morning. He politely declined, saying his car should be done near then and it was just across the street from the store, and that he'd planned it that way. I stifled my disappointment. I liked being near him.

He was an instant friend, which was kind of cool. It felt kind of awesome to be able to talk about chess with him, too, so it made sense that I'd forgotten all about what had happened that morning, driving back home, feeling happy and light for the first time in ages.

I bounded up the front porch, forgetting all about who was inside and what awaited me.

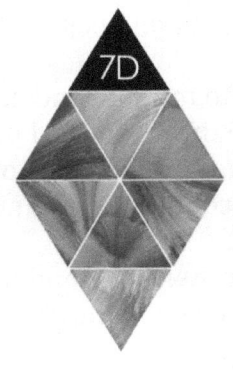

CHAPTER FOUR

I practically skipped through the door.

Immediately an arm came across my throat hard. I slammed to the floor, the wind knocked out of me. Sterling crouched close. I gasped for air but none would come. My lungs burned for air.

I guess Sterling is home.

"Just where in the hell have you been?" he asked. I shook my head, unable to answer. "I heard tell you were out whoring around."

I couldn't focus on anything as my lungs began working again and I gasped for oxygen, choking in large gulps of air.

"J.P. saw you in the park today with some boy when you shoulda been looking for work."

Still unable to talk, I could only stare at the crumbling ceiling, begging myself not to cry.

"You ain't gonna live in *my* house for free, you little whore. Now, get yourself up and get to the kitchen. Make yourself useful." I could hear him fall into the couch.

I turned onto my side and attempted to stand up but didn't have the strength. I pushed myself on to my stomach and brought my body up on my hands and knees so I could safely stand up without falling over.

I could hear Sterling stand up. "What are you doing? *What* are you *doing*? You trying to tempt me, you little whore?"

I fought with everything I had to stand, to face him, and backed into the kitchen.

"No, Sterling," I said, my voice sounding fatigued. "Just trying to get back up," I explained, hoping not to enrage him any further.

"Show that side of yourself to me again and I won't be responsible for what happens next."

He fell back down onto the sofa.

I ignored him and stumbled into the kitchen, begging God there were cans of something, anything, in the pantry I could put together for him.

Sterling had been making comments to me like that since I turned sixteen, but they'd become more frequent, more suggestive after I graduated. It scared me. *He* scared me.

I found some rice in an old canister in the back of our pantry, sort of hidden. I grabbed that and some severely freezer-burned chicken that had fallen out of the original bag and sat at the bottom of the freezer door shelf. I threw it in a pot with a bunch of stale spices and the rice and prayed it would turn out edible.

Sterling sat on the couch, watching the crappy

television. About ten empty beer cans littered the coffee table, and a cold one was in his meaty hand.

When the rice was done, I plated it, took a deep breath, tiptoed through the living room and placed it on the table, then attempted to walk out quietly.

"What the hell is this!" he yelled, making me stop in my tracks. "You trying to poison me, whore?"

I turned just in time to catch the hot plate to my temple. Instinctively, I fell to sit on the heels of my feet, my hands to my head. I brought a shaking hand down and saw blood there. Lots of it. This one was bad. Sterling stomped toward me; the weight of his body made the walls shake.

"You better get in that goddamn bathroom and clean yourself or I will fucking kill you."

He roughly shoved me with a boot and I practically crawled to the bathroom, careful not to smear blood on the walls. The last thing I wanted was to scare the girls when they came home later, from wherever they were with my mom. When I got inside, I shut the door and examined my face.

It was bleeding profusely, but from what I'd discovered, head wounds always bled a little more freely. I tied my hair back and bent to the sink, turning on the water, and letting cold water run over the side of my head. The water ran red and red and red and *red*. The adrenalin was starting to wear off and my hands shook even harder as it left. Keeping my head under the water, I dug around the floor for a towel. When I found one, I brought it up and pressed as hard as I could to the cut, then brought it away from my head so I could see how deep it was. It was pretty deep. I pressed the hand towel back to my head then rummaged through the medicine cabinet for some old butterfly stitches or something but couldn't find any.

"Damn it," I whispered.

I pulled my phone out of my back pocket and texted Ansen. I waited a few minutes and texted again. He didn't answer. I put my ear to the door, listening for movement from Sterling. It was dead quiet, so I opened the bathroom door and waited. Nothing. He wasn't in the living room, and I didn't hear him in the kitchen. Quickly, I headed for the front door and slipped out, huffing it as best I could to my Scout.

Once inside, I had a tough time getting the key into the ignition but when it landed, I turned that sucker and sped out of there, heading straight for the only grocery store in town and praying I wouldn't somehow run into Salinger.

The market looked dead as a doornail since it was due to close in ten minutes. As much as I hated the thought of going in, I knew driving to the next town was my only option and since it was an over an hour away, I also knew I couldn't afford the gas money.

Just go, Lily.

I opened the door as my phone rang. It was Ansen. *Finally.*

"Ansen," I answered.

"What's up, Lily?"

"Sterling clocked me good. Need butterfly stitches."

"*Fuck*," he answered, sighing into the phone. "At home still?"

"No, didn't have anything. I'm up at the market."

"Sit tight, Katie and I'll be right there."

"Okay, thanks, man."

We hung up and I got out, shutting the door behind me, not bothering to lock it. I sort of sprinted for the doors, but the bounce hurt, so I stopped. *Please God, please God, please God. Don't let him see me.* It was a small market, but I could hear a group of people in the back right of the store, a small radio playing. *He's probably back there,* I thought, which helped ease me a little since the stuff I needed was in the front left.

I grabbed the generic brand butterfly stitches, a bottle of peroxide, some gauze, and medical tape, racing as fast as I could without hurting myself back to the front, but when I rounded the aisle, there he was. He leaned against a display near the only open register talking to Danny Marks.

My stomach dropped to the floor, a frog built up in my throat as I approached.

"Holy shit, Lily, what happened to you?" Danny asked.

As if in slow motion, Salinger stood from his slack position and turned toward me, but I couldn't meet his eyes, too embarrassed, humiliated in front of him for the second time that day. I tossed everything onto to the belt.

"What's up, guys?" I attempted at casual.

"*Fuck*," Danny sang out. I felt my face heat up to impossible temperatures.

"Lily," Salinger whispered. As if I couldn't help myself, my face lifted toward his, but I didn't answer him. "D-did Sterling do that?"

I tried to shrug it off, but lifting my shoulder made my back and throat burn.

"That guy is such a prick," Danny chimed in, ringing up my stuff. I faced him, unable to look on Salinger any more.

He stared a hole into the side of my face, though, but I refused, no, *couldn't* look at him. I handed Danny a wad of cash from my bag once he'd totaled it all up. Twelve dollars gone. The market doors opened and in walked Katie and Ansen. They made a beeline toward us.

"Let me see," Ansen said.

I took a deep breath and dropped the rag that was almost soaked through by that point. Judging by everyone's winces, it definitely looked as bad as I thought it did. I placed the cloth back and grabbed the plastic bag full of my stuff.

"Come on, Ansen," I whispered. "You'll have to help me this time."

"Sorry about that, Lily," Danny called after me.

I half turned and mumbled a thank you, then caught Salinger staring me down, his face white as a sheet.

"Well, I'll never see *that* guy again," I said out loud when we'd exited the doors.

"Who, Danny?" Ansen asked.

"Are you mental?" I asked him. Katie rolled her eyes. "*Salinger.*"

"Oh, yeah. I told you, though."

"Yeah," I sighed, "you were right."

When we reached my Scout, Ansen opened my door for me and I sat in the driver's seat as he played doctor. I can't count the number of times

Ansen had patched me up.

"Uh-oh, mister man himself," Katie said, facing the store.

"*What?*" I asked, trying to see over Ansen's shoulders.

"Stop moving, dumb ass," he said.

"Sorry," I said.

Salinger came into view over Ansen's shoulder and I nearly gasped.

"Did that hurt?" Ansen asked.

"No," I whispered to Ansen. "Did I forget something?" I asked Salinger.

"No," he said. "I don't know why I'm out here, to be honest. Just wanted to see how you were."

Katie's mouth opened slightly and she fought a smile. She stood behind him a little and looked at me, before winking, making my cheeks heat up.

"I'm okay," I began, but he narrowed his brows. "I mean, I-I'll be okay."

Ansen stood up, unscrewing the cap to the peroxide. "Batten the hatches, buttercup," he braced me. I gritted my teeth and prepped for the onslaught over my temple. He poured the liquid and I could feel it running in rivulets down the side of my face. I looked down and saw blood and foundation pooling at my feet.

Salinger brought his hands to his hair.

"Looks bad?" I asked.

Katie's faced screwed up in mock pain. "It doesn't look good, babe. Worse than usual. What did you say to him?"

"I just existed, Katie," I explained away for the hundredth time. It was never Sterling's fault. Ever. It didn't matter who asked in my stupid town.

When Ansen was done, he taped some gauze over it to keep it clean, using the bottom of his shirt to clean off my face. I bit my tongue to keep from crying out when he brushed over a bruise.

"You can stay at my house for a few days until he cools off," Ansen offered, but I could tell that made Katie uneasy.

Ansen and I had been best friends since we were three years old, creek-water babies. He was a brother to me. Not literally, but it felt like it. I didn't want to disrespect Katie, though, so I said no.

"I've got a couch," Salinger put out there.

"No, it's okay," I said quickly just as Ansen spoke up.

"Yes, that's awesome."

"I couldn't impose, Salinger," I said.

Ansen looked at me like I'd grown two heads. "Why not?"

I stared daggers into him. "Because I'd feel like a burden."

"That's nonsense," Salinger insisted.

"I'll be okay, seriously. Thank you, though."

His brows knitted together. "It's no problem."

But I knew that was a lie. The market was a new job to him, leaving it, even if for one night, was risky, and I wasn't about to be party to that. Plus, he didn't know me.

"Lily—" he began again when I didn't respond. I interrupted him.

"Thank you so much for the offer, but I'll be okay. I promise."

"A-are you sure?" he asked me.

56

"I'm sure." I tried to appease with a smile.

"Salinger!" we heard someone yell from the front of the store.

We all looked and saw Danny signaling for Salinger.

"I've gotta go. I'm so sorry. If you change your mind, text me?"

"Sure," I said, but I knew I was never going to see that guy again, let alone text him. "Thanks."

He stared at me for a second. I didn't know if it was my imagination or wishful thinking, but it looked like he didn't want to leave. He hesitantly turned toward the store and jogged back to work.

"That boy's sweet on you," Katie carelessly spoke. It was like a pang to the heart, that statement, because I really liked Salinger. At least what I'd grown to know of him during the day. He seemed like he would make a really good friend, a good boyfriend.

"No," I explained, "he's just a really nice guy. Too good for us. Too good for me."

"Come on," Ansen said. "Let's go to Court's, get you high, get you distracted, and keep you away from Sterling for a few hours."

"Good idea," I answered.

I watched Salinger reach the doors and get lost in the shelves.

Way too good for me.

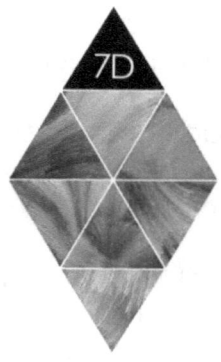

CHAPTER FIVE

Ansen rolled a fat blunt, took a hit, then passed it my way. I breathed it in deep, letting it calm me down, allowing it to erase what I felt. The anxiety, the physical and emotional pain? They buried themselves away. I settled into Court's couch.

A baby in a dirty diaper crawled into the living room with us.

"Who the hell's baby is that?" Ansen asked.

"That's my cousin's baby," Court explained.

I sat up a little. "What's it doing here?" I asked.

"I'm babysitting while she goes out with some friends."

"What the hell, Court? That baby needs some attention. And why is it up? It's like, freaking five in the morning," I told her.

"I don't know what I'm doing," she explained.

I stood and picked it up, smelled its head. "Oh my God, this poor kid. What the hell is wrong with your cousin?"

I didn't wait for her answer or even ask

permission when I took it back to Court's bathroom. I set the baby down, cleaned and rinsed the tub, then ran warm water, filling it a little. I took the baby's diaper off and discovered it was a boy.

"Hey, little one," I cooed.

I covered him in shampoo because that's all Courtney seemed to have in her tub, washed his little body, though it hurt to make the effort, washed his hair, then rinsed him clean. I searched under Court's sink for a clean towel and found a small one. It had a ton of holes in in it, but it was clean. I wrapped him in it and brought him out to the living room.

"Where's his stuff?" I asked Court.

"In that grocery bag on the counter in the kitchen," she explained.

Inside the bag was an oversized T-shirt and five diapers. "You poor kid," I said, shaking my head. "Where's his bottles and stuff?" I yelled toward the living room.

"He has a bottle, but that's it."

"Seriously, what the hell is wrong with your cousin?"

I brought my phone out. *Salinger works at the store*, I thought. My hand hovered over his name, but I couldn't do it. Instead, I scrolled up to Danny's name and rang him up.

"Yo!" Danny answered.

"Danny, it's Lily, can you bring me some, like, formula for a six-month-old baby? Some rice cereal too," I tagged on, remembering when I helped take care of my little sisters and what they ate at that age.

Danny laughed. "What?"

"Danny, I'm not joking. Go back to work and get that shit for me," I said, before realizing I'd cursed in front of the baby. I sighed. "Just get it for me."

"Fine, where are you?"

"Court's."

"Fine, see you in twenty."

"Thanks," I said, hanging up.

I grabbed the T-shirt and a diaper and went back to Court's room, laying him on her bed.

"You're such a good boy," I told him as I dried his skin with the towel. He smiled at me and I nearly keeled over. "Oh my God, you're such a charmer, little man."

Putting on his diaper proved a little difficult, but I managed it, then stuffed the T-shirt over him. The bottom hem reached his ankles and he was drowning in it, but it was clean, at least.

I brought him back out to the living room and handed him to Courtney. "There, he's clean," I said, falling into the couch beside Katie. "Danny's coming by with food and sh—. I mean, stuff."

"Hey, little dude," Court greeted him and he laughed, snuggling into her neck.

Everything ached, my back from getting the breath knocked out of me, my bones, my muscles, my throat, my head. "I gotta get out of that house," I told the room.

Everyone nodded their heads in agreement.

"What are you going to do?" Katie asked me.

I took as deep a breath as my lungs allowed. "I have no idea," I told her.

"We should all get a house together," Ansen threw out.

"Yeah," Katie joined in.

"In, like, a dope city somewhere," Court added.

"Somewhere really far away," I said.

"Yeah," Ansen added, rolling another blunt.

Except no one meant it, did they? This is what we did. We sat around, getting high, and talking about what we were going to do with our lives. We talked about how one day we were going to leave Bottle County, how we were going to make it, become successful. It was bullshit, though. We knew what our fates were going to be.

We were going to sit in Court's living room, or Ashleigh's living room, or Ansen's living room, or whomever's living room, and we would talk about how we would leave, how we were going to live different lives from our parents, how we weren't going to get pregnant, or fall further into drugs. We were going to talk about how we wouldn't do those things. It was a giant lie we all told ourselves and each other so we could feel better about our situations. Complacent is a bad place to be, even I knew that.

We lacked the imagination to self-start.

I knew I would go home in a few hours, sleep with my back to the wall, one foot on the floor, and fully clothed. I would sneak around Sterling, hoping he didn't beat me, or *worse*. I would smoke my joints to forget. I would live off my mom until she kicked me out for "tempting" Sterling or causing him to beat me to a bloody pulp. I would bounce off couches until I couldn't do that, and then I would marry some local boy and have three kids by the time I was twenty-one. No education, so I'd rely on him for everything, and when he would start to beat on me or run around on me, I'd feel trapped and he'd know it. He'd have his cake and he'd eat it too.

No one broke that cycle in my stupid town. *No one*.

So we talked of bigger lives, yes, of course, but big lives belonged to big people and we'd only ever *seen* big people pass through our little town full of little people with little imaginations.

People like Salinger, I thought, then promptly fell asleep, worn out by it all. All of it.

Danny came through at five thirty in the morning, tapping my knee to wake me up.

"Lily," he whispered, "wake up, dork."

I sat up, my body stiff. "Hey, Danny, did you bring the stuff?"

"Yeah," he said, dropping a bag on the coffee table.

I stood up, stretched myself out, and grabbed the formula, taking it into the kitchen.

The baby was asleep on Court's chest, but I knew he'd be up in a few short minutes. Babies can't stand it when someone around them is awake. They feel like they're missing out.

I made the bottle and set it on the counter. The bar in the kitchen was open to the living room and I looked up to find *Salinger* staring back at me. I felt my neck go hot. *Oh my God, what is he doing here?*

"Salinger?"

"Hey, Lily," he said, lifting a long, slender hand.

"What are you doing here?"

"The shop said they needed a few more hours, so Danny said I could tag along until it was ready."

"Oh, cool," I said, feeling anything but. "Excuse me," I added, heading toward the bathroom.

I peed then washed my hands, glanced at the mirror to see my curls had fallen and my makeup was gone. I looked super worn out. I bent over the sink and carefully washed my face, rinsing out my mouth, and brushed my hair with my fingers. It met my waist and was knotted at the bottom pretty bad, so I rummaged through Court's drawers for a hairbrush. My heart beat hard in my chest. My bruises were starting to fade, thank God, but the head bandage probably needed to be replaced.

When I came out, everyone was up. Ansen and Danny were playing video games; Katie was in the kitchen looking through the pantry. Court was holding the baby, who was half asleep, half drinking the bottle I'd made for him.

"He probably needs his diaper changed again, Court."

"Okay," she said.

I looked at Ansen. "I probably need to change this bandage."

Ansen sighed. "Fine," he said, pausing his game.

"I can do it," Salinger said.

Everyone stopped what they were doing to look at him, including the baby.

"Fine by me," Ansen said, picking up his controller again.

Salinger was tall and Court's ceilings were short. He had to duck under the haunch of her kitchen doorway to get to the stuff I'd bought last night. I watched him wash his hands, pick up the stuff, then head toward her front door. The butterflies in my stomach and I followed him outside.

He gestured for me to sit on Court's porch steps, so I did.

"How are you feeling?" he asked.

"I'm good," I told him and meant it. "I know how to adapt," I explained.

He nodded.

Being really gentle, he peeled back the medical tape. "No offense to Ansen, but the butterfly stitches are too loose. Do you mind if I redo them?"

"Go for it."

He carefully peeled the three Ansen had applied the night before and set them on top of the old gauze.

He pinched the skin there and I held up a stitch.

"I want you to sleep on my couch," he said matter-of-factly.

"You don't meant that," I said.

"I mean what I say, Lily."

"I can't," I told him.

"Why?"

"Well, because Sterling would find me, and I don't want to involve you in this crap."

"Fuck that guy," he said, his teeth gritted.

I handed him another stitch. When he took it, his fingers grazed mine. It sent shivers up my arm and settled in my chest. It sobered me and I steadied my breath.

"You got any money?" he asked.

"Not much, why?"

"There's a blitz tournament about twenty miles from here this Saturday. It's a fifty-dollar entry fee, but the winner's pool is twenty-five hundred dollars."

"Oh man, that's awesome, but I don't have that kind of cash."

"Fine, I'll pay your entry for you."

I felt my face heat up. "I don't think so, Salinger."

"Don't you want out of this town?" he asked.

Yes, I thought. "I don't think I could even if I wanted to," I said instead.

"You're scared."

I leaned away from him, but he followed me, grabbing my face to apply the final stitch. "I'm not," I whispered, his face inches from mine. The blood in my veins ran hot.

"I think you are. You're also too comfortable here. You feel like you won't be able to survive and you're resolved to this fate. It's why you hang out with people who are as resolved as you are to this town and why you all smoke your problems away."

He hit a big, *giant* nerve. I grabbed his wrist and pulled away. "Excuse me? You don't know me, don't know us."

"I know enough," he said. "People are consistent, Lily. People favor patterns because it's what they know. Your life can be changed by simply doing nothing."

His words sank into my skin, laid there, permeated deep until they reached bone. He pulled his arm from my grasp and reached for the little canister of gauze then cut a bit of medical tape. I let him cover the wound.

He sat below me on the stairs. We faced out into the dark before us.

"If you want, I'll pay your way. You'll win that

cash, I just know it, and it can open some options for you."

"Why would you do that for me?" I asked him.

"Because you're another human being, because I think there's something special about you, because I could see us becoming great friends." He looked back at me. "Is that enough of a reason?"

"Yes," I whispered. I swallowed. "But what if I lose your money?"

"So what if you do?"

"I'd feel bad."

He leaned back, resting his elbows on the stair I sat on. He looked up at me. "I wouldn't have offered if I couldn't afford it."

I took a deep breath. "Okay, then. I'll try it."

He smiled at me, a genuine smile, showing just enough of his teeth to send my stomach into loops. "I know the event organizer. The deadline to enter was a few weeks back, but I think if I vouch for you, he'll let you in."

"Okay, I'll be there."

He shoved my knee with his elbow, sending shivers down my spine. "Good."

Danny took Salinger to get his Jeep and I spent most of the day with Court and her cousin's baby at Court's house. Her cousin didn't come to pick up her son until three the next afternoon. I chewed her out for leaving her baby that long without anything to eat or more diapers. The girl started cussing me out, her baby shaking on her hip with every dramatic arm swing she threw my way, and I felt a pang of horror knowing what the future held for that poor baby.

Court rolled her eyes my direction and shrugged in a silent sorry to me. I decided I'd overstayed my welcome and bailed. When I went home, I noticed Sterling's truck was missing. All the pent-up anxiety that'd built up on the drive over alleviated at once.

"Mom, I'm home!" I called out.

She came out from the kitchen into the small living room. "Where have you been, child?"

"At Court's," I said, not giving any further information.

She would have pretended it didn't happen or tried to lessen it to make herself feel better, and I didn't feel like getting incensed over watching her do that, so I dropped it.

"Where are the girls?" I asked.

"In their room. Can you watch them? There's another shift available at the plant and I volunteered for it."

"Sure," I said. "How you gonna get there?"

"Walk, I guess."

"Why didn't Sterling leave you his truck?"

"I don't know where Sterling went. He hasn't been home since last night."

She glanced at my head, but didn't dare ask what happened. She already knew.

"You can take my car," I offered.

"Thanks, baby," she said, catching my keys when I tossed them her direction.

This was nice, yes, but it also made things a little dangerous if Sterling came home drunk because I didn't have a way to escape. I was betting on him not to start anything since he loved to keep up a good appearance in front of my sisters.

That was the most hilarious part to me about Sterling. He loved his girls. I mean, he really loved them. He was walking whiplash. He could backhand me across a room one second, flip a switch, and love and kiss on his girls the next. He didn't like to upset them, so he tried to hold back when they were home. If I was being brutally honest, it was partly why I loved to babysit them. If my mom wasn't home and it was just me taking care of them, he would ignore us for the most part. It was a reprieve.

When he first started dating my mom, I was around seven. He was really nice to me. He'd bring me stuff, candy, and generally was a lot of fun, but as soon as my mom got pregnant with Eloise, he slipped a ring on that finger and turned into a completely different person. It was frightening to witness someone shed a facade like that to reveal the true version of themselves.

Eloise, Callie, and I ate some ramen, watched a little television, then I bathed them and put them to bed. I changed my bandage then went into my room, closing the door behind me. I slid my tray from underneath my bed and rolled a joint. Even the crack of the lighter as I lit the end made me calm down. I took two deep hits then laid the blunt back down.

I felt my nerves and muscles relax. I put the tray back under my bed, left a foot on the floor and laid back against the wall my bed sat on.

My phone indicated a text, so I picked it up.

Caught the director. He fought me a little, but I told him I would vouch for you personally. You're in, Salinger wrote.

That's amazing. Thank you so much and I can't wait.

Five minutes passed before my phone indicated another text.

What are you doing? he asked.

My heart raced.

Just sitting here. What are you doing?

Wanna hang?

I smiled. I couldn't help it. I'm babysitting my little sisters. Maybe tomorrow?

Yeah. I want to take you into the city. I know of a cool park with a few marble chess tables. We can practice for Saturday.

Sounds good. What time? I asked, feeling happier than I cared to admit.

I don't know. Noon?

Sounds good. I'll meet you at the market at noon?

See you then

I laid my phone down and enjoyed the butterflies Salinger gave me. He made me forget stuff. For the first time in a really long time, I looked forward to something.

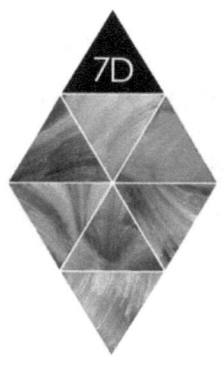

CHAPTER SIX

If I were to guess, I'd place Salinger's height around six foot three. He had thin hazel eyes, high cheekbones, and fair skin. His hair was pitch black, straight as an arrow, and fell just below his ears. He parted it down the middle and tucked both sides behind his ears.

That afternoon, the afternoon we were to play chess, he wore a pair of worn jeans and a T-shirt with a cardigan over it with a pair of white Adidas. I immediately thought of how I wanted to steal his cardigan, wrap it around myself, smell it. He was so amazing.

When I pulled into the parking lot, he came bounding up to my car and opened my door for me.

"Thanks," I said as he helped me down.

"Hey," he greeted with a smile. "How's your noggin?" he asked, lifting my hair to inspect the damage.

"It's better."

"How do you feel?" he asked. "Up for some

chess?"

I looked up at him. I was a good foot shorter than he was. I *was* underweight. He was right when he guessed I didn't eat very much, but it wasn't from lack of trying, I assure you. Also, because of this, I had small boobs and cheekbones that stuck out a little too much, lending me a gaunt feel. I did have good hair, though. That, at least, I had. It reached my waist and was a smoky lilac color. I'd curled large waves into it before I left and used almost all of the last of the makeup I had.

The summer before, I'd gone to the thrift store in Smithfield, the next town over, with Katie because it was a more affluent area and the stuff there was much nicer than what we could find nearby. I wore a pair of black, fitted overalls, tapered at the legs, with a split hem, that I'd bought that day. I paired it with a white T-shirt. I didn't have any money, but I tried to make what I already owned work. I had a bunch of different necklaces I'd collected over the years and piled them on top of each other, hoping to distract from the fact they were cheap. I topped it off with a pair of black ankle boots Katie had let me borrow. I hoped it worked.

"I'm good. I'm ready," I told him.

He led me over to his Jeep, placing a hand on my lower back, making my skin tingle there and butterflies crowd my stomach. He opened my door for me and helped me in. He rounded the front and got in the driver's seat.

It was more than an hour's drive to the park with the marble chess tables, but it was worth it. The park was stunning with lots of fresh, bright green grass, tall, billowy trees shaded the chess area, which sat on gravel and stone. Wood folding chairs sat on a cart that read Woodcreek Recreation Center. Both of us grabbed a chair and picked an ideal spot, settling in.

Salinger had his own chess pieces he'd brought with him. They were heavy, looked to be made of stone, and were stored in a leather folding pouch that tied together with bits of leather string. I reached out, running my newly manicured fingers, thanks to Katie, over the worn leather and each piece laid side by side.

"That's beautiful," I told him.

"Thank you," he said, placing the pieces between us. "They were my great-grandpa's."

"That's cool."

"Yeah, he was a cool dude. Fought in Korea where he met my great-grandmother. They got hitched when they were both nineteen and he brought her back over with him." He sat back in his chair and stared up into the trees. "They were married seventy years. When she died, he passed two weeks later."

"Couldn't live without her then."

"Couldn't live without her," he confirmed.

"That's beautiful too," I told him.

He smiled in answer and it stopped my heart a little.

We started playing one another but kept up the conversation.

"You look really pretty, Lily," he told me, his gaze roaming the board.

For some inexplicable reason, that made my eyes

sting. I blinked hard to work through it.

"Thank you," I whispered.

"When did you graduate?" he asked me, making a move.

"Last year."

"Last year?" he asked, his voice an octave higher in what I assumed was disbelief.

"Yeah," I laughed.

"How old are you?"

"Nineteen," I answered. "How old are you?"

"Twenty-three."

"Cool."

"You're so young," he remarked, which made me laugh.

"Only four years younger than you."

He shook his head. "No, I meant you're so young for having so much talent at this game."

I beamed a little. "Thank you." I cleared my throat. "Checkmate."

He laughed. Like, genuinely laughed really loud. He fell back in his chair and ran a hand through his hair then down his face. "Let's go again," he said, sitting back up, the biggest grin on his mouth.

We set the board back up.

"What time is the tournament?" I asked him.

"Ten in the a.m. Want me to pick you up?"

I imagined Salinger pulling up to my shack of a house, getting stared at by Sterling, then my being on the receiving end of an elbow to an eye when I walked back in after the tournament.

"Nah," I said, trying to stay casual, "I'll just meet you there. Text me the address."

"Cool," he said, nodding his head.

His index finger landed on a pawn but he thought better of it then wrapped his long fingers around the back of his head. He perused the board.

"I really like playing chess with you."

"It's a rush," I said. "Way more fun than with a computer."

He looked at me, a crooked smile fell across his face. "What's your last name?"

"Hahn. Yours?"

"Park."

I nodded and made a move.

"Where are you from?" I asked.

"I was born on an army base in Germany. My dad was in the military and we moved around a lot."

"Is that why you don't like to stay in one place too long?" I asked him.

He blew out a deep breath. "Uh, no. I hated moving around that much and I never got used to it."

"What?" I was confused. "Then why keep moving around now?"

A small smile fell across his lips. "I just haven't found a place that feels like home yet. I give them a year and then I find somewhere else."

"You've never been anywhere any time and felt as if you were home?"

"No," he told me without further explanation.

I waited until his eyes met mine and when they did, my heart sped up. "Neither have I," I confessed.

"It's sort of an empty feeling, isn't it?" he asked me.

"Yes," I offered. "So you keep searching," I observed.

A gust of wind blew the treetops around us and

he glanced up at them. "Always searching," he told the trees.

"I've never bothered looking," I revealed.

"You should change that."

"No money. No idea where I'd go."

"It's a risk, I admit it, but risk can be adventurous."

It was quiet for a few minutes as we concentrated on playing.

"How do you know Noah?" I asked.

"I answered his ad for tutoring online. He needed help in a math class so I helped him out. We stayed friends."

"That's cool."

"Yeah, Noah's awesome." He looked up from the board. "Is, uh, well... You and Ansen seem close."

"Yeah, we grew up together. He's like family."

"Ah, I see. He takes good care of you."

"Yeah, when he can. I try not to rely too terribly much on him. His girlfriend Katie is a good friend of mine too, and I don't like making her uncomfortable."

"I get it."

"Any siblings?" I asked.

"None," he answered. "You?"

"Yeah, I have two little sisters. Eloise and Callie. Eight and six."

"Cool," he said.

"They're Sterling's daughters."

He looked up at me, his jaw gritted.

"I see," he said. "Does he, uh, does he—"

"No, he doesn't touch them, um, if that's what you're asking."

Salinger's whole body sat eerily still. "And your mom?"

My face flamed white hot. "Uh, well, no," I gulped.

"I see," he said. He was trying to keep his voice steady, I could tell. "So it's just *you* he can't keep from hurting then?"

It was my turn, but my hand stilled on the king's knight my finger rested on. I audibly swallowed. "Yes," was all I could answer.

"And what does your mom think about it?"

I started to feel uncomfortable, so I shifted in my chair. "Salinger, I—"

"Tell me," he said, sitting back, forgetting the game, "at what point in your life do you think you're going to do something? At what point will you say enough is enough?"

"I'm not a project, Salinger, remember?"

"Is that what human beings are to you? Projects?"

He caught me off guard. "No, I just mean—"

"And what would you do if you were me, huh?"

"I'd mind my own business."

"That's alarming," he observed.

"No, it's not," I told him. "I live with this very real reality. You shake things up and you make it worse for me."

"No, Lily, when I shake things up for *him*, he will know not to lay a single finger on you again."

"You can't; you're going to get me killed," I whispered.

"Sterling, or whatever the hell that asshole's name is, he's going to fear the ever-living hell out of me because that seems to be the only thing men like him respect. So today, when I drop you off at your car, I want you to let me follow you to your house. I wanna have a talk with him."

I started to hyperventilate. "He'll kill you."

"No, he won't."

"He'll kill *me*."

Salinger leaned forward. "*No*," he whispered with quiet intensity, "he most definitely will not."

"Stop," I begged.

"No, *you* stop. You think this guy won't graduate to worse? Because he will, and one day he'll lay you out and you won't get back up, Lily."

My eyes burned. I knew he was right, but I had no where to go and no money and I knew if I'd left I'd be completely alone because I'd have to leave Bottle County just so he couldn't find me or have the sheriff drag me back home.

"Drop this," I insisted.

"No."

"Drop this right now, Salinger," I said, my face and neck growing hot.

"Then stay the night on my couch, at least, just so we can figure out a plan for you."

"No," I said, going back to the game.

"You're not even going to try to help yourself?" he asked me.

"If I stay the night anywhere but home, he beats me worse the next day. I'd rather avoid it."

"Then don't go back home *ever*. Just stay with me or whatever. I'll actually help you."

"You mean help me into *your* bed, right?" I asked, saying *exactly* what I was thinking. He acted like I'd hit him. "Please, Salinger, wipe that look off your face. That's how *all* men are."

"That's most men," he said, defending himself. "I'm not most men, Lily."

"How would I know that? I don't know you. I just met you. You want to know how many times a boy has told me he loves me but when I refuse to sleep with him, bails? Do you know how many times a boy has promised to help me then realized I couldn't or wouldn't give anything to him and left? Do you know that percentage?" I asked him.

"No," he whispered.

"One hundred percent. One hundred percent of them."

"And Ansen?" he countered.

"He's the exception to the rule," I dismissed. "And even Ansen would drop me like that," I snapped, "if Katie called on him. That's the way it should be, though. I'm not complaining. I'm just saying even the exception to the rule isn't infallible."

"But you can admit they exist, though, don't they, exceptions to the rule?"

"Yeah, but they're so rare, so impossible to find he might as well be the only one."

"Not true," he argued, "he's not the only one. There are lots of good guys out there and they're waiting, wading through life, and waiting. You're looking in all the wrong places."

"I've looked everywhere."

"No, you've looked in this shallow pool you call Bottle County. You've looked nowhere else and you want to know something else?" he said, folding his arms across his chest, "those good men, they're just waiting for you to make them even better. Men are malleable, way more malleable than you could possibly imagine. If you promise loyalty, the good ones will move mountains for you. The only thing unchanging would be their own loyalty and whatever moral compass they live by. Other than those two things, you would own them. That is how men work and that, as you said, is how it should be. God, if girls only *knew* the power they possessed."

He stared at me, his eyes searching my face. He was wondering if he'd rambled too far, I could tell. You could also tell he was a little embarrassed, but I liked what he'd said. His words broke open a tiny piece of a cold, hard sky for me.

"And are you a good one?" I prodded.

"I am," he declared, his cheeks tinged pink. He unfolded his arms and leaned over the board, searching the pieces there.

"You seem confident in that."

"I'm sure of it."

"How do you know?" I asked him. "How do you know this isn't just a romantic ideology you adhere to by mouth but the minute something distracts you, you'll run to that instead?"

His stare met mine, serious and cutting. "I know, Lily Hahn, because I have gosh damn integrity."

Adrenaline shot through my body at his candor. "I think I believe you," I told him.

"You don't have to choose to believe it. You're going to see it for yourself."

My stomach dropped to my feet. Without another word on it, he bent back to the game and my stomach settled down.

I wanted to know him, wanted to know if he was

going to be good on his word. I'd never really seen integrity before, and I wanted to know what it looked like.

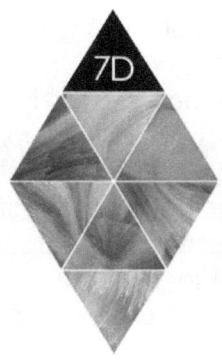

CHAPTER SEVEN

The next day, the Friday before the tournament, Salinger had to work a double because they were behind or something at the store. We'd planned on meeting to practice but that wasn't possible, so he texted me throughout the entire day instead.

I'd refused to go home with him. I needed to time to think. He respected that but begged me to lock myself in my bedroom and text my address if it looked like Sterling was going to snap. I promised, but it wasn't necessary. Sterling never came home that night. I'd blissfully lived without him anywhere near me. It was heaven.

I spent most of the day practicing chess at the library on the computers there.

The director's name is Ron, fyi, Salinger texted.

I took a deep breath, growing more and more nervous as the hours passed.

He's cool? I texted back.

Yeah, cool A few seconds passed. Cool but kind of a ball buster too

Great, I thought, before starting my hundredth game that afternoon. *I need to stop. I'm making this harder than it has to be.*

I'm done practicing. Feel like if I keep going, I'll just psych myself out, I texted back.

I totally get that lol Plus, this is just a fun tournament anyway. No pressure, Lily, seriously.

That helped me.

I stood up, stretching my body out, and took a deep breath, exhaling slowly.

"Hey, beautiful, what are you doing here?" someone asked beside me.

I turned to find Trace.

"Hey, what's up?" I asked, trying my hardest to smile. "I'm just playing a little chess online."

Trace snorted and I rolled my eyes.

"You still mad about the other night?" I asked him.

"Nah, you know me," he said.

I did know him. He probably didn't even know what I was talking about.

"Better question. What are *you* doing here?"

He laughed. "Freaking probation officer says I have to fax in some paperwork from my last court appearance. This is the only place I know that still has a fax machine."

Classy. "Ah, yeah, I get it."

"Yeah, it's dumb. Hey, what are you doing tonight?"

Freaking out and hoping I don't let down Salinger. "Nothing much."

"Really? If you're up to it, you should head over to my house. I got a couple people coming over. It's gonna be a good time."

Yeah, right. "Sounds good. Since it's close, I might stop by."

"Good," he said, walking backward toward the door. "Hope to see you there." He winked.

I went home around four that afternoon and Sterling still wasn't home. I almost shouted I was so happy. *If I'm lucky, he'll be gone the whole night long and I'll get to go to this tournament thing with a clear mind.*

I trudged up the run-down steps to find the house still empty. I went to my room and cranked up the small hand radio I'd had since I was little, dancing around my house a little, feeling better about myself than I had in a really long time. It'd been over twenty-four hours since I'd smoked weed, and I didn't even miss it. I just felt *good*, lighter somehow.

I stared at the hand radio. It was my dad's. He left when I was a baby. I didn't remember him at all, and Mom could barely speak of him. Only the occasional "your dad was into Aerosmith" if one of their songs came on the car stereo or "your dad was allergic to kiwi" or something equally innocuous. The only other thing I knew about him was he was not from Bottle County, so no one in town knew much about him. I would beg Mom, especially when I was really little, for something, *any* kind of information about him, but every time I did, I could tell her heart would shatter in a million pieces and she didn't know how to hide the expression of pain on her face. I learned to keep my mouth shut.

It was obvious she'd loved him, and I wanted so badly to know what had happened, why we were alone.

We'd had a small, comfortable life, albeit short lived, before Sterling came barreling through.

I heard keys jingle in the lock of the front door and stopped short. They were heavier than my mom's keys. I'd learned to differentiate. I yanked my window up and slid through, closing it, then sank into the side of the house. I heard heavy boots land in my room. I laid flat against the rotted siding.

"I know you're here! Your car's still out front!" Sterling yelled. I tried to sink as deep into the siding as possible and held my breath. The music from my radio went silent. "Wasting batteries, that little bitch," I heard him grumble under his breath.

He stomped near the window and I nearly ran but stayed where I was. I didn't want to run unless I knew for sure he had seen me. I knew it would mean a worse beating if I did, so it was a last resort. "One day," I heard him promise himself under his breath. "One day I'm going to get her. Tempting little bitch drives me crazy."

I heard him stomp out of my room and slam my door. I started breathing normally again and fell to the ground. I waited for the adrenalin to taper off, rounded the side of the house, and inspected the back door and deck. When I felt it was clear, I hauled ass to the fence that separated our yard from Trace's and hopped over.

I held against the wood there, checking for Sterling once more before running through Trace's yard, through his gate, and to the front of his house. For a split second I thought about calling Salinger but thought better of it. Tomorrow was the tournament and he was already working a double. The last thing I wanted to do was give him more anxiety than he probably already had.

Instead, I climbed Trace's front porch steps and landed on his doormat, knocking on his door. The door blew wide. Trace looked pissed until he saw my face and his expression softened to something I didn't want to interpret.

"Well, well, well, looky what we have here," he said out loud like a dork.

A bunch of boys I went to high school with came into view. "Well, if it isn't little miss Lily," Kevin King sang.

"Lily's here!" someone yelled out, though I couldn't see them.

Trace kicked open his totally pointless screen door with the torn screen and I walked inside.

"I knew you'd come," Trace remarked. "Me and the boys were just playing a few games. Want to join us?" he asked.

"Sure," I said, following him into his living room. It had a window that faced my house. I walked over to it and tried to see if I could get a glimpse of Sterling. I didn't see anything and my heart began to settle.

Seven boys sat strewn about on sofas and chairs and the floor, so I chose a corner on the floor facing the television.

"Why'd you come over so early?" Trace asked as everyone watched him and Kevin play some war game.

"Just trying to get away from Sterling," I told him.

Everyone nodded. They *nodded*. Like they knew. Like they understood. It put a sour flavor in my mouth. *Is this really my reality?* I asked myself.

Something happened on the screen and all the boys yelled then laughed, startling me. I stared down at my phone.

"Fuck you, Kevin!" Trace yelled loudly then laughed.

I looked at them. All of them. Two of them had bottles of liquor in their hands already. Most of them were high. Cigarette smoke filled the room. I couldn't breathe. Not from the smoke, no. I was choking on our situations. I was suffocating on our status. We were none of us going to do anything. We were none of us going to *be* anything.

I started laughing to myself. The boys looked confused, but I didn't care. I was wasting my time on the chess thing. Life was one big colossal joke.

"Want a hit?" Trace asked, passing a blunt my way.

He watched me in a strange way. I could only interpret it as excitement?

"Sure," I said, taking it.

He leaned closer, watching me intently. "Careful, mama, it's strong as hell," he said, his eyes narrowed at me.

"Beautiful," I whispered, taking it down to almost nothing. Trace smiled at me the way I'd imagined a snake would.

"Oh shit," I heard deep and muffled before passing out.

CHAPTER EIGHT

Salinger

I was wiped. Sixteen hours straight at the market and I couldn't wait to get some sleep. I hopped in my Jeep but before I started her up, I checked my phone to see if Lily had written. She hadn't. I ignored how empty that made my stomach feel.

You all right? I texted her.

When I got back home, I threw my keys on my table and fell on my sofa, waiting on a response, but my body betrayed me and I fell asleep watching some rerun on television.

I woke up around three in the morning, a little dazed, but remembered I hadn't heard from Lily yet so I checked my phone. No response.

I wished I knew Ansen's or even Katie's number so I could have found out if she was with one of them. I fell back to sleep looking forward to seeing her at the tournament later.

My alarm went off around eight a.m. so I hopped

in the shower and got ready. My nerves were a little on edge, but I didn't care. I was more excited about seeing Lily than competing. I'd texted her the address to the tournament the afternoon before and didn't really have any reason to contact her yet, but I couldn't help myself.

Can't wait to see you there. You're going to kill it, I wrote her.

I got in my car and started making my way. Pure adrenaline coursed through my veins.

Lily was amazing. She had her issues, for sure, but she was freaking talented and so freaking pretty. The boys in her town were dumb as hell. They literally couldn't see what was right in front of them.

The tournament was held at the recreation center next to the park we had practiced in and the parking lot was full. I searched the rows of cars, though, and couldn't find her. *Must be running behind*, I thought. I got out and practically sprinted for the front doors. Inside there were people milling about, so I pushed through and found the registration table.

"Hey, Mickey," I greeted. "Working the table today?"

"Yeah, you in?"

"Yeah," I answered.

He rummaged through a binder, found my name, highlighted it, then handed over a lanyard with my name on it. He also gave me a piece of paper with my first tournament time.

He was ready to turn to the next person when I caught his attention.

"Think you could look up another player for me?

Tell me if they're here yet?"

I wanted to ask just in case I missed her car.

"Sure, what's the name?"

"Lily Hahn."

He searched the binder then looked up. "Not yet," he said, shaking his head.

"Thanks," I said, waving at him as I turned toward a trophy case on the opposite wall.

I leaned against it and scrolled through my phone, landing on Lily's name, and pressed her number. It rang at least ten times before going to voicemail, so I tried again but got the same result. My stomach flipped. I scrolled through again and rang Noah this time.

"Hello," he answered, his voice rough from sleep.

"Noah, it's Salinger. Do you know where Lily is?"

"Lily?" he asked. I could hear him sitting up. "Uh, yeah, someone told me they saw her last night at Trace's."

"Trace?" I asked. "Is she okay?"

"Think so."

"Okay," I answered. My heart plummeted to my feet. "Thanks."

"No prob. Hey, don't you have that tournament today?" he asked.

"Yeah," I told him as they opened the doors to one of the rooms and called for my rating level. "Listen, I've gotta jet. They just called me."

"Oh, okay, good luck."

"Thanks, man."

I hung up, put my phone on vibrate, and entered the room.

"Hey, Salinger!" Ron called out to me. "You

ready?" he asked, offering his hand.

"Yeah," I said, shaking it.

"Looking to see this girl you wouldn't shut up about. See if she's as good as you claim," he teased.

I felt my face flame. "Yeah, about that," I began, placing a hand on the back of my neck, the other in my front pocket. "It doesn't look like she's coming."

Ron laughed then realized I was serious. "Wait, *what*? What the hell, Salinger? I pulled some freaking strings for you. Seriously. You vouched for her."

I shook my head and could only shrug my shoulders. "I'm so sorry," was all I could offer in explanation. "I made a mistake."

"Damn," he said, starting to walk away, "I've got to do some rearranging now."

"So sorry, Ron!" I called out.

"It's okay!" he lied. "Good luck in there!" he said, pointing behind me.

I nodded and turned.

I won the whole damn tournament, pocketing $2,500.

But what the hell. The tournament wasn't about me. It wasn't official, and I didn't even care to compete. It was about Lily, and she kind of screwed me over.

Whatever.

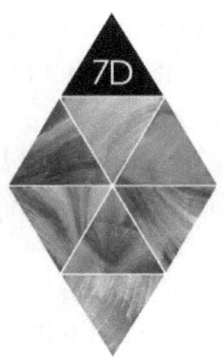

CHAPTER NINE

Lily

I was awake but my stomach roiled. I kept my eyes shut and breathed deeply. The sun poured through the window and bathed my skin, making me feel hot. *I wish we had an air conditioner*, I thought. I cracked one eye open and stared at the ceiling, not recognizing it. *What in the world?*

"Oh shit!" I yelled, shooting up.

"Shut up!" someone complained.

Vomit threatened to make an appearance, but I took a deep breath through my nose. I reached for my phone in my back pocket and brought it toward my face. It was three o'clock in the afternoon.

"Oh my God," I whispered. "Oh my God. *Salinger.*"

I climbed over random people and made my way

toward Trace's front door, practically falling outside, and landed on the front porch. I blinked to clear my vision and rang him up.

"Come on, come on, come on," I whispered.

His voicemail picked up. "Salinger here. Leave a message."

"Salinger," I begged, "I am so sorry. Oh my God, I am so sorry. I—" I began but felt overwhelming shame since I had no good excuse. "I am so sorry. I know you, uh," I took a deep breath, "really put yourself out there for me. I'm so sorry. I'm just," I exhaled, "so sorry."

I hung up the phone and toppled onto the top step of the porch. "I can't believe this," I complained to no one.

Ansen drove up at that moment with Katie in the passenger's seat.

"Idiot!" Ansen called out.

"Noah called us," Katie explained. "Salinger was looking for you. You missed the tournament."

Tears came flowing down my face. "I know," I quieted.

I stood up and met them at their car. When I got in the backseat, I handed my phone to Katie. "It's on its last leg," I explained.

She plugged it in and turned toward me. "Call him," she encouraged softly.

"I did," I told her and shrugged my shoulders. "I've screwed this up before it even started, Katie."

"You don't know that," she tried to appease.

I leaned back into my seat. "I like him so much. Why did I do this?"

Ansen looked at me through the rearview mirror. "Why *did* you do this?" he asked.

"I sabotaged myself? I don't know." I shook my aching head. "I've never handled a simple joint this badly before. I feel like I've been hit by a truck."

Katie took a deep breath. "Okay, well, now we do damage control. You'll come to my house, shower, borrow some of my clothes or whatever. We'll go to the market tonight and see if he's working."

"I don't know if I can face him," I admitted.

"Grow some balls, Hahn," Ansen encouraged. "Swallow your pride."

I took a deep, shaky breath and nodded.

I showered at Katie's and she washed some of my things while I was in there. I had a splitting headache and my stomach was so unsettled. *I think he laced that blunt*, I thought.

"We have to quit smoking," I told her.

She nodded. "I know, babe."

"Do you mean that?" I asked her, my hand resting on her forearm.

"Yes," she told me. "I just don't know how."

"Neither do I," I told her.

"We'll figure it out," she said, setting me down in a chair while my underwear and bra and clothes were in the dryer.

She dried my hair and curled it for me, which relaxed me.

"Thank you," I told her. "You're a good friend."

"I know, mama." She winked.

She did my makeup for me and did her best to cover up my yellowing bruises. Ansen laughed at something on the television and Katie rolled her eyes playfully at me.

"I'm glad Ansen has you," I told her.

"I'm glad I have Ansen," she said.

"You're lucky," I admitted.

"I know. He works hard and he's kind to me," she said with a smile.

I put my underwear and cutoffs back on but borrowed a shirt and kimono from Katie.

"Do you feel pretty?" she asked, fixing a curl.

"Kind of," I answered.

"Good," she said. "That helps, I think."

"It shouldn't matter," I laughed.

"Regardless, it makes you feel confident, and there's nothing wrong with that."

"True."

She smiled at me. "Let's go then."

"Let's," I told her.

We pulled up to the market at nine because I knew that was when he usually started work. Ansen squeezed my shoulder when I got out of his car and Katie waved.

"We'll be in the back of the lot making out," Ansen told me and I laughed.

Katie shook her head but laughed as well.

I took a deep breath and walked into the store.

"Damn, Lily," Danny offered.

I nodded at him. "Is Salinger here?" I asked.

"Yeah, in the back," he said. "Coming to break his heart?" he joked.

"I'm here to apologize."

"Well, *I* forgive you," he flirted then laughed.

I waved over my shoulder at him and made my way toward the music in the back. My stomach dropped to my feet when I saw him breaking down boxes, his back to me. There were five other guys there with him, most of them I'd gone to high school with. I'd caught their attention and I pointed at Salinger. They nodded their heads toward me and Salinger turned around.

I swallowed my nerves. "Hi," I said.

He didn't answer me, just stared and finished breaking down a box. He tossed it on the floor with the others. "Hey," he greeted quietly, making my blood race through my veins. I was so unbelievably aware of myself it was painful.

"I, uh, did you get my message?" I asked.

"I did," he said, picking up another box.

He was the only one working, though. The others had stopped what they were doing and were watching us.

"I'm so sorry, Salinger," I told him sincerely.

"No problem," he replied, waving it off, making me feel really guilty.

I felt my eyes start to burn, but I held back. "I really am."

He tossed down the box he was working on and stood tall, literally looking down on me. "What happened?" he asked.

"I, uh, I was over at Trace's," I began to explain, "and I got, uh, I got high and I think it was laced with something. I don't remember."

His brows narrowed. "Hmm," he said.

Two tears slipped through. "I'm pretty embarrassed."

"Listen, no problem or whatever," he blew me off.

One of the boys I went to high school with, Alex, spoke up. "Someone showed us some pictures, Lily."

"What?" I asked, shocked.

"Yeah," he continued, "there are pictures of you

circulating around."

"What's in them?" I asked, my heart racing. I wrapped my arms around my waist.

"Well, like, not cool stuff, Lily. You were so high you didn't realize they'd set you up like a prop, dressed and, like, *undressed* you."

"Oh my God." I blew out a breath, bent over slightly, then righted myself. "Do you have them?" I asked him, my arms still wrapped around my waist.

Salinger watched me intently, his brows still knitted together.

Alex walked over to me and pulled his phone out of his pocket. He scrolled through at least twenty pictures of me, some in really violating positions.

"Oh my God, stop, I'm going to vomit."

"Do you even remember what happened last night?" he asked me.

I had no idea. My hands climbed to my shoulders and I hugged myself, wondering what *wasn't* recorded.

What in the hell is going on?

"You should probably press charges," Salinger suggested, looking on me with pity.

All of them, but especially Salinger, looked at me like I was the biggest mess they'd ever encountered. Salinger gazed at me like he didn't want anything to do with me. I was mortified.

"Are you okay?" Salinger asked, trying to be nice, but it humiliated me worse.

"I-I'm fine," I whispered and turned.

I could feel his stare on my back as I fled. Danny watched me come toward him, his expression leant to one of disbelief.

"You okay?" he asked as I ran past him.

I bolted through the parking lot toward Ansen and Katie but, true to their word, they were too busy with one another to notice me.

Gutted, I turned toward the street and made my way toward my house. I was desperate to see my mom, desperate to fall in her arms and have her fix me.

"Just fix me," I begged no one. *Fix me. Someone fix me.*

***

It didn't look like anyone was at home when I finally climbed the steps to the house, but there was a note taped to the front door. It was my mom expressing her disappointment for leaving my car but not leaving the keys so she could take it to work that night. She went on to say that Sterling was dropping her off and the girls were next door.

I crumpled the paper in my hands and threw it to the side, punching my keys in the lock and opening it. When Sterling took my mom to work, he would go to the gaming room down the street. That was what she was really pissed about. She knew she'd be working her fingers to the bone only for him to spend it at the digital slots before she'd even really earned it.

"What a loser," I thought out loud.

I took my phone out to text Trace.

I saw the pics. Your ass is grass. You didn't think I'd find out? What's wrong with you???

I sat back on the sofa, crying with everything I had, so disappointed that I'd lost any chance with Salinger. If I'd only just called him. *My whole world would be different right now*, I thought. My mind went back to Salinger's face at the market. *Lost interest.* That was the expression he gave. If *I've lost interest* had an expression, that was it. And that. Completely. Wrecked me.

I laid down across the sofa and breathed deep. You know that feeling when you've lost one hundred percent to something? Like, you're literally out of chances to get something you want so, so badly? That was Salinger for me, and it felt really awful because it wasn't even like it had been out of my control. I knew I'd had a chance. I knew it would have worked out if I'd only just been good on my word. *I should have just called him that night. I*

wouldn't have been vulnerable to Trace and I still
could have avoided Sterling.

For all that beautiful talk about integrity from him, I forgot he deserved the same. I forgot to fight.

"Nothing I can do about it now, can I?" I told myself and headed for my tray under my bed.

I brought it out to the living room and sat down. I wiped my eyes on my sleeve and turned on a video game. I rolled a blunt, cracked the lighter, and tried to forget.

I exhaled smoke from my lungs and laid my roach on the glass tray on the crowded coffee table, picked up the remote and clicked buttons. My head rolled onto the back of the couch and stayed there, my feet propped on the table. My phone rang, but I ignored it, then it stopped only to ring again. It annoyed me enough to look down to see it was my mom.

"Of course," I complained.

I tossed my remote on the cushion next to me, grabbed my vibrating phone off the table, and hit answer, noting it was after midnight.

"Mom?" I asked.

"Lily, Sterling and I are broken down by Granger's Steakhouse. Can you come get us?"

Granger's was in the next town over. It'd be over an hour before I got back home.

"Mom, I'm busy. What happened?"

She sighed. "Lily, don't do this. Turn off the game or leave whatever party you're at, get in your car, and come pick us up!"

I felt my blood race hot through my veins. "Can't you figure this out? You can't know how disappointed I feel right now. My day has sucked so bad and—"

"Lily!" she huffed then paused. "You haven't been disappointed yet, Lily. You're too young to know that pain yet. Just wait, though. *It'll come.*"

Her words hit me hard for some reason, but I shook them off easily.

"You need a new car already. Just spring for one," I told her.

I could practically hear her shaking her head, and I rolled my eyes.

"We can't afford it, and I'm tired of having this argument with you. Come pick us up. It's gone dark and there aren't any lamps on this stretch of highway. Hurry up," she ordered and hung up on me.

I hit end on my phone and threw it back on the table, picking up my remote again. "Annoying," I told no one before pressing pause.

I rolled a blunt and took two more hits. Next thing I knew, I'd passed out on the couch.

***

Bang! Bang! Bang!

I startled awake to someone hitting our front door with a fist. Panicked, I thought of Sterling and my mom, so I hauled into my room and slid my tray beneath my bed. I shook my head to wake up and to prepare myself for the incredible fight I was about to get into.

Why wouldn't they just use their keys? I thought, still a bit groggy.

Bang! Bang! Bang!

"Smithfield Police!" someone yelled through the door, making my heart race.

I threw the door open, fully awake at that point. "Can I help you?" I asked, confused.

"I'm sorry to disturb you so late," an older cop soothed, "but may we come in?"

"Of course," I said, opening the door wider.

They stepped inside and I shut the door after them.

"Can we sit down?" he asked.

My blood coursed so quick and so hot, I felt sick to my stomach.

"Uh, sure," I said, offering the crap wool sofas we owned.

They waited until I sat then did the same for themselves.

"Please, what's going on?" I begged, shoving my hands between my legs.

"First, I just need some information," he asked.

"Yes, sir," I answered.

Oh my God, this is about the pictures. Someone must have turned Trace in.

"So sorry, but this is a formality. Would you mind stating your full name?"

"Uh, yeah," I barely spoke, "I'm Lily Hahn."

The older office nodded as if I confirmed what he'd expected.

"Thank you," he said, then scooted toward the end of his seat. "Miss Hahn, uh, I don't know how to tell you this, but we answered a call early this morning about an accident."

"*Accident?*" I spoke out loud, feeling really confused.

"Yes, this evening your mother—" he began, but I didn't let him finish.

I stood and slowly backed up into the wall. "Don't," I said. "Is she hurt? Is she hurt?"

"Miss Hahn," he tried to offer, standing himself.

"She's hurt, right? Just hurt, right? Only hurt."

"Miss Hahn," he said, edging toward me.

"Oh my God, she's not hurt, is she? She's not. I can tell by the look in your eyes. Is-is she *dead*?"

"I'm so sorry," he offered. "She and a man named Sterling were hit by an oncoming car that didn't see them."

I screamed then. Something unrecognizable lifted from my chest. I will never forget that scream, never as long as I live will I forget my own scream. I fell to my knees, bones cracking hard against the rotted wood floor. I barely registered the two officers helping me to my feet and over to the couch.

I just remember the screaming.

I couldn't stop crying.

It was all so unthinking.

More officers poured into the house, trying to be of service, but it was of no use. There was no action they could perform to bring her back or alleviate the absolute worst pain you could possibly imagine.

That pain was permanently etched in that second.

"No!" I kept yelling over and over, folded into myself, unable to stomach the pain in my chest.

The older cop sat beside me, his forearms on his knees. He looked at me, his mouth moving, but I wasn't registering his words.

"Miss Hahn," I finally heard, as if he'd been saying it over and over. "Listen to me." I flinched and his face softened. "Do you have anyone you can contact? Anyone you can stay with?" he asked.

"What?" I whispered.

"Do you have anyone you can contact?"

"Contact?"

"Yes, Miss Hahn, anyone you can stay with?"

"Oh my God!" I yelled. "My sisters! My sisters!"

"Where are they?" he asked.

"Oh my God. Oh my God."

"Miss Hahn, would you like us to contact them for you?"

I shook my head, my hand gripping his shoulder. "I don't know where they are."

"How old are they?" he asked, concern etched in his brow.

"Eight a-and six," I could barely say.

My hands shook as I picked up my phone. *Where are they? Where are they? Mom wrote down where they were on her note. The note I'd just tossed aside.*

I stood once again but lost my balance. I toppled forward, unable to support myself.

The last thing I remember was hitting the wood floor.

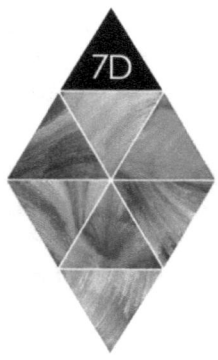

CHAPTER TEN

I sat on the dirty floor of our old, decaying home. I'd woken to paramedics checking me out after I'd fainted and waved them off of me. Officers flitted around me, handing me the pronouncement of death forms, quietly asked me to sign the consent for autopsy forms, and let me know that the coroner would call to let me know when I could arrange to have my mother and Sterling picked up for funeral arrangements.

"How do I even do that?" I asked them.

The older cop patted my shoulder. "Just call a funeral home, sweetheart."

I nodded and they left.

So I sat on that dirty floor. I laid back, unable to move, no wish to move and just let the tears flow and flow and flow. I wondered where the girls were. I wondered how I was going to tell them.

Someone had left the door open, not realizing they were the last to leave, so I stared out onto the porch through the screen door and watched the sun crest the earth, shining light on what I'd done to my mother, bathing me in the most profound guilt I had ever and would ever feel again in my entire life.

I dragged air into my lungs and exhaled, wishing the pain would bend, if even for a moment, leave for even the briefest of seconds just so I could know air again without searing pain.

I watched the sun rise higher and higher until Ansen came. So entrenched in my pain, I could hardly decipher what he was saying, yelling, when he got out of his car. Like a whirlwind, he and Katie sprinted up the front porch steps. Ansen swung the screen door open hard, sliding into the room on his knees, and gathered me up. Katie was bawling, tears and mascara flowing down her face as she met my other side, wrapping me in her arms.

They spoke to me, but I didn't hear them.

"The girls," I whispered. "The girls."

Ansen stood up, pushed through the door, and headed across the street to Alta Mae's house, guessing they were there, I thought. Katie pushed the hair out of my eyes.

"Lily, can you hear me?" she asked. I turned toward her, but my head felt heavy. "We heard what happened, baby," she said, hugging me close. "It's gonna be okay," she lied. "It's gonna be all right."

"No, Katie," I said, finding my voice. "It's not."

Her face contorted as if fighting back a sob but she couldn't help herself and it came out as a near wail. She tucked me into her and got a hold of herself.

"What are we gonna do?" she asked.

"I don't know," I told her the truth.

I heard my sisters before I saw them.

"Oh my God," I said, shaking so hard I could barely stand.

Katie helped me and brought the bottom of my shirt up to wipe my face, to try and look somewhat together.

"How is this happening?" I whispered to no one.

Ansen held both girls' hands and tears fell so quick and so hard, I couldn't see well.

I blinked them away as Ansen brought them in.

"What's going on?" Eloise asked, already nervous. I felt sick.

"Come sit down, my love." I could barely speak.

"Lily," she gritted out, breathing deep, "why are you crying? Are you okay?"

"Lily, are you sick?" Callie asked.

Ansen sat down on the sofa and both girls sat on each side of him.

I sat on the coffee table across from them.

"I have something to tell you," I began, and Ansen instinctively brought them tight against him as if he could protect them from the inevitable.

***

The girls were devastated. I refuse to write about it. Hearing them cry for their mommy over and over again is probably the worst thing I've ever experienced.

It's all my fault, I kept thinking.

We, all five of us, sat on the couch staring at a random television show no one was watching. The girls had cried themselves to sleep and leaned against Ansen and me.

I turned to my oldest friend. "What should I do?" I asked him.

Katie watched us both, her eyes red and swollen; her hand gripped the shoulder of Ansen's shirt. As if just touching him kept her from floating away; I wondered what that felt like. *Having someone to lean on must be such a tremendous comfort.*

"I don't know what you should do, Lily."

"How am I going to feed them?" I asked.

Ansen breathed deep. "You're going to figure it out, Lily, like you always do. You're going to figure it out."

Tears sprang forth. "I have no money, Ansen."

"D-do you own this house?" he asked.

"Yeah, I mean, it was in Sterling's name, but it's paid off. It's not worth much."

"So you just take it one day at a time then," he said.

"How? How do I even do that?"

"Lily, stop, you're just in shock. You'll take it one day at a time," Katie encouraged.

"I don't think I have it in me to do that," I admitted out loud, staring at the sun pouring through the blurry glass of our ancient windows.

"Yes, you do," Ansen said.

But he didn't know, did he? How could he? *I* certainly didn't.

I did know I needed to see what burying my mom would cost, though, so I could come up with the funds somehow, get an idea of how much I needed. I picked up my phone and searched for funeral homes in Smithfield. Not knowing what to do, I chose the first one that popped up on the list and clicked their website, searching for their number. I called and a woman's soft voice answered.

"Legacy," she practically whispered, setting my nerves on edge.

"Hi," I greeted, unsure how to speak, to be honest. "I, uh, I need to bury my mom and stepfather."

"I'm so sorry for your loss," she began, but it felt rehearsed. It made me feel ill. "We recommend coming in for a consultation. We'll take very good care of you," she offered quickly when I didn't answer right away.

"Uh, I don't have much money. I was calling to see what my cheapest options are."

"I understand," she said, "of course. Our cheapest options start around five thousand."

Two tears slipped down my face. "Each?"

"Yes, ma'am."

I will never be able to come up with that, I thought.

"I see."

"Would you like to set up an appointment?" she asked.

"No, uh, I'll never be able to afford that. Is that standard?" I asked.

"That's very reasonable, yes, ma'am."

"I see," I said, overwhelmed.

"And you don't do anything cheaper than that?" I asked, feeling ashamed.

There was a pause. "No, ma'am."

"So what do people do when they can't afford to bury their family?"

She lowered her voice. "Many people look into cremation. If you work directly with the crematory, you can work out a more affordable option, usually around a thousand dollars."

Two more tears fell. "Okay, thank you so much," I told her.

"You're welcome," she said, her voice softer, kinder. "Good luck to you and, again, I'm so sorry," she told me, but that time I thought she meant it.

"Thank you," I choked out and hung up the phone.

"How much?" Ansen asked.

"She said I could work with a crematory directly and that it would be about a thousand dollars."

"But that doesn't include burial or services or anything?" Katie asked.

I shook my head, afraid if I spoke, I'd break down completely.

"I see," Katie said, unable to offer more.

"I can't afford any of that," I told them.

"My great-uncle, when my great-aunt died, couldn't afford to bury her and the county arranged something. It was a state-run cemetery, I think," Ansen said.

I nodded, wondering what in the world I was going to do.

Someone knocked on the front door, so I carefully wedged out from underneath a sleeping

Callie and cracked open the door.

Trace.

I stepped out onto the porch and closed the door.

"It's a bad time, Trace," I whispered.

"Listen," he said, running a hand through his hair, "about the pictures."

"Trace, that is so far off my radar right now. I don't want to talk about this."

"Listen, Lily, I didn't really know what I was doing or whatever—" he tried to appease.

"Trace," I said, fighting tears, "I'm barely holding it together. My mom a-and Sterling died last night and I'm trying to figure out how I'm going to keep my sisters alive and myself from falling off the deep end. I'll talk to you later."

All the color drained from his face. "Oh, shit. I'm sorry. I'll, uh, yeah, I'll catch you later then."

He bounded off the porch and I turned back toward the door, sneaking back inside.

"Who was that?" Katie asked.

"Trace," I answered and sat back down, placing a still-sleeping Callie back on my lap.

"Asshole," she whispered. "What did he want?"

"Wanted to talk about the pictures. D-did you hear about them?" I asked her. She nodded once. "I sent him away."

She nodded her head again. I laid my own on the back of the couch.

"Go to sleep," she said. "Ansen and I will be here. We'll take care of you guys."

I faced her and two tears slipped down my cheeks. "Thank you," I whispered.

***

I woke to Ansen tapping my shoulder. He held my phone toward me. "It's the coroner," he offered.

He took Callie off my lap and laid her to the side. I stood, my bones literally cracking; my muscles felt heavy and sore. I took the phone and went to the front porch again. It'd grown dark, which represented something different but just as awful as the light had proved.

"Hello?" I asked, my voice deep from crying.

"Yes, is this Lily Hahn?" a woman's voice asked.

"Yes, ma'am," I answered, already crying.

"I'm Dr. Sonia, the coroner for Smithfield," she introduced herself. Her voice was soft and quiet. "I've completed the autopsies and just need you to come confirm identity."

My heart stopped. "What? Why?" I asked her.

"It's procedure, Miss Hahn. I'm so sorry."

"Let me have the address?" I asked.

She told me where I needed to go and I hung up. Katie came outside to check on me and I reached my hand out to her.

"What do we need to do?" she asked.

"I have to identify my mama, Katie."

Katie started crying and she brought me close, hugged me tight.

"She's dead because of me," I sobbed.

Katie shook her head against my neck. "Stop it, Lily. Stop it."

"It's my fault," I insisted.

"Stop," she said. "I refuse to listen to that. Come on," she continued, opening the front door so I followed her inside.

"I'm taking Lily into Smithfield," Katie said.

"Why?" Ansen whispered when Eloise stirred.

"She has to identify them," she explained.

"Maybe I should go?" Ansen asked.

"No," I was quick to say. "If the girls wake up, I'd rather you be here since they've known you forever."

"Of course," he said.

He hugged me and kissed Katie and we headed toward Ansen's car. Katie drove me. It was a silent drive. Deafeningly silent. I listened to the guilt call out to me, pushing me closer and closer to insanity. It was cruel and incessant.

"I might break, Katie. Will you be there with me?"

"Right by your side. I won't leave you."

"Thank you," I told her as we headed toward our exit in Smithfield.

The morgue was cold and sterile and absolutely horrifying. They had me identify Sterling first. He looked like himself but not; it was hard to explain. I confirmed that Sterling was who he was and I felt nothing for him. He meant nothing to me in that moment, absolutely nothing. I didn't know if that made me a bad person, but it was as natural a response as it could have possibly been.

Dr. Sonia silently walked to the back of the room and gestured to another body lying on a table. I gripped Katie's arm as we followed her over. When we reached the body, draped with a clean, crisp white sheet, I nearly vomited. I could follow the outline of my poor mama's face, could see the lines of her worn shoulders. Those shoulders cared for me, cared for my sisters, endured Sterling. They carried the weight of the world.

"Are you ready?" Dr. Sonia asked softly.

"Yes, ma'am," I lied.

As if in slow motion, she tipped the top of the sheet back. I glimpsed my mom's hair, dark like my natural color, but shorter. When her face was exposed, my breaths came so fast and hard; I felt like I would faint again. Katie wrapped her arm around me tight.

"Is this Cathleen Byrnes?" the doctor asked.

"Yes," I whispered.

She covered my mom's face instantly and the nausea doubled. I took deep, short breaths through my nose and Katie steered me toward the door and into the small entry room of the morgue.

"What funeral home will you be going with?" Doctor Sonia asked.

"I-I can't afford to have someone bury her or Sterling," I admitted.

Dr. Sonia nodded as if she'd heard it before. "I understand. Are Sterling or your mother ex-military?" she asked, pulling out forms from a filing cabinet.

"Sterling is but Mama is not."

The coroner nodded once more and reached for another set of papers from another cabinet.

"Take these home," she said, her voice quiet. "Fill these out," she said, pointing to one set, "and take them to the courthouse. The address is here," she said, tapping the top of one of the papers. "These here," she said, pointing to the next set, "are for past military. The VA usually handles these cases. Fill these out and mail them to the address on the form. They'll take care of the rest."

"I see," I said, my stomach sinking, "thank you."

"Of course," she offered, curtly but kindly.

Katie and I tumbled out of the morgue and rode the elevators up to street level, practically sprinting toward Ansen's car.

"Get me out of here," I begged her.

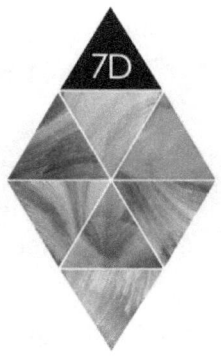

CHAPTER ELEVEN

I didn't waste time. I did everything the coroner instructed me to do. I mailed off Sterling's stuff and visited the county of Smithfield's Department of Health and Human Services.

That night, I'd given Ansen half my graduation money so he could go to the store and buy instant ramen and milk and cereal and anything cheap but filling he could find.

"I saw Salinger there," he said when he came back.

The mere mention of his name sent a pang through my chest and stomach.

"You didn't say anything to him, did you?"

Ansen looked ill. "Was I not supposed to?"

"I guess it doesn't matter," I said.

"He was really worried about you," he said.

"Wanted to know if he could come by."

"What did you say?" I asked, petrified of his answer.

"I said it was probably not a good time."

I sighed in relief. "Good," I replied.

"What happened?" Katie asked. "When we dropped you off?"

"I have no chance with him anymore," I told her.

"Why?" she asked.

"I'm too dysfunctional for someone like him."

"We all are," she said.

We stared at the girls asleep on the couch. They'd clung to me the entire day.

"How does one become functional?" I asked them.

"You're asking the wrong person, baby girl," Katie answered.

I couldn't sleep, so I stared at the stars the entire night, both girls beside me.

The next morning, Ansen and Katie went home to clean up, get a change of clothes, and promised to be back later. Since the girls were still asleep, I slipped away for a moment to take a shower myself. I turned the water on and waited for it to get hot. The tub creaked when I stepped inside it, threatening to break through the bottom, I thought. I could see the strings of the fiberglass peeking through, so it was just a matter of time, I knew it.

I wet my hair and peered down at the few soaps and bottles we had. My mom's bottle of Suave stared back at me. I picked it up and cracked open the lid, smelling its contents.

"Oh my God," I whispered. "I killed her. I killed Mama."

I bawled until the water turned cold, stayed beneath its torturous spray because I felt I deserved it. I only stopped because I heard someone knock on the door. Thinking it was Ansen and Katie, I turned the water off and hastily dressed, my hair still dripping down my neck.

The girls were up, kneeling on the sofa and checking for who it was out the window.

"Who?" I asked them.

"I don't know them," Eloise offered, making my heart race.

"Who in the world?" I asked no one.

I opened the door to a stocky woman and a police officer. "Can I help you?" I asked her.

"Miss Hahn, may I come in?"

"I'm sorry, I wasn't expecting anyone. Are you with the county? Is this about the burial?"

"No, ma'am. I'm with Child Protective Services."

My gut sank to the floor. "Wait, *what*?"

"CPS, ma'am," she offered again.

"*Why*?"

"There's been a complaint. May I come in?"

"No," I told her. "You may not."

She looked up at the cop and he looked back at her. "Ma'am," the cop offered sternly, "we can do this the easy way or we can do this the hard way."

"The hard way," I demanded, so sick of being blindsided; I was ready for a fight. "Where's your warrant?"

The woman sighed, as if she'd been expecting it, as if she was above it all. She pulled a piece of paper from her bag and held it up for me.

"What do you want?" I asked, not budging from my spot, blocking their entrance.

"Let us in, please, Miss Hahn," the cop said, stepping forward.

Going against every fiber of my being, I stepped to the side and let them walk in. The woman glanced around her surroundings then brought pen to paper.

"What is your name?" I asked her.

She looked pissed that I'd even asked but offered it anyway. "My name is Faye Briar."

I stole a look at the girls. "Eloise, Callie," I began, "step into your room for me for a second?"

They obeyed me, holding hands as they went. A

knock came at the screen door, as I'd left the front door open, hoping they would leave soon. There was another woman there, this time in scrubs.

"This is a nurse for the county, Miss Hahn."

"Wh-why?" I asked, my voice cracking.

Oh my God, whatever they'd laced that joint with is still in my system.

"Someone has called into CPS claiming your sisters were in danger."

"Bull. No one called."

The Faye woman rolled her eyes. "I've come to understand that your mother and father are recently deceased?" she asked.

"Very recently," I said. "We're still in shock."

"I'm sorry for your loss," she offered dryly. "You are the only family of the girls?" she asked.

"Yes."

"Your parents didn't have any extended family?" she asked again.

"Sterling is not my father."

"Excuse me?" she asked, flipping through paperwork.

"He's my stepfather and no, we have no other family. They're all deceased."

"I see," she said, clearing her throat and looking up from her papers at me.

"Excuse me, but I'm a little confused. How are my

121

sisters in danger?" I hedged.

"We've gotten word that living conditions were unsuitable and that you were addicted to a controlled substance."

I balked at her. "I am not. Who made the accusation?"

"I'm not at liberty to say," she offered, shifting her briefcase to the other hand. "We're here to assess the situation and submit a drug test."

"I refuse," I told them, rocking back and forth on my heels. My arms were crossed, gripping my shirt, damp from my wet hair.

Faye looked me up and down then made a notation on her pad. "That's fine," she explained, and my heart slowed down. "Just know that until you submit a drug test, the girls will be placed in a home."

"Oh my God!" I cried, my hands going to my head. "You can't do that. Our mom just died. You can't do that!"

"Miss Hahn, please calm down."

The nurse stared at our decrepit ceiling and avoided eye contact. The cop laid a hand on his gun.

"Please don't do this to us. Please. They'll be scarred for life as it is. Please don't do this," I said, bringing my palms out.

The Faye woman nodded at the cop and started

toward my sisters' room.

"No," I said, and he stopped. "You don't understand." I wiped tears away, trying to gain some composure. "I was at a party. I admit I was smoking marijuana. I admit it. That's all I do. I don't do anything harder but when I smoked it, I realized too late that someone had laced it with something." Faye looked uninterested, but she was feverishly scribbling across her pad of paper. "I think they were trying to or maybe they did, I don't know, rape me or something." The cop looked down at me, his eyes narrowed at me. "You gotta believe me." All three adults sat there, their body language rigid and all business. "Oh my God, I'll take the test. I'll take it just so I can see what they drugged me with. I have witnesses that will corroborate my story."

The nurse walked to my mom's kitchen table, the same one we used to sit together and draw with crayons on, and set down a big plastic folding case. She popped it open and retrieved an alcohol swab, needle, test tubes, a pair of scissors, and a small container with a taped label.

"Miss Hahn—" she began.

"If I do this, are you still taking the girls?" I asked the Faye woman.

If you tell the truth, everything will work out.

"Let's just take the test," she hedged.

"You can't take them. You don't know what it will do to them."

I sat down and swiped my face across my sleeve. "First, Faye and I will witness a urine test and after, I'll take a blood test and a sample of your hair," she explained methodically.

"Whatever, I don't care. I just need to know what it was so I can press charges against Trace and clear this whole thing up."

The nurse and Faye handed me a cup and followed me toward the restroom. I could hear the girls whispering in their room, and I felt sick to my stomach. With shaking hands, I unscrewed the lid to the urine cup, followed her instructions, and peed inside it, laying it to the side. While I wiped and put my pants back on, not even caring how humiliating it all was, she put on a pair of gloves, screwed the top back on and walked off. I washed my hands and met her back at the table while Faye watched.

I sat down in one of our rickety chairs and offered my arm, not even bothering to hide my tears any longer. She swabbed my arm and stuck me with a needle, took three test tubes' worth of samples, and placed them in a tight storage container. She placed a cotton ball and a band-aid over the site and instructed me to stand up and turn around, to lift my hair, so she could obtain a hair sample. I did exactly what she asked then watched as she placed the sample into a plastic envelope.

When she was done, and without another word, she took a disposable pipette, unscrewed the lid to my urine sample and stuck ten to fifteen test strips through, laying them on a plastic sheet she'd laid out. She put the lid back on and we all stood in absolute silence as she peered over the strips.

"Marijuana," she dryly spit out and Faye aggressively scribbled. "Ketamine," the nurse added as if in slow motion, like a punch to the gut and there was Faye with her evil pen once more.

"Can I file a police report?" I asked the cop.

He snorted and rolled his eyes. I swallowed hard. "You don't believe me."

"You can file a police report at your local station," he told me and looked away.

"I know how it looks, but that is what actually happened to me," I explained, but it fell on deaf ears.

Faye began reading from a document in her stack of papers that I know was supposed to be for my benefit, but I didn't hear a word she'd said because the cop had started to walk down the hall. I heard him instruct the girls to gather some things, that if they had a bag, they could put their belongings in them, but if they didn't, he could get a few trash bags.

"Please think about what you're doing!" I yelled at the Faye woman.

"Miss Hahn," she gritted, "you have tested positive for a controlled substance and the living conditions here are deplorable."

"I can change that!" I bargained. "I can change all of this. I know I can. Whatever you require, I can do it!"

She didn't respond. Didn't say anything.

The nurse had gathered her things and had walked out of the house toward her vehicle already. Another police officer appeared, throwing the screen door open, and stepped inside.

"You're going to scare them!" I said. "You can't imagine what they've been going through. Don't do this. Don't do this!"

"Please calm down. We're trying to do what's best for them," Faye sputtered out and walked toward their room.

I buried a fist into the thin wall of my parents' old house. It began to rain heavy and sudden on our shoddy tin roof, the sound hollow and horrible in my ears. I fell to my knees in front of the hall wall. My palms met crumbling wallpaper as their door opened, so I stood. They each held the hand of Faye Briar, a perfect stranger.

"Lily?" Eloise asked quietly as she passed me. My

fingers grazed her hair as the woman led them toward the front door. Both girls tugged their hands back, visibly panicking, and reached for me.

"Lily!" Callie screamed, making me want to vomit.

"Lily, help us!" Eloise begged, tears streaming down her face.

I stormed forward, reaching out for them but the two officers reached for my shoulders, holding me back. An unholy noise escaped my lips when the door shut behind them and my knees met floor once again. I bellowed at the ground, slamming my fists. "What have I done? What have I done?" I asked no one.

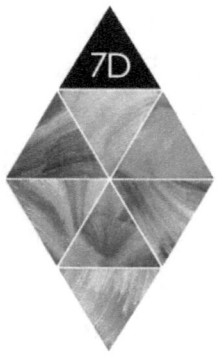

CHAPTER TWELVE

Katie and Ansen showed up an hour later after I called them. When I saw them, I busted through the screen door, popping it off its hinges, and ran to Katie's arms. She met me with open arms and held me. Ansen guided us inside.

"What happened?" he asked, throwing his keys on the coffee table.

"They took them, Ansen." I sat on the edge of the sofa and wrapped my arms around my stomach. "I feel like my world is ending," I confessed.

"Tell me exactly how it happened," he demanded, his face red.

I relayed each moment to him and he shook his head.

"Why would you willingly take the drug tests, Lily?"

"Because I told them I was drugged. I wasn't afraid of it. It was the truth."

He brought his hands to his face and dragged them down in frustration. "Lily, you should have waited until the drugs were out of your system."

"They said they were going to take them if I didn't submit a test!"

"But they took them anyway, didn't they!" he yelled back.

Tears streamed down my face. "It didn't matter if it was today or next week or weeks from now. They sampled my hair."

"Yes, but we could have hired an attorney by then," he said. "We could have arranged for something else. Reported that fucking asshole Trace!"

I stood. "Oh my God, that's who reported me," I said, connecting the dots. "It was Trace! He knew he was about to get turned in, knew it would happen. He's trying to make it look like it was all me."

Katie rocked back and forth, side to side. "Would Trace do that?" she asked. She turned toward our back door and peered over the fence into Trace's yard.

"He would," Ansen said. In the blink of an eye, Ansen threw open the sliding door, scaled the back porch deck, and started barreling his way through our knee-high grass toward Trace's.

Katie and I screamed at the top of our lungs.

"No!" Katie yelled. "Ansen!" she desperately screamed.

I ran through and caught up to him, Katie right behind me. We yanked on his sleeve and shoulder together, but he was bigger than us. Katie raced in front of him and held him with her palms, tears streaming down her face.

"Ansen," she breathed and he stared at her. "Not like this. Please, let's just go back inside. We'll go to the police station and file a report."

Ansen's eyes appeared glassy. "I won't do anything," he gritted.

Katie shook her head at him. "Yes, you will. Let's do this the right way. Let's figure this out in such a way that no one else gets hurt worse than they already are."

Ansen pointed at me. "More hurt than that?" he asked her, his chest dragging in large gulps of air.

"Hard to imagine," Katie admitted, swallowing a sob, "but if you caught a charge, it would make Lily's case that much less convincing, don't you think?"

With that, Ansen visibly calmed. She led him back inside and I followed, the adrenaline leaving my body quick and painfully.

"Let's go," Ansen said.

I grabbed my bag, a million thoughts racing through my mind, and we piled into Ansen's car. The police station wasn't very big or busy. My heart raced as I headed inside. There was a cop sitting behind a sliding glass window so I stood in front of it. He looked at me but didn't acknowledge me right away, busy writing something down. When he was done, he set his pen down, and slid the window back.

"Yes? Can I help you?"

"Yes, I'd like to file a police report."

"What's this about?" he asked.

"Three days ago I was drugged at a party. I don't know what happened after I passed out, but I have photos others took where my clothes have been removed."

The guy nodded his head. "Okay, let's have you come across here," he said, pointing to a door with an automatic locking mechanism.

"I'll be back," I told Ansen and Katie who sat in the lobby.

"We'll be right here," Katie assured me.

I heard a buzz, indicating the door was unlocked so I opened the door and walked through.

"Just this way," he said, pointing toward a section of cubicles. "Take a seat here," he said, gesturing to a plastic chair inside one of the cubicles. "A detective will be with you shortly."

"Thank you," I said, taking a seat. My knee bounced up and down quickly. The nerves, the anxiety, the sheer awfulness that had been my last few days taking residence in that obsessive bounce.

Five minutes later a man sat down across from me. "Detective Johnston," he said, sliding in his chair. He reached for a pen and pad and faced me. "I understand you'd like to file a report?"

"Yes, sir," I told him.

"What happened?" he asked, not yet making eye contact.

"I was at a party three days ago. While I was there, I was offered a blunt, but it was laced with ketamine. I didn't know this and when I passed out, I believe the boys there did something to me."

The detective finally looked at me, then through me. "You willingly smoked the blunt, though?"

"Yes."

"*Well*," he offered, not finishing the thought.

"Well, what?"

"Well, I mean, how do you know it was even laced with ketamine? You could have just passed out on your own."

"First, I know because I was tested and it was positive for ketamine. Second, I was under the impression it was only marijuana."

"But you willingly took it."

"It doesn't matter if I did or not, Detective, they took advantage of me."

He shook his head. "But wouldn't you agree that since you admit to willingly taking the blunt, that you also ran the risk of someone taking advantage?"

My blood ran cold. "Sir, are you saying that because I took a hit of a blunt, which I was led to believe was only marijuana, that it's my fault boys undressed me, possibly worse?"

"You admit to breaking the law. If I were you, I'd chalk this up as a life lesson and let it go."

"Is this a joke?" I asked him.

He looked at me sternly, set his pen and pad down, and scooted his chair up really close, intimidatingly close.

"How do you know these boys even did anything?" he asked.

"I don't know for sure. I just know that I have pictures of them after they've undressed me, without my consent, and them doing pretty gross things to me."

"Let me see these photos," he said.

I took my phone out and showed him the forwarded images. He scrolled through them quickly and handed the phone back.

"I'll admit they shouldn't have done that," he said, "but this just looks like a bunch of boys being stupid. There's no proof they did anything worse than this."

I pointed to a picture of my naked breasts being held by a laughing Trace.

"Is this not enough to press charges?" I asked.

"Well," he hedged, leaning back. "Listen," he began, picking up his pen and tapping it on his pad, avoiding eye contact again. "I think it would be best if you just brush this off as youthful indiscretions and maybe next time, when a boy offers you a blunt, you control yourself and not take a hit from it."

I stamped down the rage I felt. "Regardless," I told him, "I want you to take my statement."

"Now, now, *listen*," he said, getting close again. "What's your name?" he asked. He knew my name. All the men there knew my name. They'd all pulled Sterling off me at least once.

"Lily." I played along.

"Lily, if you drag this out like this, you'll be in trouble yourself. Do you really want that? A drug charge?" he asked.

"Of course not."

"Well, you see, if we take the statement, that's what it will come down to, do you understand?"

"Yes."

"And you still want to do that, do you? You'd ruin these boys' lives because of something you willingly took? I mean," he explained, barking out a short laugh, "I can't tell you how many times boys just do stuff because they think it's funny, and I think that's what's going on here, okay? Let's not make this worse than it already is."

"Sir, are you going to take my statement or not?" I asked him.

His face was growing more and more red by the second. "Did you not hear what I said?"

"I heard it."

"And you still want to proceed forward?"

"Yes," I insisted.

"Boy, you are a handful, you know that? Never in my life," he blustered.

He made a big show of grabbing a pen and the statement form. He handed it to me and I took it.

"You're creating more problems for yourself," he continued, but I didn't hear him.

Seventy-two hours prior, I would have been tired enough to let him influence me, but I didn't have time for that poor excuse of a man. It wasn't even about me getting justice, though that was important; it was mostly about clearing my name so I could get my sisters back. It was the least I could do for my mom.

He took the statement and I asked for a copy. He nearly bit my head off when I asked, but I didn't flinch. I was done being intimidated.

I was done with men like him.

What this detective didn't realize was that I knew exactly what he was all about. I'd seen his kind, grew up with his kind, been *beaten* by his kind. I knew blustering and the bully coercer. I saw him for what he really was. He didn't realize it, but I saw through him.

So he took my statement. He gave me my copy. I walked out of there with my head held high but my stomach sunk low, straight to the clinic to get myself checked out.

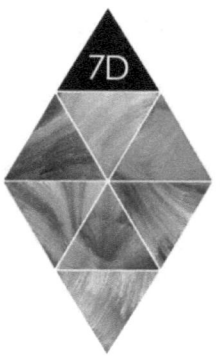

CHAPTER THIRTEEN

The health clinic I visited right after filing my statement found no evidence of rape, much to my relief. It didn't excuse the stupid, disgusting, violating things they'd done to me, that they'd documented in the photos, but it did help ease my mind a very little. I got tested for STDs regardless, though, as it was part of their procedure.

I found a legal aid in Smithfield and made an appointment the next day. The woman assigned to my case was gentle and kind, overwhelmingly helpful, but she didn't sugarcoat things for me. I told her my predicament; she laid out a course of action and I promised to follow it faithfully.

By the time I'd left that afternoon, I had her promise that she would petition the courts on my behalf for visitation and custody, and I promised I would have a job soon and start improving the house so it was suitable for the girls to come back to. She also arranged for me to take voluntary drug tests once a week. I agreed immediately.

On my long drive back, I passed Granger's. I pulled over and vomited on the side of the road, overwhelmed by it all.

"No, I don't have time to mourn right now," I told myself. "Later," I promised, choking back tears.

I hadn't heard from the county yet concerning my mother's cremation and made a mental note to check with them as soon as I had an opportunity. Sterling's local veteran's chapter had already rang me up and left a message for me with the promise they'd take care of everything, but I didn't call them back. I didn't care.

I went home, straight for the shower, and readied myself.

Bottle Co. Market was busy for a Thursday night. I slowly perused the lot for a free space. I found one in the back and hopped out, taking a deep breath to steady my nerves. I started walking but startled short when I caught a glimpse of Salinger's Jeep. I shook my head and kept walking.

Inside, the entire front of the store stopped still and stared at me. *They know*. Their stares were mixed with pity and sadness. One of Mom's friends saw me and burst out crying. She came up to me and hugged me hard.

"I'm so sorry," she said.

I nodded, fighting back tears, and thanked her. I left her where she stood. I couldn't do that right then. I was in a hurry. I needed to get my sisters back.

I knocked on the door of a closed room labeled "Manager" at the front left corner of the store.

It opened and the manager, Casey Goodwin, who was just a couple years older than I was, came out.

"Hey, Lily," he greeted with a small smile.

"Hey, Casey," I began, but he cut me off.

"I was sorry to hear about your mama," he offered. *No mention of Sterling.*

I nodded. "Thank you. Listen," I began, unable to give that any further thought or I'd crumble into a pile on the floor, "I need a job, Casey. Anything. I'll take anything."

Casey nodded in turn and patted my upper arm. "Of course, of course. I have night crew open, if you're up to it? Hours kind of suck, though."

"I don't care," I told him. "I'll take anything," I answered, trying not to think on the fact that I'd be working side by side with Salinger.

"Okay then," he said softly. "Come on in here and we'll fill out some simple paperwork."

I followed him into his small office and the door closed behind us. He gestured toward a chair and I sat.

"When would you like to start?" he asked.

"As soon as you'll let me," I told him, meaning it. Any movement felt like progress and a wonderful distraction.

"Well, I've got a girl who called in sick tonight, but if that's—"

"I'll do it. What time?"

"Shift starts in an hour."

"Done," I agreed, eager.

"Fine, finish this up, leave it on my desk, and go

home. Get some clothes on that you don't mind getting a little dirty."

"Sure, of course," I said and feverishly filled out the form.

It felt like my hundredth form that week and I felt a little ill. I breathed deep.

"Lily," he said, staring at me. "If you need some time, I'll hold the position for you."

I brought my eyes to his. "No, Casey, this is perfect, thank you."

"If you change your mind, just let me know."

"Thank you," I told him as he left his office.

When I was done with the paperwork, I laid it across his desk and hauled to the parking lot to get my car so I could go change.

"Done," I said, checking off the first invisible box of the list inside my head.

I returned that night in jeans, a T-shirt, a pair of Converse, and my hair in a ponytail, ready for work. I met Casey in the front.

He looked at me. "That was quick."

I nodded once. "What do you want me to do?" I asked.

"Come here," he said, leading me to the back of the store, to shipping and receiving as he called it.

There was one of those old-fashioned time clocks. He showed me a card he'd made with my name on it and I time stamped it.

"There you go, girl," he said. "I'll have one of my guys teach you the ropes this week."

"Cool," I told him.

Not Salinger. Not Salinger. Not Salinger.

"Just follow me," he said.

We walked to the back right of the store and came upon all the boys from the other night, the ones who had witnessed my meltdown with Salinger. My face flamed red, but I stood resolute.

That's when I saw him. Salinger. He was bent over, breaking down boxes, and stood when he saw Casey and me approach. My heart beat harder in my chest than I'd ever felt it. A mixture of sorrow, pain, and humiliation flooded my entire body and I felt the urge to bolt, then the urge to run to Salinger, which made no sense to me.

He looked at me, his face blank.

"Salinger, this is Lily. She'll be working the night shift with us. Show her the ropes?" Casey asked him, not realizing we already knew the other.

Salinger nodded once. All the other boys stood dumbstruck, staring at us.

"Chop, chop, gentlemen!" Casey yelled, which broke their trance and they started moving again, breaking things down and loading shelves.

Salinger came to me as Casey turned for the front of the store.

"Hey," he greeted.

"Hey," I spoke, but it was soft and quiet.

"I was sorry to hear—" he began, but I stopped him short.

"Thanks. If it's okay with you, I don't want to talk about it. Can't, really. I just want to do the job."

Something passed across his face then, but I didn't know how to interpret it. He nodded his reply and turned back to the shelves. "Follow me."

He showed me the most efficient way to stock the shelves and how to face the product. I picked it up quickly, only needing a few pointers here and there, but kept up with him for the most part. The work was tedious, but I was grateful for it. Grateful for the distraction, for the means to fix my life, for the way I could bring my sisters back home.

I took a deep breath for the hundredth time that day.

We worked our way down the store, my body tired beyond belief, and arrived at the frozen section.

"This one kind of sucks," Salinger offered.

"That's okay," I replied.

But as I started unloading boxes of frozen pizza, ice stuck to my hands, and within an hour they were freezing cold, numb, and my skin turned red. I shook them out every few seconds, but it didn't help. Salinger watched me then went to the back.

"Come on, Lily," I whispered to myself.

A pair of thin leather gloves appeared in front of my face. I looked up and saw Salinger holding them.

"They help," he explained.

"Thank you."

When we were done, we broke down all the boxes and laid them on a cart, ready to recycle. All the other boys made their way to the back, but Salinger held me back. I turned to see Casey making his way toward us.

"How'd she do?" he asked Salinger.

"Really well. She kept up with us the entire time," he answered.

Casey looked shocked. "That's amazing, Lily. Not even full-grown men can keep up with the crew, especially their first night."

"Thank you," I said, my chest feeling tight for some reason.

"The better question, though, is how you feel about it? Think you want to do this every night?"

"Yes," I answered, too tired to feign optimism.

"Good," he said with a nod.

"Get home. Get some rest. See you here tomorrow at nine."

He held his hand out for me and I shook it.

"We've got to clock out," Salinger said when Casey walked away.

"Okay," I said and followed him to the back.

I noticed all the guys stood in the thin light of the morning sun, smoking cigarettes and hanging out.

"We always go to breakfast together," Salinger said, punching his card.

"Cool," I said.

"Wanna come?" he asked.

"No, thank you," I told him. I needed every dime I had.

He nodded. "See you tomorrow, Lily."

"See you," I responded and watched him walk away.

Keep it together, Lily.

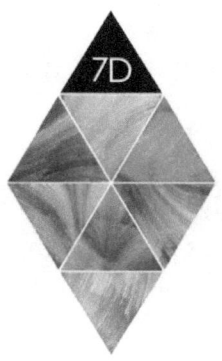

CHAPTER FOURTEEN

I worked the night shift every night for the next seven nights. I grew accustomed to sleeping during the day. I never heard from Legal Aid. When I called the county about my mother, they had no news for me. They both promised me they'd have more information the following week.

After my shift on the eighth night, they handed me a paycheck for the previous week. While I walked to my car, I ripped it open.

Two hundred sixty-three dollars and some change.

I mentally calculated what I'd need to eat the cheapest way I possibly could, what I'd need for gas, and thought about how I could make the most impact on the house to make it suitable to bring the girls back again. When I reached my Scout, I leaned across the hood, feeling the metal cooled by the night air, and rested my forehead on its surface as I tried to gather enough mental courage to put one more foot in front of the other.

I was hanging by a thread. A very thin thread.

Keep it together, Lily.

"Lily," I heard to my left.

I opened my eyes to see Salinger standing there.

"Hello, Salinger," I said, not bothering to stand back up.

"Lily, you're struggling."

I took a deep breath and met his eyes. "I'm fine," I told him.

"You're not sleeping or eating. It's obvious."

I summoned enough strength to stand back up. "You wanna know what pain like that does for someone who deserves it?" I asked him.

He flinched. "Nobody deserves that."

"I do," I told him.

He breathed deeply through his nose. "Lily, that's really unhealthy."

I laughed and dug for my keys out of my bag. "I killed my mom."

"She died in a car accident," he stated.

"That night," I confessed, "she called me. We fought a little back and forth. She told me to come pick her up because their car had broken down. I was pissed about what Trace had done and mad at life in general. I smoked a little and passed out on the couch, too idle in my own pathetic world to think past its borders. I woke to the cops banging on my door." I stuck the keys in the door handle and turned them. The door creaked as I pulled it open and I rested my hand at its top. "I made a conscious

144

decision not to pick her up, too lazy, too pissed, too selfish to obey her simple request after she'd worked her fingers to the bone for who knows how many hours that day while her piece-of-shit husband gambled away everything she'd probably earned." I watched Salinger swallow. "I took my sisters' mother and father away, and I've gotta do something about it."

I got in my car and closed the door; my hand shook as I tried to fit the key in the ignition. I looked up and saw Salinger staring at me, his chest rising and falling with each breath. Slow in his movements, his left hand fell on the hood. He rounded the front of the car; his hand slid across the metal and stopped at my door. I watched his long fingers wrap around the handle and open her up.

"Scoot over," he said, so I did. He slid in the driver's seat and held out his hand. "Keys."

I gave them to him, too tired to argue, and I trusted him. He drove us toward Smithfield, just outside Bottle County to one of the older apartment complexes there but they were still decent, clean, and well maintained. He pulled into a space near a bottom corner apartment at the front of the complex and parked my car.

"Come on," he said, stepping out, and offered his hand to me.

I took it. When my skin touched his, it felt electric, which made me feel incredibly guilty. I was relieved when he dropped it. I rubbed the skin of my hand across the thigh of my jeans so the feeling would leave, but it never did. My arm still tingled. That tingle wound up the skin there and pooled in my belly.

I followed him to that bottom corner apartment. He held the door open for me and I walked in. It was dark, so he leaned across me to flip the lights on. The crack of the light was overwhelming since the sun hadn't yet risen. His apartment smelled clean and looked it as well. There were shelves and shelves of books, several guitars hung on the walls, and chessboards *everywhere.*

"Have a seat," he offered and gestured to a leather couch sat in front of a decent television.

His simple apartment wasn't huge, but it was like a completely different world compared to my own house. I felt a sudden awareness of myself standing in his apartment.

"Why did you bring me here?" I asked him.

He went through to his kitchen, which was open to the living and dining rooms, and opened his fridge. I heard the hum of the motor it was so quiet in his house.

"Are you thirsty?" he asked.

"Yes," I barely spoke.

He brought me a bottle of water and sat on the arm of a chair next to the sofa I'd taken the liberty to sit on. He unscrewed his lid and took a swig. I did the same.

"You're obviously not sleeping and you're on the verge of breaking, I can tell."

I didn't argue with him.

"I want you to forget," he began. I opened my mouth to tell him that was impossible, but he stopped me. "Not everything. Just a change of scenery, a temporary escape. You can shower here.

I'll make you something to eat. You can have my bed and I'll take the couch."

"I don't know if I can do that," I said, my eyes burning. "I can't impose on you like that."

"It's not an imposition," he said.

He stood, went to a room off the living space, and returned with what looked like one of his T-shirts, a pair of shorts, and a pair of socks.

"I've got everything you'll need in there," he said, pointing to a shower off a bedroom, *his* bedroom, I assumed. "When you're done, come out, I'll have something to eat for you."

"Are you sure?" I asked.

"Very sure," he answered. His expression was kind but gave nothing else away.

I took a shower, washed away the night's work, breathed in the heat of the water, and let it clean out my congested lungs. Since losing my mom, watching my sisters get torn away from me, and the new job, my body was stiff, the muscles rigid every second of my days and even my nights. *I don't think I'll ever know carefree again, and it's just what I deserve.*

I put on Salinger's clothes, though I was swimming in them, and padded back into his living room.

He stopped when he heard me come in. His eyes started at my face, adrenaline flooding my body, and followed down to my feet then back up.

"It's," he swallowed, "they're a little big on you."

"Yes," I agreed in a whisper. "Thank you, though."

"Of course," he offered.

He went back to his stove, picked up his pan, and brought it to the table. He laid out an omelet on a plate. He stared again then knocked his chin up, encouraging me to sit.

"Smells really good," I told him, trying to smile, but it barely reached my eyes.

"I like anything I can throw in a pan as a big mess and have something edible by the end." One side of his mouth ticked up in a sarcastic smile.

He sat and we started eating together.

"You're doing really well at work, Lily," he told me.

"Thanks," I said between bites.

"Who is taking care of your sisters while you're with us?" he asked, obviously not knowing what happened.

I laid my fork down and my eyes filled with tears.

"Lily? No, no, don't cry. What's wrong?" he asked. He looked frantic. He stood and looked at me, his hands on top of his head. "Don't cry. What's wrong?"

I shook my head to get control of myself. "I'm just tired," I told him. "Sit. I'll tell you where my sisters are."

He did as I asked and sat back down.

"What's going on?" he asked.

"That night," I said, letting out a shaky breath, "the night before I didn't show up?" He waved it away like it didn't matter, but I couldn't let it go. "I'm sorry," I told him.

"It's okay," he assured me.

"No, it's not, but I am sorry."

"It's fine. It's water under the bridge."

I nodded. "Thank you," I told him and wiped a few tears away. I hadn't realized how much that had laid heavily on my shoulders until he forgave me in that moment, and I was grateful he accepted my apology. "The night before, I did something stupid. I, uh, as you know, I went over to Trace's because he and a bunch of our friends were partying over there. I was, uh, running away from Sterling. He'd come home and I hadn't expected him, so I thought instead of going over to Ansen's or calling Katie or whatever, that I'd just hang at Trace's until enough time had passed that I could sneak back over. Anyway, while I was there, Trace offered me a joint."

Salinger nodded but his body language was a little cut off, making me feel sick to my stomach.

"I, um, I took it," I admitted, my eyes glassing over. "I shouldn't have done it, but I'm an idiot and he offered an escape, so I took it." I took a deep breath and let it out, tears spilling over. "It was laced."

Salinger unfurled his crossed arms and laid his hands on the table. "For sure?"

"For sure. I didn't know it was, but I shouldn't have taken it in the first place."

"Fuck that guy. Don't you dare blame yourself for that," Salinger whispered.

"It was ketamine," I said, ignoring him.

"He told you it was ketamine?" he asked.

"No, uh, I had a drug test done."

"Good."

I shook my head, biting my lip to keep from bursting into tears. "No, it wasn't."

"What do you mean?"

"Something I said must have made him uncomfortable because when he found out that Mom and Sterling had died, he called CPS. I think he was trying to discredit me, make it look like I'm an addict trying to blame him or something, just in case I did turn him in."

"Fuck!" Salinger said. His hands balled into fists.

"I know." I laughed without humor. "He must have thought I was going to turn him in or something."

"The men in this worthless town."

"CPS showed up, tested me, and took the girls, Salinger."

"Oh my God," he said, grabbing for me. "I'm so sorry. So sorry."

I let him hold me because I needed it. I didn't deserve it but I needed it.

"First thing's first, you need to file a police report," he said, pulling away.

"I did. I already did," I explained, wiping my face clean.

"We need to get you an attorney."

"Already have one through Legal Aid."

"What did they say?" he asked.

"That I need to take a voluntary drug test every week, fix the house up so it's livable for the girls. They're working on visitation. Sh-she suggested I get a physical examination. To, uh, to rule out—" I said, but couldn't finish.

He nodded.

"Sounds like you did everything you were supposed to. Are you, uh, are you going to get, you know, checked?"

"I already did."

He audibly swallowed.

"There wasn't... I mean, he didn't," I began.

"You don't have to say any more."

I nodded.

"Are, uh, are you quitting weed?"

"Absolutely. I—" I paused. "I am worried about the damage this is doing to the girls."

"You're going to get them back. You're going to give them stability, probably better than they've ever had it, Lily, and you're going to come out of this happier than you could possibly imagine. You're going to do all this."

"How do you know?"

"I just do," he said. "Eat your eggs."

I nodded and did as he said.

We finished eating and put our dishes in his washer. He took the couch and I slid onto his gray sheets. They were soft and clean and smelled like him. I fell asleep instantly.

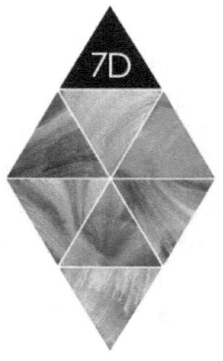

CHAPTER FIFTEEN

I woke to knocking on Salinger's door and the sound traumatized me. I shot up in bed and started breathing fast and heavy. *It's okay. It's okay. You're not at home*, I assured myself. I steadied my breaths then swung my legs off the bed. When my feet hit carpet, I heard Salinger open the door.

"Hey, babe!" a girl told him, and my heart started beating for a very different reason then.

"Lyric?" he asked, his voice scratchy from sleep.

"Yeah, who else would it be, crazy?" she asked him.

I heard her, like a tornado, whirlwind her way through his apartment, laying stuff down on his counter, it sounded like, and dropping a pair of keys somewhere. I had no idea what I needed to do in that moment, paralyzed by indecision, but Salinger saved me.

"Uh, I've got company, Lyric."

There was a dramatic pause and I felt like sliding under his covers to hide.

"What?" she whispered.

"Yeah," he said, "quiet for a minute. She might still be asleep."

"*She?*" Lyric spit out.

Another pause. "Uh, yeah, *she*. What's wrong with you?"

"Nothing, I'm just, I'm surprised is all. I didn't, I wasn't sure if you did that kind of stuff."

Salinger laughed. "You're jumping to a bunch of conclusions."

"*Oh*," she said, sounding relieved.

It bothered me, what he said, but I didn't have the right to be offended. I had my chance with him and blew it. *You also have much bigger fish to fry.* That sobered me.

I heard Salinger walk to his bedroom door. Adrenaline shot through my veins. He knocked lightly. "Lily?" he asked.

"I'm up!" I said, clearing my throat. "Coming now."

"Lily?" she whispered, sounding confused.

"Yeah, Lily," he explained. "Remember that bad-ass chess girl from Noah's party?"

I heard nothing.

"What?" Salinger asked.

"*Her?*" Lyric whisper-yelled.

Oh God. I am so unbelievably uncomfortable right now.

I stood and glanced in his bathroom mirror just off his bedroom, next to his bed. I ran my fingers through my hair, leaned over, and rinsed my mouth with water. I opened the door to see Lyric and Salinger having a silent argument. Salinger stood when he heard me, though, and smiled.

"Sleep okay?" he asked me.

When Lyric saw me, her mouth gaped wide. "Are you wearing *his clothes*?" she asked.

I looked down at myself. "Yeah," I answered.

She fixed her expression. "Oh, that's cool. Sorry for interrupting or whatever," she offered, but judging by her facial expression, it was anything but cool for her.

Salinger furrowed his brows. He looked tired of her.

Lyric couldn't find her next words. Instead, she stood, swung her hair forward. "Well, I brought dinner," she said quickly, awkwardly handling a bag placed on his counter. "I'm sorry, I only brought enough for two," she said, pursing her lips.

I shook my head and waved my hands forward. "No, man, it's cool. No big deal."

Salinger took a step toward me. "I can make you something," he said.

I smiled at him but shook my head. "I should probably get going," I told him. "Gotta get ready for work and all that." I went back to his room and gathered all my clothing then came back out. I walked backward toward his front door. "Are you, uh, okay to get to work?"

He ignored me. "Are you sure you can't stay?" he asked, looking baffled.

"Yeah, thanks for the invite, though," I told him, backing into a wall. "Whoa, sorry," I dumbly apologized.

"I can take him to work," Lyric said, answering my question for him.

"Cool," I said, ducking my head as I turned toward his front door.

I gripped the door handle, but it wouldn't turn. I unlocked it, but it still wouldn't turn.

Salinger's hand landed above me. "Hey," he said softly. I turned. We were inches from one another. "Are you sure you can't stay?"

"No, uh, thank you," I told him.

He stayed close to me. I could see the muscles in his stomach shift through his shirt as he reached above me and unbolted a safety lock above my head.

"Thank you again," I said, "for everything."

I turned and twisted the knob. This time the door opened and I escaped into the early evening air, walking toward my car, but not before turning back to see if he was still there. He was. He was watching me, leaning against the jamb of his door, tall and stunning. He made my heart race, and that made me feel so selfish. I shook my head to clear the feelings.

I waved and he nodded his head slowly in acknowledgment.

I circled back around and practically sprinted back to my car. I heaved all my stuff inside and got in. He watched me until I was no longer in view. When I reached the first red light, I plugged my phone into my car charger. The clock read six o'clock in the evening. I'd slept ten hours at Salinger's and it had helped, really helped me.

The phone powered on, indicating a voice mail. I pulled over, put the Scout in park, and looked to see who it was from. It was my attorney.

"Sylvia?" I asked no one.

Frantically, I pressed play.

Lily, it's Sylvia from Legal Aid, the message played, *we met with a judge this afternoon. They feel it might not be best for you to have visitation with the girls as of yet, love. I'm so sorry, but don't give up. This happens*, it continued on, but I let the phone drop on my seat, done.

I made it home safely and that fact stung, imagining what happened to my mama because of me. I dragged my feet inside and fell on my bed.

I was losing hope.

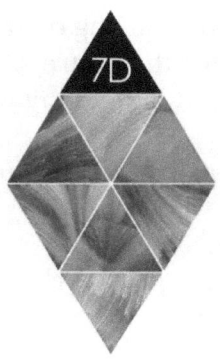

CHAPTER SIXTEEN

I stared at the ceiling, not bothering to glance at my clock.

"I'm never gonna win," I told the yellowed tiles.

I mulled over my options, wondered if the girls were better off where they were, wondered if I was worthy of them, wondered if I'd be able to meet their needs. I wasn't afraid of the responsibility, but I was unsure of what I was capable of. I didn't have the best examples growing up. I could recognize dysfunction, knew it so, so well, but I didn't know how to approach function.

I cried myself to sleep, overwhelmed with loss, overwhelmed with the maze I was caught in. The maze of what was right. Every turn I made seemed to be a dead end. I was caught in the myriad twists and turns of the labyrinth of what we all need, but only a few know how to achieve.

I woke to someone sitting on my bed. I shot up, my hand reaching for the figure sitting beside me, but the person caught it, held my wrist, and didn't let go.

"Lily," Salinger said, calming me, "are you all right?"

"I'm fine," I lied.

"You didn't show up to work and we were all worried. Danny sent me."

"I'm sorry," I whispered.

"What's going on?" he asked.

I fell back against the wall. "Nothing," I lied.

The quiet felt deafening. "Don't lie," he whispered into the dark.

He still held my wrist.

"What do you want?" I asked him.

"I want action." He breathed deeply through his nose. "I'm tired of idle, tired of those who blow their smoke, tired of doubt. Get up," he whispered. "You don't have to be perfect. You don't have to be the best at everything you do, don't have to be flawless, but you do have to try. Just try. Even if trying yields you nothing, keep moving before you petrify, Lily."

"I don't know if I have the strength," I told him. My voice cracked with emotion.

"But you do. The world is heavy and I can't imagine the weight you feel on your shoulders, but you're going to do it."

"How do you know?" I asked him. "No one can know that."

"I know this. I just know it. I feel it in my gut," he whispered, bringing my hand to his belly, then dropped my hand. "Let me help you lighten the load."

"I can't let you do that. I have to do this all on my own."

"Why?" he asked.

"Because I caused all this."

"There is no way you could have known what would happen."

"If I'd done what I was supposed to, she'd be alive; she'd be with the girls right now."

He stood up and flipped on the light. It took my eyes a moment to adjust, but in an instant, he picked me up and held me against him.

"Wrong," he whispered into my hair. "It was an accident. Just that."

"If it was only an accident, why do I feel such guilt?"

"Most people make mistakes and nothing happens. Most people have the opportunity to mess up and learn from it. Your mistake has the cruel and unusual punishment of an accident attached to it, but it was only that. It was *only* an accident."

"I can't navigate this," I admitted.

"You can and you will."

"Maybe," I told him.

He nodded once then looked around my room. "We'll need to fix so much."

"You mean *me*."

He looked at me. "No, *us*. We. I'll help you with this. We'll get everything sorted, get it repaired and cleaned. They won't even recognize it when we're done with it."

Tears started to stream down my face. "Sorry," I said, wiping my face.

"No worries, kid," he said.

"Let's go to the market," I said.

"Are you sure?"

"Yes."

Salinger drove me in to work and we stayed the remainder of our shift. All the guys were quiet but cool toward me. Danny waved when we showed up, and I smiled back.

The next morning, while Salinger took me back home, I got an email from the county. They were to cremate my mama at nine a.m. the following morning and her ashes would be interred the day after at eleven.

"The county will cremate my mom tomorrow," I told him. "Funeral's the day after."

I emailed Sylvia and let her know so the girls could go, if they were able, then texted Ansen and Katie and let them know as well.

"I'm not ready for this," I told the passenger-side window.

"You're not supposed to be, Lily. You're normal."

When he said that, it brought me strange relief. I took a deep breath and steadied my nerves. Instead of turning into the little country road I lived on, though, we kept going toward Smithfield. I didn't bother asking where we were going. I didn't care. I didn't want to go back home, and I think he sensed that in me.

I couldn't tell whether Salinger was becoming my friend. He was selfless, yes. He took care of me when I needed it, but I couldn't tell if he was doing that because he felt an obligation to do it or because he actually wanted to be my friend and we just started off on a really strange footing, where all hell broke loose and he was only prodding me along until I could find some stability.

Katie texted me back and let me know she and Ansen would be there and that she had a dress for me. I sent her a thank you but not much more than that. I didn't—no, couldn't—say anything else.

"When I was little," I told him, "before she met Sterling, my mama would take us to church. There was an old priest there. Really nice guy. He would let us shop in the little church's pantry even after hours because he knew my mama worked during the times they were open. At Christmas, he gave us gift cards to Wal-Mart and we had a decent meal because of him. I even got a little doll."

"That's amazing."

"He was. I-I wonder if he's still alive."

He shrugged his shoulders. "What made you think of him?"

"I wonder if he'd be able to make the funeral. If he could give her a proper burial?"

"You should call the church," he prodded.

"Should I?"

"Go on," he said, turning onto the highway toward Smithfield.

I searched for the church on the phone and found their website. I saw pictures of the old building and it looked a little worn out, but stood tall, for the most part. I called their published number and a little voice, a woman's voice, answered. She let me know that Father Robinson was there and put me on hold. When he answered, his voice sounded exactly the same to me, and it made me happy to know he hadn't. I told him all about me, and he remembered us immediately, which made me tear up a little. He said he could make the funeral, that he could push some things around, but he would definitely be there. At the end, I tearfully thanked him, not just for offering to be at the funeral, but for what he'd done for us when I was young.

"He's coming?" Salinger asked.

"Yes," I answered with the first genuine smile I'd had in a long time.

We pulled into a hardware store, which I hadn't been expecting. "I think getting some stuff done on your house will help you feel some progress toward bringing your sisters home."

I nodded. "I think it would."

Inside, he took me to the back of the store where he knew they kept all their clearance stuff. We found a bunch of boxes of outdated tile. It was plain and white, but I thought a black grout with it would look okay and he agreed. There was a new showerhead someone had returned and a standard white bathtub with apron, as well as some returned buckets of paint. We rummaged through and found a pedestal sink really cheap. I added it all up and found I could afford everything but the sink.

"I'll have to get the sink later," I told him.

"It's only thirty-five," he said.

I shook my head. "I literally don't have the cash. I'll have to wait until next week."

"No, we get it today. I'll pay for it."

"Dude, you're helping me so much as it is, I can't let you do that."

He smiled at me. "We'll never find a deal this cheap again. I'd rather just get it now."

"Okay, I, uh, I can pay you back when we get paid."

"Don't worry about it. I won some cash in that tournament. If you'd come, it would have been yours anyway, so—"

My mouth fell open a little. I swallowed back tears.

"Oh shit, Lily, no, don't cry. Jesus, I hate it when girls cry. I can't take it. Please, don't worry about that stupid tournament. I just meant you definitely would have won, so I don't really even consider that cash mine. Please," he begged me.

I shook my head and gathered myself. "No, I know, it's okay. It's okay. I just feel really bad about it still."

He brought his hands to his face and dragged them down his skin. "Jesus, I am such an idiot. Please, don't feel bad. It feels like a million years ago, and I literally don't even care about it anymore. It was free money, and I just wanted to gift some your way. That's all."

"Okay, let's just go before we both end up in tears then."

He smiled and nodded. We loaded everything up in the back of his Jeep. It barely fit. I had to sit behind him on the way home since the tub was so long we had to bend the passenger seat forward to get it in. It was crowded, but I was pretty amazed we'd gotten everything for so cheap. It helped that I wasn't picky.

When we got back to my house, we brought

everything inside. The white of the tile, the sink, and the tub in juxtaposition to the yellowed floors and walls was shocking.

"There's so much to do to make this livable. I don't know how I'll get it all done."

"One room at a time," Salinger said.

We spent the morning demoing the existing bathroom, which was cathartic. Since there was only one bathroom in the entire house, though, we were forced to relieve ourselves at Alta Mae's, but she didn't mind. She told me she was proud of me working hard to get my sisters back. I kissed her cheek and let her know if she needed me, I'd be where I always was.

We finished the demo because I found out the bulk trash was coming that Friday and they only came once every two weeks and we knew that was our chance to avoid hiring a dumpster, something I definitely couldn't afford.

Around ten, Salinger and I were starved and tired, so I made some ramen for us. He was too sleepy to go home, so he slept on our lumpy couch.

I was unbelievably grateful to him. I knew I couldn't have moved forward the way I was without him.

We worked our night shift, and spent the next morning, the morning my mama was cremated, installing the tub and laying tile. I would randomly burst out crying, but Salinger never made a big deal of it. He'd hand me some toilet tissue and I'd blow my nose and we'd get right back to work. By nine that morning, we'd tiled every single wall to the ceiling. The floor tile we'd found was pitch black and hexagon with a white grout. There wasn't much available that day, but the bathroom was so small, it was enough to cover. The wall tiles were those cheap square ones you see, but with the black grout it didn't look terrible.

"I'm proud of us," Salinger told me, grout all over his hands.

I nodded, overwhelmed with emotion. "Thank you so much," I told him.

"Let's get the sink in and toilet in," he said.

"Aren't you tired?" I asked.

"Yeah, but if we get them in, we can turn the water back on and take showers here."

"Won't it take a bit?" I asked.

"Maybe an hour. Let's do it."

He brought the toilet in and set it down carefully on a stack of towels I'd set on the floor.

"I'll be right back," he said, running out to his car. He brought back in a plastic bag full of stuff. "We left this in there the other day," he said, taking out things I didn't recognize.

We watched a ten-minute video on how to install a toilet and followed their instructions perfectly. Before I knew it, we were caulking the base and moving on to the sink, which took a little bit more time than we'd anticipated, but we were done around one o'clock.

"I can't believe we did this," I told him.

"Does it make you feel better?" he asked.

"It makes me feel like there's a light at the end of a very long tunnel. I can't see it yet, but I can sense it."

"Exactly what I wanted to hear."

"Thank you so, so much, Salinger."

He stood beside me, stared into my crazy new bathroom and nodded. "Of course."

We slept for a few hours then went into work. I tried not to think about the fact that when I clocked out, I didn't get to go home to move forward or get some sleep.

I had to go home and put on Katie's black dress.

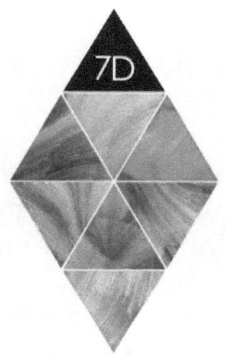

CHAPTER SEVENTEEN

"I can't do this. I can't do this. I can't do this. I'm not ready to do this."

"Lily," Salinger whispered, "you don't have a choice."

I stared over the muddied path, the mist that laid close to the ground. "It's all my fault and I don't how I will live with this kind of guilt," I choked out.

I swallowed; my bottom lip trembled. I turned from him and looked back onto the grass near the trees. They stood there, the girls, side by side, and I felt like vomiting.

"What have I done to them?" I quieted to no one.

Salinger answered anyway. "Nothing, Lily. You didn't do anything."

I looked at my lap, unable to gaze at them any longer. "You're right. That's exactly what I did. I did nothing. I did nothing. Nothing. When I should have done something."

"It was an accident."

"Nothing is an accident, though, is it?"

"Not true."

I ignored him.

"I need to forget this. I have to forget this. I don't want to remember this." I closed my eyes and took a deep breath. "Will you stay near me?"

"Of course," he whispered.

We sat still and silent for a moment.

"When I'm with you, it's easier to forget."

His head lolled back and forth on the back of his seat. "You're not supposed to forget, Lily."

"I want to, though. I don't want to remember ever. I can't even look at them"

"And what does that get you? What does forgetting do for you?"

"It takes away the guilt."

"Wrong," he argued, "it only makes it worse later." He turned his head toward me and I looked up at him. "Eventually you'll remember, and it will hit you hard and fast. Face it now and head-on or it will resurface when you least expect it. It'll paralyze you."

I opened my door and the fresh smell of dirt assailed me, making me feel sick. I felt Salinger behind me as we climbed the small hill to my mother's graveside. When I crested the hill, there stood a few of my friends, including Ansen and Katie, the old priest, two adults, dressed well with their hands on my sisters' shoulders, and my sweet sisters.

I ran to them. Fell on my knees before them and brought them to me. They held on to me with everything they had and I did the same.

"I've missed you, Cal," I told her, kissing her head. I moved to Eloise. "I've missed you, Wheezy," I told her as well and kissed her head. "I'm working so hard on bringing you back home. I'm going to bring you home."

They didn't respond, just held on to me as tight as they could, shattering my heart into a million pieces, into so many fragments I didn't think it could ever be reassembled the same. I breathed into their necks and gathered enough strength to stand.

I held their hands, refusing to look at their foster parents.

"Oh God, whose blessed Son was laid in a sepulcher in the garden—" the old priest began.

I squeezed my sisters' hands for the entire funeral, never letting go, not once, and when our mother was interred, the stone placed, I fell beside them once more and held them for as long as they would let me. They had to pry me away from them.

"I will come for you," I promised them. "I'll bring you home."

I watched the two strangers take my sisters away. I thanked the priest.

Ansen, Katie, Noah, and Court hugged me and I thanked them for coming. They told me they were taking me to lunch and I couldn't say no.

And Salinger was there, always near me. He told me he would stay near me and he delivered on his promise.

He poured me into his Jeep and we followed Ansen and Katie, Noah, and Court.

Lunch was pleasant. Quiet, but pleasant.

"I have to go," I told the table, thinking of the sadness in Callie's and Eloise's eyes. "Thank you for being there for me. Thank you for lunch."

I started walking out and felt Salinger right behind me. He didn't say anything, just steered me toward his car and held the door open for me. He drove me home. I took off Katie's dress.

And I got to work.

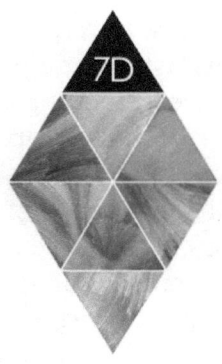

CHAPTER EIGHTEEN

I took the paint buckets and decided what discarded paint colors would look best and where. Salinger helped me paint the entire inside of the house and cabinets and it transformed it. I cleaned windows, pulled all the weeds, planted seeds, used old river rock to border the beds, and mowed the lawns myself with Alta Mae's old hand mower. I looked online for alternative fence options and decided to do a horizontal plank fence because it required less wood, would cost less, and still looked good.

Over the next few days, Salinger took me to my voluntary drug test at Legal Aid. We picked out marked boards at the hardware store, boards they couldn't sell at their full amount due to small imperfections, and dramatically reduced in price. Over the following two weeks, the store workers helped us gather enough of that cheap wood to tear down the front and back porches and rebuild. Noah and Ansen helped us with that. I power washed the old siding of the house, removing all the old paint, then painted the entire house a pretty blue with cream trim. That cost me an entire week's paycheck, but it was worth it to see it all come together so well.

We played chess every single day together and I started to feel a little more human again. I missed my mom ferociously, but I was learning to compartmentalize. I had a set order of things I wanted to accomplish—finish the house, get visitation, get the girls, mourn our mom, deal with Trace.

Faye the social worker came to inspect our progress and even she wasn't able to deny the improvements we'd made. She recognized my clean drug tests as well and promised to evaluate visitation rights.

That morning, after we'd worked, Salinger and I were feeling so good about ourselves, he treated me to take-out.

"Enough ramen already, Lily," he'd said and I didn't disagree.

We sat in my living room, enjoying how different it all looked and felt.

"Only a few things left now," he said.

"Yeah," I sighed, feeling calmer than I had in a long time. "The floors, right? Maybe some new beds for the girls, and that's it."

"Yeah," he agreed, flipping through the television stations.

"Thank you for all your help, Salinger."

"Of course," he said, and flipped up his laptop.

"Just checking to see what grade I got on this pysch paper." He leaned into the screen. "Nothing yet."

I smiled at him. "You're pretty amazing," I told him.

"Not at all," he said.

"Are you kidding? You work five days a week, go to school, and you're helping me with all of this stuff. You're just... You're amazing."

It started raining and I shrieked then jumped up.

"What's going on?" he asked.

"Well, uh, we've got a few leaks. I'm grabbing the rain buckets from the hall closet!" I called out, running to the hall.

"How bad are the leaks?" he asked.

"Pretty bad," I said, shoving a few buckets in his arms.

"How bad?" he asked.

He followed me all over the house, helping me place them where the leaks were the worst. We glanced between the rooms, checking for new leaks.

"Uh, this is insane," he said, glancing all around the living room, where we'd ended up.

I blushed red. "Yeah, a little."

"We need to replace the roof."

"Okay," I said, running my hands through my hair. "What is that going to cost?"

Salinger looked a little sick. "I can't do a roof, Lily. Too much. You'd have to hire someone, and that can be thousands of dollars."

I nodded. "I'll save then."

"That would take you months," he whispered.

"I don't have that much—" I began, but I was interrupted when we heard someone knocking on the front door.

I scaled the buckets and opened it, but there was no one there. Attached to the new screen on the screen door, though, was a taped note. The door creaked as I pushed it open, pulled the note off, and brought it inside.

"What is it?" Salinger asked.

"I don't know," I told him. I peeled open the envelope and took out its contents.

It was a note. I scanned the message.

"It's... I think it's from Trace."

Salinger searched my face. "What does he want?"

I handed it over to him.

"*You went to the cops after I told you I didn't mean any of it. What the fuck is wrong with you? Stupid skank*," he said, reading it out loud. "Is this guy for real?" he asked me.

"They must have followed up on my statement. I didn't think they'd actually do that."

"I think they have to or they'd lose their jobs. Plus, you know, it was the right thing to do?" he bit.

"They're all so tied into their good ol' boy club, I didn't think they were afraid of following procedure or whatever. I only did it so I could have something on record for when I try to get the girls back, not that he doesn't deserve to be prosecuted, but I'd given up on that happening."

"No shit. I hope he gets jail time, the asshole. That's probably it, though. The state is probably looking into those statements."

My hand went to my mouth and I bit at my thumbnail. "I can't think about this right now."

He searched my face. "I think you should, Lily."

"I can't right now. I'm close to getting the girls home," I said, falling back onto the couch. "I just have to lay low for a little while, try to find a way to get the cash for the roof."

Salinger sat beside me, picking up his kimchi, and crossed his long legs on the coffee table. "Maybe stay at my apartment for a few days while I have a talk with this moron?"

"Maybe," I said, biting my nail again.

"You know," he said, swallowing a bite of food. "I know a way you could pay for the roof and floors."

"How?"

"You could go to five or six regional chess tournaments, make some cash in a couple weeks, if you don't mind traveling. You win every tournament you enter, you'd have more than enough, I'd think."

I sat up a little, my heart racing. I tucked my legs under my rump. "Traveling? Like where?" I asked him.

"You could go all over the US, but we can stick to local stuff for now. We'll register you with the USCF. I think it's like thirty-five bucks or something. Anyway, you can start building your rating."

"What is USCF?"

"The United States Chess Federation."

I nodded. "I need a rating?"

"Yeah."

"What are the levels?" I asked.

He set his food down. "So, before your first official tournament, we'd choose a tourney that had a wide range of rating players and as high as we could find so we could get your initial rating up as high as possible."

"Why?" I asked.

"Because once your initial rating is set, it's hard to advance as quickly. You can only jump so many points each tournament. The last thing we'd want is for you to have to bump up slowly because you started out with too low a rating."

"Okay, go on."

"Every time you compete against a player, you have an opportunity to improve your rating."

"Who decides who I compete against?"

"It's done through a computer program for optimal pairings. If there's a lot of players up, like most of the regional stuff, they'll use a Swiss-system tournament. So you'll get paired with people who are at your same rating level, and you can work your way up from there. You never play the same player twice and the player with the highest aggregate points wins the tournament."

"How do you earn ratings?" I asked.

He took a swig of the beer he'd been nursing. "Okay, so, say you play someone who's got, for instance, a similar rating number as you do and you win. You'll get around thirty points, but if you lose, you actually go down thirty points. If you play someone at least three hundred points above you, and win, you'll get sixty points. Lose? They deduct nothing. Lose against someone three hundred points below you, though? And they'll deduct that sixty. Get it?"

"Yeah, what if it's a draw?"

"If it's a draw against a someone with similar ranking, pretty much no change. If you win against someone at least three hundred points below you,

you'll get nothing. A loss against someone three hundred points above you yields you no change in rating either, though."

"I got it," I said, staring at the coffee table. I brought my eyes up to him. "What is your rating?"

"I'm sitting around twenty-four hundred," he said, trying to fight a smile.

I smiled for him. "Is that good? What are all the ratings?"

"Anything two thousand and up is considered an expert. Twenty-two hundred is a Chess Master. Twenty-four hundred is a Senior Master and the minimum you have to own to compete in the National Tournament."

"Does it go higher?" I asked him.

"Yeah, a twenty-five-hundred rating is a Grandmaster. The current world champion sits at 2836."

"That's freaking amazing."

"It really is, especially since you can beat me without even trying, Lily." He smiled so wide and shook his head before taking another swig. "Freaking amazing."

While he flipped through channels, I took out a pen and paper since it was all I was allowed to use in terms of communication with the girls. I wrote them a letter telling them how much I loved them, how I hoped they were doing as well as they possibly could be doing, and how I was fixing up the house. I even included pictures so they could see our progress. I wanted to give them hope. I wanted to show them I loved and cared for them. I wanted to let them know I was fighting for them.

When I was done, I sealed the envelope, placed a stamp, and walked toward the door to my bag near the window. I put the letter in my purse and just as I turned I saw Trace pacing outside my house.

"What the hell," I whispered.

"What?" Salinger asked.

"It's Trace. He's outside in the rain. He looks *crazy*."

Salinger stood. "Stay in here," he said, opening the front door.

I followed him but stayed in the doorway.

"Who the hell are you?" Trace asked Salinger.

"What are you doing here?" Salinger asked, ignoring him. His hair grew drenched and stuck to his neck.

"I want to talk to Lily," he answered.

"That's not a good idea," Salinger told him.

"Lily!" Trace yelled over Salinger's shoulder. "Come talk to me."

"What the hell was that note all about?" I yelled down my new porch.

The sound of rain punched against the thin tin of the roof.

"Come on! Come out here!"

"She's not coming down here, dude," Salinger said.

"I don't understand why you went to the cops, Lily!" Trace yelled up at me.

I crossed my arms and leaned into the jamb of the door, my foot propping open the screen door.

"Trace," Salinger said, "you took some pretty fucked-up pictures of her when she was obviously passed out. That's really fucking creepy, man."

Trace's hands went to his head. "I didn't know what I was doing!" he screamed at us. "I don't even remember doing that."

He made like he was going to come up the porch, but Salinger swung his hand out and pressed it gently against Trace's chest. "No, stay where you are."

Trace backed off. "You gotta believe me, Lily!" he yelled up at me.

I opened my mouth to say something, but Salinger beat me to it.

"Why are you stressing about this?" Salinger asked him.

"Dude, they're trying to charge me with sexual assault."

"You did!" I yelled at him in disbelief.

"I didn't know I'd done it. I swear!" he answered me.

"You're lying," Salinger told him.

"Fuck you, dude, you have nothing to do with this!" Trace bit back at him.

"Any time a dude takes advantage of a girl, I make that my business. What did you expect when you came over here, huh? Even if she *wanted* to drop the charges, she couldn't. The state picks them up even she doesn't want to prosecute. They can't have creeps like you running about town, can they?"

Trace looked like he wanted to murder Salinger. He sucked in air as if he tried to control himself, fisting his hands.

"Don't, dude," Salinger said. "I'll drop-kick you before you even reach me. Just go home. Leave her alone. Take your misdemeanor and chalk it up as a life lesson. Maybe, you know, not take advantage of girls you drug? You know, maybe not drug them either, you prick?"

"She willingly took that blunt!" Trace tossed more my direction than Salinger's.

Salinger bit out a caustic laugh. "You think we're stupid? You fucking knew it was laced and kept your mouth shut. You drugged her! Think about how fucking gross that is! And we know you called CPS, asshole!" Salinger seemed to be losing his cool, so I scaled down the steps quietly. "You drugged her and accosted her and then have the fucking audacity to try and discredit her by calling CPS after she *just* lost her mom? You really are low, you know that? Scum of the fucking earth right here!" he yelled to no one, pointing at Trace. "If you were smart," he spoke softly, eerily. "If you had even a brain cell left in your pathetic head, you would get out of here while you still had the chance before I show you exactly what I think of you."

"Go ahead," Trace said, puffing up his chest and bouncing on his feet. "Let's go. I *want* you to hit me."

Salinger pulled forward toward Trace. Trace's eyes blew wide, not expecting Salinger to react that fast, I guessed. I luckily caught Salinger's shoulder and brought him back toward me. We toppled down on the new steps, the edges of the wood still sharp and square, though. They scraped my back and stung pretty bad, but I kept my mouth shut. He fell between my legs and I wrapped both arms around his neck and chest.

"Stop," I whispered in his ear. I could feel Salinger's chest rise and fall with each deep, hurried breath. "This is what he wants. He'll try to use this." I raised my head. "Trace! I'm calling the cops," I said, holding up my phone. "Should we add stalking? Threats?"

"Stupid bitch," he bit out, making Salinger jump forward only for me to try to reel him back, which proved a struggle for me.

Trace took the hint then, knew I wouldn't be able to hold Salinger back for much longer, and started hauling ass down the block.

"What a coward," Salinger said, still struggling with me. He managed to stand.

"Stop," I said, my heart pounding. I looped around him and placed both my hands on his shoulders, pushing him back. "Get inside."

We loped up the steps, back into the house, and I went straight for our '50s refrigerator, searching for an ice pack for what I suspected was a fast bruising back.

"You must be so tired of my shit," I whispered into the quiet.

Salinger had closed the front door and was leaning on it, watching out the window. "What does that mean?" he asked, still staring into the yard.

I tied the bottom of my shirt right below my ribs and hissed when I placed the ice pack against my lower back. Salinger's face turned my way.

"What's wrong?" he asked.

"Nothing," I lied.

He stomped around the filling rain buckets to reach me. He led me back into the kitchen light and examined my back.

"Jesus, what is this from?"

"Why are you friends with me?" I asked him.

"Is this from falling back onto the steps?" he asked, examining me closer.

He went to the bathroom and rummaged through its little closet. He came back with a handful of bandages and a towel.

"Come here," he said, quiet.

He leaned me over the countertop and tucked the towel he'd brought into the back waist of my shorts then ran the faucet and brought a dry rag under the running water. He wrung out the water and carefully pressed it against my back.

"It's bleeding," he said. "Not bad, but still."

He pulled the cloth back and leaned close to me. He blew the skin there. I closed my eyes, trying to ignore the butterflies that simple act gave me. He affected me and I had started to wake back up to it. I didn't want that. Didn't deserve that. Couldn't think about that right then. My breaths came heavy and quick.

His index finger found a loop of my waistband. "You okay?" he whispered against the skin there.

Oh my God. "Yes," I answered, letting out a shaky breath.

He stood upright and pulled out three small Band-Aids. Each time his warm skin grazed mine, I had to swallow. The butterflies grew more and more frenzied with every move he made, and I found myself silently begging him to finish before I fainted. He was sensory overload. I glanced at him over my shoulder, noticed how careful he worked, noticed his hands. He was *everything* overload.

When he was done, he stood and carefully

slipped the towel from the inside of my waistband. He threw one end of the towel over his shoulder then held both ends; the veins in his forearms popped out. I stood as well and faced him. He was six inches from me and my heart raced harder. I looked up at him.

"There you go," he whispered over the tinkling rain. It had slowed to a drizzle.

I swallowed once more. "Thank you."

His hair was still wet, so he brought the towel up and absorbed some of the water from his neck.

He smiled something crooked at me and I had to look away from him.

"Why are you my friend?" I asked him again.

"I don't know," he answered, but it didn't confuse me.

I didn't understand it either. Salinger's waters ran deep. Depths I could never reach. I'd never be able to hold my breath that long. He inhabited those depths. I could see him down there, peaceful, placid, quiescent, idle in the sand there. I trod above him, desperate to be near him. He would wave for me but my hands were too busy for him, too busy trying not to drown.

He was a perfect person. I'd have never believed that if you'd told me people like him existed, but he was. He was perfect. He was selfless. He helped me, was a friend to me. He let me do things but sort of shoved me up when I would start to falter. He didn't do drugs. He went to school. He was smart. He read. He studied. He worked hard. A jack of all trades. *A chess master*. He was interesting. He had values. I'd never met anyone like him.

He was careful around me, though. He trod carefully. Never went too far. Always controlled himself.

I knew what that meant. Men were only careful around you if they weren't interested. Men were consistent in that, I thought. At least that's what I'd experienced, and that fact killed me a little inside.

"Why are you friends with me?" he asked me.

He'd volleyed it back, but there was something else there. His eyes begged me for something, but I didn't know what.

"Because you are here for me."

"That's it?" he asked, staring at the tops of his boots.

"No," I whispered, "because—"

I like you. I like you because you push me, because you pointed me in the direction I should be going and gave me a little push. I like you because you were intolerant of the things no one should tolerate, because you speak your sharp mind, because you constantly strive for improvement. I like you because you are gorgeous, more than gorgeous, actually, because your skin on my back felt like heaven, because you are exactly my type, because you smell incredible. I like you because you are kind and compassionate. I like you because you treat other people's problems like they're your own. Nobody does that anymore. Nobody helps others for no reason anymore. I like you. More than I should. More than I deserve.

I stared at him.

"Because?" he asked.

I swallowed. "Because you're the best person." I answered him, but only partially.

If I'd said how I'd really felt, he'd run for sure. I think he thought me a novelty. Me with my chess ability. Me with my out-of-this-world problems. Whatever he'd felt for me romantically before was, for sure, gone the night he'd seen me at the store. The thought of that night made my cheeks warm, my eyes sting. I shook the emotion clear.

Like sand through my hand, he'd slipped through, but that was okay with me. As long as I could have this version of him, I'd be happy.

Any version of Salinger was a good version. I had to learn to accept that.

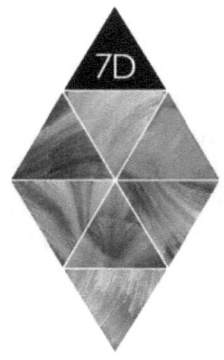

CHAPTER NINETEEN

"Tomorrow's our day off," Salinger mentioned toward the end of one of our shifts the following week.

"Yeah, I can't wait to sleep in."

He smiled at me and my heart stopped a little. "What's so funny?"

"You won't be sleeping in," he said, ripping up a box.

I knew he didn't mean anything by it, but my heart began to beat erratically. "What do you mean?"

"I have this friend," he began. *Oh, God, please don't try to set me up with someone. You're killing me*, I thought. "He's a little eccentric, but he's the most brilliant player, beside yourself, that I've ever met. I think he could prep you for tournament." I breathed a sigh of relief.

"What's his name?" I asked him.

"Bernard Calvin."

"Cool."

He studied me, trying to gauge something. "Never heard that name?" he asked.

"Never," I admitted, already feeling embarrassed. "Should I know him?"

Salinger laughed, chucking boxes of cereal onto shelves five at a time. "Maybe a little, Lily. He's only the best living chess player in the world."

"Oh, shit, really?" I was right to feel embarrassed.

He stopped and looked at me. "Just a lover of the game, I think. You just like to play."

"Yes," I confirmed, filling in boxes next to him.

"I like that," he told the shelves. He looked down toward me. "I'm not that much fun for you to play, I suspect." My cheeks tinged hot. *Yes, you are.* He misinterpreted the blush, though. "I knew it."

"No!" I insisted.

"It's okay," he said, brushing it off with a wide smile. "I can't tell you what an ego check you are for me sometimes. There I am, trying my absolute damnedest and you're half-watching television then take three seconds to decide your move when I'm taking five minutes."

"That's not true!" I sobered my panic. "Seriously, I've never had so much fun as when I play with you, Salinger."

His eyes widened briefly then he turned and grabbed another cardboard box full of cereals. I hid my face behind my hair, feeling a little vulnerable.

He cleared his throat.

"Me too, Little."

"Little?"

"Yeah, it's my nickname for you. Do you hate it?"

"No," I told him.

"That's what you are to me, you know. A little mystery. A little unpredictable. A little hard to read. A little storm. A little Lily who packs a great, big clash."

My stomach clenched. "Are those good things?"

"A *little*." He smiled.

My blood ran hot throughout my entire body and I avoided eye contact.

"Where is this Bernard Calvin?" I asked him, desperate to distract myself from him.

"He lives in New Orleans. He's a little eccentric. There's only a few people who know where he lives, and I'm one of those he trusts. Keep that info quiet, though?"

"Of course," I promised.

He trusts me.

"He was unseated as world champion twenty years ago, but it was proved the opposing team cheated. He never came back after that."

"Unreal."

"What do you think? Wanna take a little road trip?" he asked me.

"Um, I don't know."

"Come on," he encouraged, "it's only three hours away. We'll be back the same night. He and I have been talking tournaments you should enter to set up your rating."

I was scared; I won't lie. I'd never really left Bottle County, save for the museum trips as a kid for school. For all the talk my group rambled on about in our promises to one another, there was the comfort that none of us were actually serious. I thought on the buckets of rainwater on the floor at home, the floor itself, and the girls.

"Okay," I said.

"Good," he offered, another crooked smile on his glorious face.

After work, Salinger showed up at my house at four in the morning. I had a little bag packed, just in case, as did he.

"You ready?" he asked me, his voice deep from the early morning hour.

"As I'll ever be," I said.

I allowed a smile, a real smile, and he looked shocked. The expression fell into a smile of his own.

"You're smiling," he whispered.

I bit my bottom lip, trying not to cry. "I know," I whispered back.

"You're thinking you don't deserve to smile. You're thinking you have no right?"

I bit my bottom lip harder to stave the tears and nodded.

"Don't."

A few tears slipped despite my effort. "I can't help it."

"Lily," he said. He put his hand on my shoulder briefly and squeezed, "if you can't help it, then we'll just navigate it until you can."

I nodded and wiped away the tears.

"Let's hit the road," he said, throwing his Jeep in reverse. He brought his arm around the back of my seat to check behind us.

The clean smell of his shampoo and his soap assailed me, made my eyes roll back a little. It brought me back to the present and I felt a little blindsided. My hands dug into my seat's armrests.

"You hungry?" he asked.

"No," I told him truthfully, "not used to eating this early, I guess."

"Neither am I. Not really, anyway," he agreed. "Let's see how far we can get then."

We headed down the highway. It took us fifteen minutes to leave Bottle County, I'd counted, and Salinger pointed at the sign as we left it behind us. I leaned out of my window, letting the warm, crisp air drift across my skin and hair. The early morning sky was still blanketed with stars, and they shone so bright, so clear above us.

I giggled a little, took off my belt, and stood through his moonroof. The wind was loud. Its song whipped around me, promising me a future unknown.

"I'm alive!" I shouted into that wind and let it carry my words behind me, informing my past what it didn't seem to remember anymore.

After a moment, I sat back in my seat, my hair a tangled mess around my face and shoulders. I buckled back in and attempted to tame it down.

Salinger looked at me, his mouth wide with a smile. "Let it be!" he yelled over the wind still enveloping his car from the open windows and roof. "Let it live."

I laughed then remembered myself and my smile fell abruptly, a new tear slipped past without my permission.

"No!" he said, glancing at the road then back at me. He brought his hand up and brushed it away with his thumb.

I sucked them back and took a deep breath.
"Take me to the ends of the earth," I shouted at him.

"I promise," he called back.

He signaled for me to roll up my window so I did.
He did the same then shut the moonroof. The entire
car fell insanely quiet.

"I realized I don't know what music you listen
to," he said, breaking up the calm.

"I have eclectic tastes," I told him. "What about
you?"

"Same," he said, handing me his phone. "Just not
a fan of country."

"Same," I agreed.

We had old cars and hardware was a necessity,
so I plugged his phone in for him and scrolled
through his music.

"Which playlist?"

"There should be one in there called *Lily*."

I melted in my seat for a moment. "Y-you have a
playlist named after me?"

He smiled at me and I melted further. "Yeah, it's
music I just wanted you to know I liked. It felt
important that you knew."

I felt my skin grow hot but couldn't say anything.

"Hit play," he prodded, so I did. He let it go for a
minute. "What do you think?"

"I love it," I told him.

"Is that the truth?" he asked.

"Yes," I said and meant it.

We spent the whole time trading music back and
forth, peppering the conversation with tactics and
endgame strategies for good measure. By the time
we'd met city limits, I was disappointed we hadn't

had more time to talk. We were always so busy with work or fixing up my house or his schoolwork that we never got to dig much deeper than survival. I really liked him, liked what he was into.

We'd arrived in the sleepy French Quarter in New Orleans in a little more than four hours. It was quiet but the state of the streets indicated it hadn't been that way for long. It looked like it'd barely survived but it liked it that way.

"It's so pretty," I whispered, leaning out the window, admiring the architecture.

We pulled in front of a period home with mint siding and cream, elaborate trim. It was one story but truly ornate with a green stoop and mustard-yellow door. Salinger pulled around into the back alley and sidled into its very narrow driveway in front of a closed garage door. He put the car in park.

"You ready?" he asked.

A belly full of nerves, I nodded my answer.

"Listen, so Bernard is, um, he's a character, a pistol, if you will."

"Is this, like, an eggshell situation?" I asked.

He smiled. "Yes, but as long as we play it cool, catch him in a good mood, he'll be fine."

"This isn't helping me."

"You'll be fine. You need this. You need to play someone stronger than me. Play the best so you can follow their footsteps."

He got out of the car before I could respond to him. He grabbed both our bags, not wanting to leave them in the car, I guessed. I followed him through a pretty wooden gate into the most gorgeous garden I had ever seen in my life. Small paths wound throughout the entire yard around small pockets of reaching flowers and led to the garden center where a small table and set of chairs sat on top of flat stone underneath an iron canopy full of vine.

We climbed the small set of concrete steps. I stood on a step behind Salinger as there was only room for one at a time. He knocked and I pressed a hand to my throat from nerves. We heard shuffling behind the door. It opened and there stood a small man, thin in most areas but his middle, hair sticking up at strange angles. He wore brown leather slippers, a plain white T-shirt, a pair of navy Bermuda shorts, and a navy-blue-and-maroon-striped robe draped over his shoulders that met him mid-calf.

"You're early!" he grumbled, turned away and started walking, but left the door open.

We scrambled in behind him, down a very narrow hall, past a tiny laundry room with ancient-looking machines, a small half bath covered in what appeared to be marble original to the home, and through a pair of dark wood French doors into a cozy sitting room, complete with plaster ceilings.

Bernard Calvin had stacks and stacks of newspapers lining the walls that rose to the chair railing. He didn't own a proper sofa, just several old single chairs scattered throughout the room but all facing a small television tucked into a corner of a wall. In the center laid a chessboard on a marble table, with a game already set up. There was pipe smoke everywhere from a burning pipe nearby on an ashtray that sat on a little table next to a comfortable-looking chair pulled up to the chess table.

"I wasn't expecting you this early," he complained, lifting up random bits of paper on tables and searching underneath each one.

"What do you need, Bernie?" Salinger asked him.

"My damn glasses!" he fussed.

Salinger leaned forward and picked up a chain dangling around Bernard's neck. On it was a pair of thick reading glasses. He looked at Salinger like he blamed him for not realizing they were there. Salinger hid a laugh with a poorly constructed cough.

"Come with me," Bernard rumbled and made for the front door that sat at the end of the hall connected to the back door we'd entered from.

"Bernie, aren't you going to put on some shoes? Take off your robe?"

"Why would I do that?" he squawked.

"Never mind then," Salinger replied. "Where are we going?"

Bernard stopped so suddenly I didn't react fast enough and ran into Salinger's back. He reached his hands back to steady me.

"To get something to eat. What else?" Bernard explained with impatience in his tone. He leaned around Salinger's shoulder. "You must be the girl. Are you hungry?"

"Yes, sir," I whispered, unable to find my voice.

He studied me for a moment. I didn't know what he was looking for but whatever it was, he'd decided what he'd decided and it was obvious I couldn't do anything about it.

"Good then," he finally offered and opened the

front door, leaving it open behind us.

"Don't you want to lock it?" Salinger called after him.

He moaned something unintelligible and waved Salinger's comment away. Salinger snorted and closed the door. We practically had to sprint to catch up to him. He meandered through streets, mumbling to himself, and reached a little shop called the Café Du Monde.

"Come on," he said, waving us on, "I haven't got all day."

"You don't work, Bernie," Salinger teased him. "You *do* have all day."

The old man whipped around, his robe flowing around him as he did so. He raised a finger up at him and frowned the most comical frown. He opened his mouth as if to say something, thought better of it, and dropped his finger.

When Bernie opened the door to the shop, people looked up only to widen their eyes then raised their newspapers or hid behind their coffee cups or found the ceiling very interesting. I wanted to laugh but didn't dare. He scared me. He amused me, but he scared me a little more.

Bernie bypassed the line, which shocked me, but not a single patron complained or even gave a dirty look. He was expected and he was tolerated, it was apparent.

A young man reached over the countertop and handed Bernie a large bag along with *seven* coffees to go. *Seven?* All were wrapped elegantly and ready for transport.

Bernie grabbed the bags, slapped cash down on

the countertop, and turned.

"See you tomorrow, Bernie!" the boy shouted after us as we fought to keep up with the old man.

Bernard grunted in reply and, like a tornado, left Café Du Monde behind him.

Salinger glanced at me as we raced down the street back toward Bernard's house and lifted his shoulders in question. I opened my mouth wide in disbelief and tried not to laugh.

"Taking too long, ya rascals," he griped.

We picked it up and edged closer to him. He threw the bags in Salinger's hands and signaled for me to meet his stride, so I did.

"Salinger said you're pretty good. Is that true?"

"I don't know," I answered him.

Bernard stopped abruptly again. "You don't know?" he asked, finally meeting my eyes for the first time that morning.

"Only enough to know I've beaten every software I've ever played a-and Salinger," I explained.

When I said his name, Salinger playfully reacted like I'd punched him in the face. *Sorry*, I mouthed.

"Hmph," Bernard said and started forward again.

We walked into his house to find four other old men sitting in the chairs I'd noticed in Bernard's sitting room.

"It's about time!" one of the old men shouted, standing up. "What do we have here?" he said when he noticed Salinger and me.

"Carl," Bernard said, pointing to an African American gentleman with a shock of white hair tucked under a golf cap.

"How'd you do?" he said, tipping his hat.

I smiled at him.

"Gus," Bernard said, pointing to another little old man. Gus was either a little younger or in better shape than the others. He stood up and shook my and Salinger's hands. He wore trousers with a button-up and suspenders.

"Abe," Bernard said as he introduced the third old man. Abe looked of Spanish descent and wore a guayabera shirt along with a pair of linen pants and sandals. He had a glint in his eye that told me he was probably up to no good a lot as a young man.

"Nice to meet you, *hija*," he said, taking my hand with a smile.

"This is Ralph," Bernard said, pointing at the fourth and final gentleman. Ralph was wheelchair-bound and dressed the smartest with a bow tie, jacket, and button-up, and topped off his ensemble with a straw fedora. I didn't know how he fit in the room, but you could see where they'd carved out a spot for him.

All the men there, you could tell, were comfortable and must have spent most of their days there with grumpy Bernard.

"A pleasure," Ralph greeted us sweetly.

Salinger and I scaled the newspapers to shake his hand.

"Clean this damn place up already, Bernard," Carl chimed in, plopping into a chair and surfing through the scant, blurry channels Bernard's old TV would produce.

"Oh shut up, will you?" Bernard complained.

He gave Salinger a little push and indicated to him that he wanted the bags dropped on the small foyer table in the hall right outside the crowded sitting room. Carl and Abe grabbed some paper plates and opened the bags, doling out beignets and passing them over to Ralph, Gus, and Bernard.

"There you are, *hija*," Abe said, offering me a plate.

"Thank you," I told him.

Carl offered me a chair at the side of the room and I started to sit.

"No! No!" Bernard yelled.

"What?" I asked, frightened.

"Sit here," he said, pointing to the chair across from him at the chess table.

My heart beat in my throat. "Okay," I said, sitting down.

"You play?" Carl asked me, sitting nearby.

"Yes, sir."

"Salinger's told me she's the best he's ever played, including me."

Bernard raised an eyebrow at Salinger.

"Just wait, old man. You'll see."

"Oh, I can't wait to see this," Ralph said, rubbing his hands together.

"Whoa, whoa, that's a lot of pressure," I said, feeling a little hot.

"Don't worry, baby girl. You're here for fun. Have fun. Don't over think it," Gus told me before taking a bite of his beignet.

I took a deep breath and let it out slowly. "Okay, let's go then."

"You don't mind if I play white, do you?" Bernard asked.

"Of course not," I told him.

Bernard spun the board around with ease, like he'd done it thousands of times.

"What is the first move, though," Gus teased Bernard, "if it's answered properly?" he finished, winking at me.

I looked to my left, at Salinger. He gave me a small smile and a head nod to encourage me.

"Need him, do you? Lack confidence, do you?" Bernard asked. He avoided eye contact and sat back, cleaning his reading glasses with the edge of his robe.

I swallowed.

"Nice, friendly, casual game, mind you. I just want to see what you're made of," he commented.

Nf3 Bernard scooted to the end of his chair. Without hesitation, he moved.

Nf6 That was his favorite move. I could see it in his eyes, in the slight tilt of his mouth.

I took a solid breath, left the room around me, and glanced at the board. I saw my usual grid, my invisible lines, the pure potential. I ran hundreds of tactics instantly through my mind, but pushed them aside. *Wait*, I thought. I repaid in kind.

c4 He smiled at me and moved his pawn.

g6 I knew this opening. I flipped through my mental catalog and processed all potentials then moved.

Nc3 He expected this. His next move, I expected as well.

Bg7 *Bishop*, I thought.

d4 Bernard yawned, mumbled about the time of morning, and picked up a pawn.

O-O *King's Indian.*

Bf4 Bernard's eyes narrowed ever so slightly, but he said nothing.

Abe and Gus leaned into one another and said something, though I couldn't hear it.

Bernard countered.

d5 *What are you doing, Bernard?* Finally, I moved to the center.

Qb3 Bernard took a sip of coffee then moved.

dxc4 He was trying to throw off my pawn structure. I closed my eyes and imagined the board, shifting pieces in my mind and predicting tactic.

Qxc4 I further entrenched my pawn. Bernard moved.

c6 This was what I expected.

e4 I brought out another pawn. As did Bernard.

Nbd7 Bernard thought he owned the center. I could see it in his face. I took a deep breath.

Rd1 Bernard looked at me like I was an idiot.

Nb6 I countered.

Qc5 He leaned back in his chair a little and made his next move.

Bg4 My turn.

Bg5 "A pin is mightier than the sword," Abe whispered, and the other men chuckled beneath their breath.

We ignored them and I waited for Bernard. He moved.

Na4 His center made vulnerable to me. I moved my knight.

Qa3 Bernard cleared his throat, the first sign he felt slightly uncomfortable. He moved his queen.

Nxc3

bxc3

Nxe4 Instinctively, I scooted farther to the edge of my chair, took a deep breath, and moved my knight.

Bxe7 He didn't move, didn't blink. I'd backed him into a slight corner and he was analyzing.
Adrenaline raced through my veins. He aimed for his bishop.

Qb6 My fingertip edged my queen. I steadied my nerves and moved her.

Bc4 Some small part of myself recognized the incredible silence in the room, but I shut it out immediately. Bernard took his bishop on a trip once again.

Nxc3 I rested my forefinger on my knight, confirmed the move with myself, and took his pawn.

Bc5 He took his bishop and aimed for my queen.

Rfe8+ I shifted a rook.

Kf1 He moved his king.

Be6 A bishop for me.

Bxb6

Bxc4+ He responded in kind.

Kg1 King.

Ne2+ Knight.

Kf1 King.

Nxd4+ Knight.

Kg1 King.

Ne2+ Knight.

Kf1 King.

Nc3+ Knight.

Kg1 King.

axb6

Qb4 Queen.

Ra4 Rook.

Qxb6

Nxd1

h3

Rxa2

Kh2

Nxf2

Re1

Rxe1

Qd8+

Bf8 Bishop.

Nxe1

Bd5 You could hear even the slightest movement. It was deathly quiet.

Nf3

Ne4

Qb8

b5

h4 He moved a pawn. He was grasping at straws. He looked up at me, the first time he'd made eye contact since we'd begun and his face was unreadable.

h5

Ne5

Kg7

Kg1

Bc5+ I placed a bishop. There was a single sharp intake of breath, but I didn't know from whom it came from.

Kf1 He scrambled his king. He knew he'd lost. He knew, but he respected me enough to finish it out.

Ng3+ My knight.

Ke1 His king.

Bb4+ My bishop.
Kd1 His king.
Bb3+ My bishop.
Kc1 His king.
Ne2+ My knight.
Kb1 His king.
Nc3+ My knight.
Kc1 He moved his king.
Rc2 I placed my rook at his queen.
"Checkmate," I whispered.

The room came back all at once and I relaxed my muscles, beyond relieved.

I breathed a sigh of relief then glanced around the room, starting with Bernard, and noted each of their faces were blank. I stopped at Salinger. His eyes were wide, his mouth slightly agape.

"I've never seen anyone beat Bernard," Carl said, breaking the silence. "And I've known him twenty years."

"Young lady," Gus told me, "that was nothing short of brilliant."

I felt my cheeks burn and looked back at Bernard. Slowly, his mouth started to twitch, then moved into a smile. I jumped when he started to laugh, gut laughed, fell back in his chair and laughed hard.

The other men were unsure of how to react to him but everyone eventually, except for Salinger, began to laugh along with him and when that laughter died down, Bernard sighed, stood, and offered his hand.

"Miss Lily," he said, his voice slightly shaken.

"Yes, sir?" I answered him and took his hand.

"Very good game, young lady. *Very* good game."

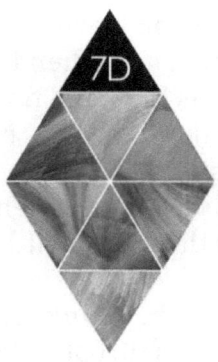

CHAPTER TWENTY

"Where are you from, girl?" Bernard asked me over lunch. "Who are your parents?" he asked without giving me an opportunity to answer his first question.

I felt my eyes burn but I kept myself together. "I don't know who my dad is, but my mom is, or," I swallowed the lump in my throat, "*was*, a blue-collar worker in a manufacturing plant in the town over from where I grew up."

"Oh, is she not working there anymore?" he innocently asked.

I tried to smile at him. "No, sir, she's passed on."

Bernard looked sad but fixed his expression. "I'm sorry to hear that."

"So sorry," the other men grumbled, casting pitiful stares my direction.

I started to feel panicky and rubbed my palms on the thighs of my jeans over and over. I felt antsy, like

I needed to stand up and leave. Salinger had sat next to me at the table and, just when I was going to stand to bolt, I felt his left hand find my right and his fingers wrapped around the tops of mine. He squeezed them gently.

"Lily needs to find a tournament still to establish her rating," he told the men, swiftly changing the subject.

I turned toward him. *Thank you*, I mouthed.

Bernard cleared his throat. "I know the perfect one," he mumbled, staring at his reading glasses. He found something on them and cleaned them with the edge of the robe he still store.

My heart settled in my chest then remembered that Salinger still held my hand and it picked back up again. I stared down at his fingers, just stared at them. He looked down at our joined hands. I heard him swallow and I looked at him, his Adam's apple rose and fell with the movement. He lifted his hand from mine and rested it on the tabletop.

None of the men had noticed what was going on, too engrossed in their own conversations, but I was hyperaware. How could I not be? His hand was warm, lean, but strong, and slightly callused from the work we did.

I kept my hands under the table but turned them palms up. I studied them. They weren't nearly as rough as Salinger's, but they were starting to look it. I felt a deep burn resonate through my chest. My mom's hands were callused like that, callused from years and years and years of hard labor. *I miss her*, I thought. The burn in my chest rose to my eyes and threatened tears. *No*, I demanded of myself. *No. That wasn't the deal. It's finish the house, get visitation, get the girls,* then *mourn Mom, and deal with Trace. Stop.*

Salinger found my left hand again, this time palm up, and threaded his fingers through mine.

He leaned over and whispered in my ear. "Where are you, Lily?"

A sharp intake of breath and I turned toward him, inches from his face. "Here," I lied.

He didn't answer me, at least not right away. Instead, I watched his eyes search my face, like he was memorizing me from a proximity he'd not experienced. He leaned into my ear again.

"Lie," he quieted, letting go of my hand, leaving it lonelier than it'd ever felt, and sat upright again.

"What about Austin?" Bernard asked the table, unaware of the personal chaos I wrestled with.

"I thought about that," Salinger contributed, like he hadn't just melted me to my seat. "I'm just worried, since it's her first tournament, that she runs the risk of being overwhelmed."

"Nonsense," Bernard commented, flippant. "She's a natural. She'll wipe the floor with everyone there." His hand went to his forehead and scratched through the messy hair at his temple. "Let's see, who do we know will be there for sure?" he asked no one. He snapped his fingers. "Aurek, I think, is the top player there that weekend."

Salinger folded his arms across his chest and casually laid back in his chair. "Aurek is phenomenal, but she'd beat him. She'd leave there with at least a twenty-five-hundred rating."

"At least," Abe said, taking a drink from his tea.

"Aurek's a bit of a ball-buster, though," Carl

chimed in.

"Not like our girl here," Gus added with a wink my way.

I smiled at him or tried to. I wasn't sure it translated.

"That gives us two weeks to prep her for tournament. That's plenty of time," Bernard said.

"What does that give us, though?" I asked Salinger.

He looked at me. "I don't know. This entire weekend, next?" he asked me.

"Yeah," I agreed.

"No," Bernard interjected. "You'll need to practice every day here."

"I can't do that," I told him, feeling panicked. "I have to work. I have to... Well, I just have to work every day."

Bernard waved my comment away. "That's no good. You need the time, the practice. You'll take the next two weeks off."

I looked at Salinger.

"Lily has obligations," Salinger said, coming to my rescue.

"A girl as young as her? Please, Salinger," Bernard answered him, not grasping what we really meant.

"Surely you can take a few days off," Gus added.

"No, sir," I said quietly. I began to ring my hands. "I, uh, I'm alone and I've got some issues with my home and, well, I—" I stuttered out.

"She definitely cannot take time off. I'm sorry, boys," Salinger chimed in. He turned toward Bernard. "You'll have to do your best with her this weekend and next." He looked at me. "Are you okay staying the night out here tonight?"

"Yes, I can do that."

"I don't see what the big deal is," Bernard complained, "but I suppose we'll have to just work with what little time we have."

After lunch, we all returned to Bernard's. All the men, but especially Salinger and Bernard, tried their best to school me on a tournament-style match. I was so overwhelmed with trying to remember procedure, I lost my first game after lunch to Bernard. Then I lost my second. And my third. And my fourth.

"Excuse me," I told the room and walked out onto Bernard's little front stoop.

I poured myself down the few steps there and began pacing in front of his home. I felt rather than saw Salinger appear on Bernard's stoop, so I stopped, my back to him.

"I'll never get my sisters home, Salinger. I can't do this. The first win was a fluke. He's too good."

I wrapped my hands around my arms and turned around. He had closed the door and had leaned on it, both hands in his pockets.

"You're letting Bernard and the procedures get into your head," he said.

"No. It's him. He's too good."

"He's a brilliant player, Lily, but so are you."

"I'll lose the tournament if that Aurek guy is any good."

"He's a phenom as well, Lily, but so are you." He shifted his weight. "Bernard is a lot to take in, and you're letting him overpower you."

"I can't help it."

"You *can* help it. You're powerful." He eyed me, starting at my feet and worked his way up. "You have no idea *how* powerful."

I swallowed, tamped down the sliver of heat his gaze gave me, and shivered. A small smile found the corner of his mouth but fell.

"Stop letting him and the rules cloud your head. He's autistic, Lily. He's smart as hell but has slight issues with boundaries. When you go back in there, you set those for him. Once you have that down, disregard the rules. Just let yourself play the way you'd always play. We'll explain the rules as we go so you're not so overwhelmed. Just play the game because you love to play. We'll figure the rest out."

I took a deep breath through my nose and exhaled through my mouth.

"Come on," Salinger said and stood from his leaning position.

He opened the door and yelled inside. "I'm taking Lily on a walk. Clear her head."

"I'm starting to wonder if she won on accident!" Bernard answered, but I heard him, and the truth of it made my chest constrict.

"She didn't and you know it!" Salinger called back. "Stop messing with her head. It's cruel, Bernard!"

Bernard grumbled, "Aurek will be no different. I thought you wanted me to prepare her."

Salinger didn't answer him. Instead, he closed the front door and jumped off the stoop onto the sidewalk, grabbing me by the upper arm, and leading me away from the house.

"Let's clear your head and let's be honest, I need to cool off."

When we reached the end of Bernard's block, he let go of my arm.

"Let's walk around the French Quarter."

"Okay," I said.

The buildings were gorgeous. I'd never seen anything like them. You could tell they were built in a time when art was appreciated and each building was just that, a work of art. They took pride in the architecture and obviously built them to last. They were fascinating to look at with their ornate wrought iron railings, their painted shutters, their patina bricks, and inviting doors.

"My sisters would love it here," I told him.

"That's sweet, Lily." He paused for a moment. "I always wanted a sister. I was a pretty lonely kid. Since I was an army brat, we didn't have any real roots. I thought having a sister or even a little brother would have helped fill that insecurity for me."

"Did your mom and dad not give that to you?" I asked him.

He smiled at nothing. "Not really. Dad was always working, and my mom was always drinking because of that. I barely know either of my parents. They ignored me for much of my childhood. Dad tried a little harder than Mom, though."

"I'm sorry," I told him.

He shrugged. "I don't drink because of her."

The memory of him refusing a drink at Ashleigh's made sense to me then.

"I get that." I looked at him. "You and I are

opposites."

He looked offended and I tried not to laugh. "Why do you think that?" he asked.

"No, I just meant that your parents' struggles guided you in a way my parents' struggles never guided me. There's only one common denominator in those equations, and that's us. You're obviously smarter than I am. You learned from it. I didn't."

"Not true," he said. "My dad never laid a hand on me. Neither did my mom. I can't imagine being in that same situation and not being desperate to find an escape from that."

I swallowed. "I don't think you would have done what I've done. Besides, abuse comes in many forms, Salinger. My stepdad hit me—" I shook my head. "It's so weird to say that out loud now he's gone. A bit freeing to say it out loud, actually, like I'm starting to let the hurt go with the words." I shook my head again. "Anyway, abuse comes in many forms."

"That may be true, but I would never presume I endured anything close to the hell you lived. I can't know what I would have done."

"We all have our personal hells," I told him. "What does it matter if one is hotter than the other? I'm not in denial. I knew there were better choices. I just didn't care. I didn't have a purpose. I chose what I knew, what was easy."

"You care now?" he asked me.

"Maybe."

He didn't respond. He smiled, though he tempered it by biting his bottom lip.

"Thank you," I told him.

"For what?"

"For many things. All of it."

"No need. I don't help people because it yields me something, Little. I helped you for the good of helping. It's its own reward."

"Thank you anyway."

He smiled to himself and my stomach flipped on itself. "It's not *entirely* selfless, actually," he added, staring ahead.

"It's not?" I asked him, my heart beating hard in my chest.

"No," he admitted, looking at me briefly then back ahead of him. "I want to be your friend."

My heart skipped a beat then immediately flatlined. I'm ashamed to admit I felt disappointed by his answer. I felt dumb for feeling it, too, but I won't lie and say it didn't disenchant me. I scolded myself for feeling as much because he was being honest in every way you could possibly be honest and he was a good friend to me, a very good friend. So I decided not to be selfish. I decided I could hope all day long, but I couldn't get mad when he wanted to be my friend and only my friend. I couldn't get mad because he deserved someone better than me. I couldn't get mad because I didn't deserve to get mad. I had amends to make and I didn't have the time or the right to think of anything else, even if that anything, or rather that *anyone*, was Salinger.

Salinger with his perfect heart. Salinger with his perfect face. A face the sun seemed to find whenever it woke enough to search. It found him and bathed him in its warmth because he gave it meaning.

I wanna be just like him.

"Hungry?" he asked.

"Not really. I am thirsty, though."

We came upon a small cafe and Salinger led us inside. We ordered a couple of smoothies and headed back onto the street. We caught a street musician's performance before heading back toward Bernard's.

"I have to ask you something," I said, feeling a little nervous.

"What's that?"

"What did you and Lyric talk about after I left that night?"

Salinger cocked his head back slightly, exposing his strong jaw and long neck, and stared down toward me, a small smile on his face.

"What does it matter, Lily?"

I felt my face heat up. I was embarrassed because I felt like asking made my crush obvious. I tried to deflect. "She hates me; I can tell."

His head dropped forward, his smile fell. "She's jealous of you."

I swallowed. "Impossible. Does she even know my family situation?"

"She's jealous of what you're capable of."

"I'm not capable of anything, Salinger."

"Wrong," he said and his fingers found my forearm, wrapping around the skin there. He stopped me and I stared up at him. "You're smart, smarter than her, and you're talented, and that eats at her."

"Why? Does she play?"

"She does."

"Is she any good?"

"She's okay, but that's not what eats at her."

"How do you know?"

"She told me," he said, letting go of my arm and we continued on. "You have my attention, so that night she told me she didn't want me to be around you." My heart beat in my chest. "I asked her why and she explained she felt threatened. I told her to chill. She exclaimed she was in love with me and asked if I felt anything for her. For the fifth time this year, I told her no. She promised to calm down and we could go back to being friends. I don't believe her anymore and told her we should both cool off for a couple of months."

"Did she take it well?"

He looked at me like I was crazy and barked a laugh. "Uh, no."

"I see."

"I don't understand how hard it is to take a hint," he said, dragging a hand across the stone facade of a building. "She just couldn't be cool." This sobered me. *I won't be making the same mistake.* "Anyway, let's forget all about it."

"Yeah," I agreed.

Take the hint, Lily.

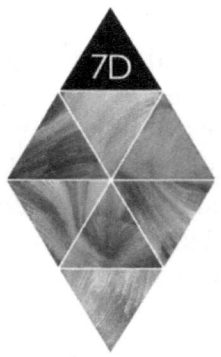

CHAPTER TWENTY-ONE

We practiced with Bernard until late into the night. We decided to stay and played the entire next day as well. By Sunday evening, I'd gotten a lot of my confidence back and beat Bernard several times while still applying tournament rules and procedures.

Pulling up to my house after not seeing it for two days felt strange. I hardly recognized it. It was actually pretty, something I'd never really experienced, even when we first moved in. It looked like someone loved it, and I guess that someone was me. It reminded me of the girls and why I was working as hard as I was.

"See the neighbors around you?" Salinger asked when we pulled into my gravel drive.

I looked around and saw that during the weekend several people had started to take pride in their homes. A few had mowed their lawns, fixed broken windows and doors, and ridden their yards of trash. Two neighbors down, the Garsides, had actually painted their house.

"Weird," I said.

"It's cool, actually," he said. "You did that."

"I definitely did not."

"You did," he insisted.

He brought my bag inside for me then stretched out on our old couch. I'd covered it with a couple of crochet throws since it didn't seem to match the house anymore. I turned the stereo on.

I brought my phone out and texted Ansen and Katie that I'd made it home all right.

"Don't let me fall asleep," he told me.

"I promise." I paused. "I'm going to beat Aurek," I told him.

"I know," he spoke into the cushion.

He was too tall for the couch and his legs extended onto the perpendicular love seat. He was a gorgeous boy. I didn't want to think that about him, but I couldn't help it. It was too obvious to ignore. I didn't blame Lyric the least bit. I started to imagine running my fingers along the skin on the back of his neck but stopped myself.

"Not because I'm better than him or anything," I continued, "because winning is my only option." He leaned up, rested on his elbows, and looked at me. "Winning is the only option."

"I agree."

"Then it's settled," I told him and he laid back down.

I went into the kitchen and raided the fridge for anything of substance. All I found were a few beers

Salinger had left over the other day.

"Salinger, do you want a beer?" I asked him. He didn't answer. "Salinger?"

I walked back into the living room and saw him still on the couch, but his breaths had evened out.

Salinger Park was asleep on my couch. He'd nodded off.

My heart raced.

I debated waking him up or risk him getting upset I'd let him sleep, though I'd promised. I thought I could suffer his wrath because I wanted him there. The house felt empty without him, so empty it made my skin crawl. I'd been the one to empty it.

Him being there brought me peace, though, more than life to the lifeless house. It was more than his mere presence there that motivated me to keep quiet. I wanted him there with me. I wanted him. For him I had tunnel vision and he was the light at the end of that tunnel.

Salinger was a very bright, beautiful light. I could admit it openly to myself, at least. I thought if I could admit it, maybe I could also live within those parameters.

So I sat there, silent and still, in my pitch-black house, nursing one of his bottles of beer, the low base of a song playing on the stereo rumbling through my chest, and watched his own rise and fall with each breath he took, feeling more and more like who I was supposed to become, because Salinger didn't just fill my house or paint the walls. He filled *me*, painted *my* insides with a purposeful life.

He was a burning lantern guiding me home.

I'm falling in love with him.

I suddenly remembered myself. I got up, poured the beer down the sink, and paced the kitchen floor. *Focus on your list. Finish the house, get visitation, get the girls, mourn Mom, and deal with Trace. Stop looking at Salinger. Stop thinking about Salinger. Stop wanting Salinger.*

I don't deserve him. I don't deserve him. I don't de—

"Lily?" I heard and startled to a stop.

Salinger was leaning on the jamb of the open doorway into the kitchen.

"What are you doing?" he asked me.

"Thinking," I explained and stuck my hands in the back of my jeans to keep them busy.

He fought a smile. "You let me fall asleep. You know what the penalty for that is?"

I tamped down the heat that pooled in my belly when he said that. "What?" I whispered.

"A quick game of chess."

"Oh?"

"Yeah," he said, tucking his hands into the front pockets of his jeans, "but there's a handicap."

My heart beat wildly behind my rib cage. "What's the handicap?"

"You have to be blindfolded."

I swallowed. "Blindfolded," I whispered.

"Yes," he said, standing upright and walking backward toward the living room and the little chess table we'd set up.

I followed after him.

"Take a seat," he told me.

I sat down, my heart beating a million miles a

minute; for some reason as he left for the kitchen. I could hear him rummage through the drawers there then he returned with a thin, worn cheesecloth. He folded it over and over until it made an appropriate blindfold. He smiled at me.

"You ready?"

I nodded and he placed the cloth over my eyes. I felt him carefully brush my hair aside and I stifled a shiver. He tied the knot.

I felt him lean into my ear. "Too tight?"

"N-no," I stuttered.

I heard him take the seat opposite mine.

"Ladies first," he said.

I carefully brought my hands up and felt for the edges of the table. I lightly ran my fingers over the tops of the pieces and chose my play. I moved my piece, placing it where I thought it should go.

"Is this close?" I asked him.

His hand found mine and he guided it to its correct spot. "There," he whispered.

When he let go of my fingers, I brought the hand he'd touched to my lap and with my other tried to wipe away the maddening drug he seemed to leave behind.

"Your turn," I said.

"Let me have your hand," he said.

"Why?" I asked, desperate for him not to touch me again.

He laughed off my question. "So you can know which piece I've played."

I swallowed nothing. "Oh."

I offered my hand to him and he took it in his, moved his piece, then let it go. I felt my breaths coming faster and I tried to steady them.

"You going to be able to remember every move?" he asked.

"Not sure," I whispered.

If I'd played this way with anyone else, I'd be able to know the table and the position of each piece at any given play easily, but with Salinger? He did things to me. He *distracted* me.

"This is good practice, I think," he said.

"How's that?" I asked, delicately feeling for my next piece and placing it.

He grabbed my hand softly once more and placed it perfectly. Instead of dropping my hand, he held on to it and showed me his next play.

"Because you always play the game in your head. It's your MO, Lily. I want to see you return to that, but with tournament rules in place."

"I see," I said, keeping his fingers with mine. Absently, I ran my thumb over the top of his hand while I felt with my other hand for my next move. I didn't know why I did it. I only realized I was doing it when I heard a hitch in his breath. I stopped, grateful I couldn't see him.

"I'm sorry," I whispered. "It was a reaction. So sorry."

He cleared his throat. "No big deal," he said, but I knew it was a lie because his fingers began to tremble. I heard him let out a slow breath. "I, uh, I think if, uh, you were to, um—" he stuttered.

"If I were to?" I asked, desperate to change move on.

"If you were to, uh, get back into that habit, you'd, um, feel more comfortable."

"Salinger?"

"Yes?"

"Are you all right?" I asked.

His hands began to shake more and he pulled his fingers from mine. I sat back in my chair and lifted one side of my blindfold to look at him. He didn't answer, only stared at me. I lifted the rest of the blindfold, pushed it to the top of my forehead. His hands gripped the edges of the little table our chessboard sat on. His knuckles were white.

"Lily, I—" he began, but there was a knock on the door. He opened his mouth, closed it, turned toward the door, and shook his head. "I'll get it," he said, standing up.

I stood up as he was swung the door open.

"What's up?" Ansen asked casually, opening the screen door and walking in. Katie followed him inside.

"Hey, guys," I said.

Ansen narrowed his eyes at me, cocked his head to the side. Katie smiled at me. She pointed at her own head, silently asking what the blindfold was all about. I pushed it off my head and laid it on top of our game.

"We interrupting something?" Katie teased.

I felt my face flame. Both Salinger and I looked away from each other. "No, of course not," I said, trying to defuse the obvious awkwardness laying dormant in the room. Awkwardness I'd laid out there. I felt so stupid.

"Whatever you say," she answered. "We brought food," she said, lifting up a full paper bag. She walked toward the kitchen, her bright white shoes with the thick black platforms clomping across the worn wood floor. "You've been working so hard, both of you, we thought you guys could use a reprieve. It's not healthy the way you two push yourselves."

"She's right," Ansen said, following her into the kitchen.

They kept up a conversation in there, but I didn't hear anything they were saying, and I don't think Salinger did either, because we were watching each other, unsure how or if we needed to approach the subject of what had happened over the chess table.

Salinger inched toward me and I followed suit until we were two feet apart. His eyes never left mine.

"We saw Trace at Ashleigh's on Friday night!" Katie called out from the kitchen.

I kept my gaze on Salinger but answered her.

"Oh yeah? He calmed down yet?"

"No," Ansen answered for her. "He's fucking lost his shit is what's going on."

I broke our gaze and walked into the kitchen, Salinger right behind me.

"What did he say?" I asked them.

Katie laid out several containers of Chinese food on the new butcher-block countertops we'd salvaged and sealed.

"He said, well—" She looked at me then Ansen. "Don't worry about what he said."

"Just tell her," Ansen prodded.

Katie sighed and put down the last box of food then folded the paper bag they came in. She laid the bag on the counter next to the food and turned my direction.

"He, well, he said he was going to, and I'm quoting him by the way, that he was going to 'take care of you.'"

"What the hell is that supposed to mean?" Salinger asked. His hand found my wrist and stayed there. I wasn't sure he was aware he'd even done it.

Ansen fell into one of our old wood chairs and ran his hands down his face. "It's fucking Trace. It could mean anything."

Salinger turned me toward him. "You need to file another report then. If several people heard him say this, it needs to be reported."

My free hand found the top of my head. "I don't know, man. It would only make things worse, I think."

"Lily, you're kidding me, right?" Salinger asked, the disbelief apparent in his eyes. "He's openly threatening you to other people. That's scary shit."

I took a deep breath. "Trace is unpredictable. If I add this on, he'll *really* come after me."

"Worse than he already has?" His tone was incredulous. "It's exactly *because* he's unpredictable you need to document everything he does."

"Let me think on it," I said, but I knew I wouldn't do anything.

Dealing with Trace was further down the list. I didn't have time for Trace.

Ansen stood up and stared out the sliding glass door. "It's so fucking shitty he lives right behind you," he said.

"I don't even care," I admitted. Salinger looked down at his fingers around my wrist. He let me go. "I don't have time for Trace. I have to fix the roof and the floor. I have to get Callie and Eloise home."

Katie nodded. "Let's no more talk of Trace then," she said and handed me a paper plate. "You're skin and bones, Lily."

"I'm stressed."

"I get it, but it's time you started taking better care of yourself. You're falling off the deep end a little bit, and I'll be damned if I watch you drop over," she replied.

"I'm getting there, Katie."

She nodded.

We all sat around the dining room table, a table I don't think I'd ever sat at once. When my mom and Sterling were alive, it was a catchall. It was where all their junk would land. Since I'd cleaned up the house, we could see the surface of it, and it was actually kind of pretty. It was an old table, for sure, but it was well kept, because it hadn't been really used in years.

"Lily is training for a tournament in Austin," Salinger told the table.

"Is this a big deal?" Ansen asked.

"Kind of," I said. Adrenaline pumped through my body at the mere thought of taking on Aurek. "I, uh, I looked my opponent up."

Salinger dropped his fork on his plate. "You did?" he asked.

"Horrible idea," I said. "I'm freaked the hell out." I brought my knees to my chest and hugged them, resting the arches of my feet against the edge of the chair. "So much is riding on this."

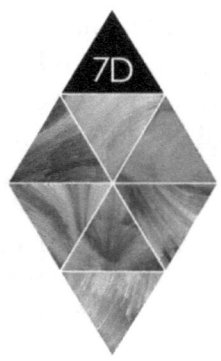

CHAPTER TWENTY-TWO

"Yes, Bernard," I told him over the phone. He'd asked me if I was ready.

We'd spent pretty much every waking moment I wasn't working or sleeping preparing for the tournament in Austin. I'd gone to Bernard's the previous weekend and had an intensive training session. I was as ready as I could possibly be.

"Remember to relax," he prompted.

I took a deep breath. "Yes, sir."

There was a dramatic pause. "Good luck, Lily," he said, but before I could respond, he'd hung up.

I stuck my phone in the back pocket of my cutoffs. I turned toward Salinger.

"Ready?" he asked.

"Yes," I answered.

We got out of his Jeep and walked side by side toward the convention hall.

"I feel like I'm ready but the nerves. Feel like I'm going to be sick," I told him.

He lifted his bag higher on his shoulders. "That's normal, Little."

I nodded.

This tournament was a $3,500 pot. Salinger had several roofers come out and the cheapest guy estimated a new roof around $8,000. I almost fell over when he told me. Apparently the house had some code issues and a lot of stuff had to be replaced because it hadn't been maintained for years. I needed to win. So bad.

We approached the ten or so doors to the hall. Salinger opened one for me and I stepped in. Cool air assailed me. The place was crowded. Really, really crowded. There were lines just to get to the registration tables. My heart started to race.

"How many games will I play today?" I asked him.

"There's seven levels this tournament. I think, like, one hundred twenty-eight opponents."

"Okay. When will I have the provisional score given to me?"

"Yeah," he said, as we landed in the registration line. "We'll have to talk to the director."

"Okay," I said.

We were both really quiet as we waited in line. My stomach was in knots. I looked over at Salinger. He appeared casual and I envied him for it. I knew I looked as I felt—anxious. I tucked my hands into my sides.

"Salinger!" someone yelled behind us.

We both turned to see who it was. It was two people I didn't recognize. They waved as they passed us by.

"Who are they?" I asked.

"That's Diego and Akeem. Really nice. If you advance far enough, you'll probably play one of them."

Just then two boys around ten or eleven approached us.

"Excuse us, are you Salinger Park?" one of them asked.

Salinger looked down at them. "Yeah, little dude."

The looks on their faces were priceless. Both their mouths gaped wide open and they glanced at each other before turning back to Salinger.

"Can we have your autograph?" the second boy asked.

"Sure thing," he said.

They thrust a pen in his hand and handed them their registration lanyards. Salinger slipped their cards out of their lanyards and signed the backs of each one.

"Wanna know a secret?" he asked them. Their eyes grew wider, if that was possible. Salinger leaned forward a bit and threw his head my way. "You're gonna want her signature too."

The boys looked at me, but they weren't convinced. My face grew hot. "Who is she?" the first boy asked.

"This is Lily Hahn."

"Never heard of her," the second boy commented.

"Don't worry," Salinger said, "you will."

"What's her rating?" the first boy asked.

"She doesn't have one yet. This is her first tournament."

Both boys looked skeptical, on the verge of laughter even. "That's okay," they said, putting their name cards back in their lanyards.

"A mistake, boys," he said, but smiled at them anyway.

"Thanks," they both said and walked away.

I glanced at Salinger.

"When this is all said and done, they'll have instant regret."

My face grew hotter. "Too much pressure," I whispered.

Salinger stared at the side of my face. "Lily."

"What?" I asked.

"Look at me," he said as we progressed in line.

I did as he asked. "Instant. Regret."

"I know chess, but I don't know competition."

"This week you've done so freaking well. I couldn't be more proud of you. And guess what happens if you don't do well in this tournament?"

"What?" I asked.

"Nothing," he said. "Nothing happens. So no worries."

"That's not right, though, is it? Or do you forget why I'm doing this?"

He looked like I'd slapped him. "I didn't forget," he explained low, inching closer to me. "How could I forget? I only mean that we will find a way to get the roof and floors done regardless, so stop worrying. Try to have fun."

I nodded, feeling a bit ashamed. "You're right. You've been so generous with me. I'll take your advice and let this be fun. I'm grateful to have you." I paused. "As a friend," I clarified.

That was awkward. I knew it was awkward. We'd never addressed the strange tension between us during our blindfolded game. I wanted him. I was certain he did not want me back. After his comments in New Orleans about Lyric, I wanted to make sure he felt comfortable with me. I just didn't know how to convey that to him.

"You are such a dork," he teased then laughed.

We made it through the line and the registrar signaled for the director to approach him when we checked in.

"Miss Hahn?" the gentleman greeted and offered his hand.

"Yes, sir," I answered, and shook it.

"I'm Charles Odelay. Let's set you up with a provisional rating."

"Yes, sir."

"Where do you believe you lie?" he asked, picking up a clipboard and flipping through pages of names.

"We believe I'm at a twenty-six hundred, but we aren't sure."

Charles Odelay looked at me. "Are you sure?" he asked. He was skeptical, and it started to make me question myself.

"Yes, sir, she is, at the very least, a twenty-six hundred. Bernard Calvin himself trained with her," Salinger said, bolstering me.

When Salinger mentioned Bernard's name, I felt at least twenty pairs of eyes train on us at once. I sidled closer to Salinger.

"Impossible," Charles replied, letting the papers he'd flipped through all fall at once. "He's a recluse.

No one's seen him in years. He's in hiding."

"She's seen him, sir. She's trained with him."

Charles stared at me. "For a provisional rating that high, we'll have to use the Elometer."

"That shouldn't be a problem," Salinger assured him.

"Meet me in private room three-oh-two in fifteen minutes," he said and walked off without another look my direction.

"What is an Elometer?" I asked him.

"It's a test. Seventy-six chess problems. It should give them a fairly accurate rating of your skill level. That will decide your provisional rating."

"Will I do well?" I asked, my heart beating a million miles a minute.

"You will do extremely well," he answered me.

The registrar eyed me but didn't say a word. He handed me my lanyard with all my information on it. Where it read *rating,* the letters TBD appeared.

The guy handed Salinger his lanyard. Where it read *rating,* his said 2412.

When we left the table, I felt those twenty pairs of eyes follow us.

That's when I noticed it.

"Salinger," I whispered, tugging at his sleeve.

"Huh?" he asked, searching the nearby map for the private room we were supposed to be in soon.

"Where are all the girls?" I asked, looking over at the lines again.

"What?" he asked, peering over to where I was looking.

"The girls, Salinger. Where are the girl competitors?"

"Girls rarely compete."

"What?" I asked, getting nervous. "Why?"

He looked at me. "If I were to guess? I honestly think it's because girls aren't encouraged to choose chess. Everyone has these strange ideas of what a gender role is supposed to be. I don't think they're supported when they show an interest."

I took in every single person milling about. They ranged from sixty to five years old, but they were all male. All of them. I didn't notice a single girl.

"What in the world?" I asked no one.

"It's not cool," he said, then tapped a place on the map. "Here," he said, distracting me. He looked at me, suddenly serious and I sobered. "Pee now, drink some water, let's go."

He took long strides toward the bathrooms. I had to run to keep up with him. I threw my bag at him and he held it for me while I peed. When I once again emerged, I took my bag from him and got a bottle of water. I cracked the lid as we rushed along the corridor toward the room Charles would hold the test.

I took a swig, replaced the lid, and tossed the bottle back in my bag. I breathed deeply through my nose. "I feel sick," I whispered.

"Deep breaths, Hahn," he told me.

We reached room 302 and stood in front of its tall wooden door inset into the wall.

"Tell me when you're ready," he said.

I took two deep breaths and reached for the handle, but he beat me to it and opened the door for me. He leaned into my ear. "Good luck, Little," he whispered, sending shivers across my skin there.

I swallowed and walked into the room. I heard the door shut behind me.

"Miss Hahn," Charles Odelay greeted. There were three other men in the room.

"Yes, sir?"

"Leave your bag by the door, please, and feel free to take a seat there," he said, gesturing to a simple table with a chair in the center of the room that faced him and the other men.

I did as he asked, and one of the men stood and brought a tablet over to me. "Miss Hahn, you will play white. Enter your move by clicking any piece then the intended target field. If you change your mind and want to pick a new piece, just choose the New Move or Clear Input button and it will clear the piece for you to try again. Good luck to you."

"Thank you, sir," I said and placed the tablet down in front of me.

I completed the example play and pressed next. I went from scenario to scenario without any issue. It was fun for me, and the nerves I'd been feeling melted away with each completed scenario. Within fifteen minutes, I was done and clicked the submit button at the end.

"Done," I said.

The men looked shocked.

"Did you finish?" Charles asked me.

"Yes." My score shown at the bottom of a graph on the tablet. "Estimated Elo rating of 2739."

My heart started beating but not from nerves, from excitement.

"Let me see that," Charles said, putting on a pair of reading glasses that hung around his neck.

He stood and made his way over to my table. The other men joined him.

"Outstanding, young lady!" one of them commented.

"It is as you said," Charles commented. He looked down at me. "It is unfortunate the highest player here is a lower rating. We'll have to start your provisional rating at his level. If you beat him," he looked at the ceiling briefly, "your rating should only land about 2565, decidedly lower than your Elometer rating, but will allow you to compete at high levels in different tournaments. Are you satisfied with this?"

"Yes, sir."

"Good." He gave me a small smile. "You're free to go. I'll set up your place in the first opponent round. Good luck, Miss Hahn."

"Thank you, sir."

I got up and walked toward the door and picked up my bag.

"Oh, Miss Hahn," Charles called out.

I turned toward him.

"How long have you played?"

"I started playing my freshman year of high school. I've only ever played online."

He pursed his lips, as if he was intrigued, and nodded his head.

"I look forward to seeing you play."

"Thank you," I said and turned back around.

I opened the door to see Salinger pacing the floor across the corridor. The door shut behind me. His head popped up when he saw me. He lifted his hands and shoulders in question.

"2739," I told him.

He fist-pumped the air and ran over to me. I smiled. I couldn't help it. When he reached me, he lifted me up and spun me around. I felt my cheeks heat up as he set me back down.

"That is incredible, Lily. Incredible."

"I'm so excited. It's higher than we thought. I guess my provisional score can't be that high, though?"

"Yeah, you'll have to start where Aurek is since he's the highest rating competing today."

"That's what Charles said. I don't mind, though. All I care about is competing in enough tournaments to get my house fixed so I can bring Eloise and Callie back home."

Salinger nodded. He looked down the hall at nothing then back at me. "You know you could probably go national, right?"

"I don't care about that."

"Maybe, uh, maybe you should consider it."

"It's not on my list."

He looked confused. "List?"

I swallowed nothing. "I have a list of things I have to get done."

"What's on this list?" he asked.

I ticked off each goal on my fingers. "Finish the house, get visitation, get the girls, mourn Mom, and deal with Trace."

"Lily, that's admirable, but—"

"But *what*?" I interrupted him.

He raised his hands defensively. "Listen, life doesn't work like that. You need to embrace what hits you here," he said, pressing a finger at my temple. "You try to force things and you can do more damage."

"I know what I'm doing," I told him.

"I guess," he said, but he didn't look convinced.

"Let's just see who we play first."

"Fine," he said and started walking back toward the main convention hall lobby.

"Listen, I know what I'm doing," I told him one more time.

"You said that."

"I can't let anything distract me from getting my sisters back."

"I know this, Lily. I'm just saying if you delay handling Trace and, more importantly, grieving your mom, it will eat you alive when you finally embrace it. It feels like you're delaying the inevitable."

He walked faster than me again, so I tugged on his arm for him to stop. He stared down at me. Tears filled my eyes. "I know what will happen if I let the loss of my mom come tumbling out of the cage I've put that grief in, okay? I won't recover, Salinger," I harshly whispered. "Do you understand that?" His gaze softened. "I won't recover. I *owe* Mama this. I owe her this. Grief this profound isn't something I'm equipped to handle when I'm the deep root of it. I *killed* them, Salinger. I ignored her when she pleaded for help." I grasped a handful of the shirt near my chest. "I *killed* her. I'm going to have to live with that the rest of my life. Avoiding it won't rid me of the eventual blame. I know I'm still left holding the gun, but you want to know the part that gets me? I didn't even notice until after the trigger had been pulled."

Tears threatened to spill over. Both Salinger's

hands found my arms and he pulled me to an alcove, away from prying eyes.

"That's *exactly* what makes it an accident," he told me, his eyes desperate.

The tears I'd fought to keep back crept over without my permission.

"What do you call an accident that could have been prevented, huh? What do you call that?" He began to open his mouth, but I cut him off. "Negligence, Salinger. I was careless and I failed to help her. Accident or not, I am culpable for this, and I will feel it every day for the rest of my life."

"Jesus Christ, Lily. You're *nineteen*. Yeah, you fucked up, but this fallout isn't normal, do you hear me? You cannot hold yourself accountable for what happened. There are too many variables. What if they'd been better parents and not required so much of you? What if Sterling had not beaten the ever-living shit out of you all the time? What if he wasn't a drunk who gambled all your family's money away and held a job like a fucking real man would have? What if your mom had chosen a different path in life? What if they had been normal? You can't hold yourself culpable for an accident that could have very well been prevented by *them* had they been the adults they claimed to be!"

Tears streamed down my face. "Great questions. Those are great questions, but I can't answer for them. Wanna know why? Because they're not here, are they? They're not here, and it was because I didn't do what she wanted. The girls don't have a mom because of *me*, Salinger."

He shook his head.

"I don't know what you're looking for, Lily."

"Just stop, Salinger."

"So this is what it's going to be for you? This is your forever?"

"Yeah, I guess."

"Why?"

"I won't ever be able to amend for this, to make it right, make it perfect."

Something flashed across his face. "Ah, I see now." He paused. "It's all an illusion, Lily. Did you know that?"

"What is?" I asked.

"Perfection. Nobody has it. The only good in perfection is the seeking of it. It's in the seeking we find hope and love and light. It's in the seeking we sacrifice for others, in the seeking we abandon selfish." I stared at him. "Every person falls back, but not every person picks themselves up." He looked at me. "Pick yourself up, Lily."

He brought me to his chest and held me tightly against him. I fought him at first, but he refused to let me go. I eased into his embrace and cried into his chest tears I swore to everything I wouldn't let fall until I'd completed the list. I'd promised myself, and I was seething at him for making me approach my grief when I wasn't ready, but I also desperately needed the hug. The physical touch of another human being. He comforted me. I didn't deserve it, but I *needed* it.

He held me for countless minutes. I both hated and loved him for it.

"This was never on the list," I spoke into his chest.

"Add it to the list then, Lily."

"Why did you make me say those things?"

"You can't blame me for that. You wouldn't have said them if they didn't need to be said. I don't agree with some of your thinking, but I'll respect you enough to disagree peacefully."

"Thank you."

He brought me away from his chest and the skin on my cheeks fell cold. He held my face, wiping the tears away with his thumbs.

"Are you gonna be okay?" he asked.

"I'm fine," I lied.

"You're not but that's all right. I'll be here for you always."

His words struck me like an arrow. He *was* always right there. He was *always* right there.

"Do you feel like I'm using you?" I asked him.

"No," he replied without an instant of thought.

They called for the first round and my stomach plummeted to my feet. We walked out into the lobby once more and followed the group inside a large room. Two rows of rectangular tables lined end to end in a long succession sat in between raised observation decks with railings. People sat in groups there. Competitors' families and friends I could only assume.

"Name?" a man with a clipboard asked me at the entrance.

"Lily Hahn."

"Table seven, seat twenty-two."

"Thank you."

"Name?" the man asked Salinger.

"Salinger Park."

Table nineteen, seat seventy-six."

"Thanks."

We came upon Salinger's table first on our left.

"Kill it," I told him and started to walk away, but he grabbed my hand and pulled me toward him.

"You got this, Little. Do you hear me? You got this."

I nodded my head and we bumped fists.

"See you in the skittles room," he said.

I watched him take his seat across from a kid half his age. Neither of them greeted one another and that set me on edge for some reason. I took a deep breath and followed the rows of tables. Table number seven was on my right and my seat was closest to the deck wall. I sat down and stuffed my bag beneath my chair, then tucked my hands underneath my legs to keep them from shaking.

After a minute, an older man sat across from me. If he was surprised I was a girl, he didn't show it. He didn't greet me or make eye contact with me. Instead, he took off his thick glasses and cleaned the lenses with the bottom of his button-up shirt. He looked all around us and pointedly refused to look my direction. I looked around me and found this to be the norm. It all felt really strange to me.

When everyone had seemed to settle in, the officials settled randomly in the room amongst the tables. Everything Bernard had mentioned to me was happening in that instant. I faced my opponent and he faced me. The director, Charles, made a flourished announcement and the officials moved closer to the tables.

"Good luck," the man said, still not making eye

contact. The offer was perfunctory. He probably barely remembered having said it.

"Good luck," I volleyed back.

The game moved quickly back and forth. We recorded our moves and the pieces seemed to move smoothly. I couldn't believe I'd remembered everything Bernard had coached me on. The man made a move I decided was fatal and steered him a particular direction. He was casual and I felt like he was unaware, but I didn't drop my guard. I wouldn't until I had his queen.

And I got her.

"Good game," he said and stood up, walking out of the hall.

I looked down at my board.

I won? I won!

I looked up and saw Salinger still at his board. He stared at his pieces. I picked up my bag to head toward the skittles room, but when I passed by him, he looked up. He raised his brows in question and I smiled at him. He winked at me, giving me butterflies, and I skittered past him. Instead of heading to the skittles room, though, like we'd agreed, I decided to head up into the observation deck to watch him finish his game.

There weren't many people against the railing near him, so I leaned over. His long fingers moved fluidly over his pieces and I felt those butterflies fly into a frenzy. The game didn't last long after I arrived. Salinger won. He smiled genuinely and told the boy he played well.

He stood and looked up at me, throwing his head the direction of the hall's double doors. We walked together, him on the convention floor, me through the parallel observation deck. I raced down the stairs and met him outside the hall.

"How was it?" he asked.

"Really fun," I told him and meant it. I smiled at him. "It was so much fun."

"Right?" he asked. "It's a rush." He looked up and down the corridor. "Let's find the skittles room."

We found a sign that read Player's Room and headed inside. There were all sorts of people running around. It was loud, so different from what I'd experienced in the tournament hall. Teenagers clumped together, older men napped, little kids chased each other around their talking parents.

"This is wild," I told Salinger.

He smiled at me in answer. We found a bit of wall and slid down it.

"How long until the next round?" I asked.

He checked his phone. "Another hour or so?"

I nodded. I laid my backpack down and used it as a pillow.

"You're too far away now," he said and did the same. Placing his backpack directly next to mine and laying the opposite direction, our faces right next to one another.

"Too close?" he whispered.

"No," I said but barely.

"Let's talk about your next tournament," he said.

"Okay."

"There's one I know of. It's part of a big chess convention. The U.S. Open Invitational."

"How big is the pot?"

"Fifty thousand dollars, Little."

My mouth dropped. I blinked slowly, trying to process that kind of cash. "When?" I asked.

"Next Saturday."

"Damn, that's close."

"I know."

"Where?" I asked.

"Richmond, Virginia."

"We couldn't drive that far," I observed.

"We'd have to fly, for sure."

I smiled at him. "I guess one of us is going to have to win this thing?"

He smiled back. "I guess so."

My phone indicated an email and I brought it out of my back pocket, up to my face. It was an email from Sylvia at Legal Aid. I sat up and opened my email.

Hello, Lily, I'm writing to let you know that we've got a court date next week, Tuesday, July 3rd, to address visitation. It would be a very good idea if you were there for this one to show good faith, present to the judge how well you're doing, and show him how responsible you've become. Wear something conservative and respectful. Come clean and well rested.

Attached you'll find the court details. Show up an hour before our scheduled time.

Let me know if you have any questions.

Hope to hear from you soon,

Sylvia

"What is it?" Salinger asked. I handed him my phone and he read Sylvia's message. "This is good."

My chest felt tight with gratitude. "I know." I let out a slow, shaky breath. "I'm getting closer."

Salinger smiled up at me and handed me my phone back.

We dominated the next five rounds. Salinger and I were in the final four. We'd been there for hours and we were both pretty exhausted. The skittles room was mostly empty. Most of the opponents who had lost in the previous rounds now joined family and friends in the observation decks.

We laid down for a few minutes, but it felt like as soon as we'd gotten comfortable, they called us back into the hall. The nerves I'd felt that morning came flooding back to me. The hall was full of people. There were two lone tables in the center of the hall and everyone crowded around them.

"Lily Hahn?" an official addressed me.

"Yes, sir?"

"Table one, seat one."

"Thank you."

I found my seat and dropped my bag on the floor then sat down, my body coursing with adrenaline.

"Peter Aurek?" the official asked a tall boy around my age. He had on dark, thick glasses and had a shaved head. He wasn't anything like I'd expected.

Salinger had tried to point him out to me earlier in the day, but I'd only caught glimpses of him, and he didn't ever come into the skittles room.

"Table two, seat one."

He didn't respond. Kept his gaze at the floor and sat down, staring only at the top of his board. He intimidated me. I whipped my head back Salinger's way when the official announced his name.

"Table two, seat two," he told him.

My heart started to race for Salinger's sake. I watched him as he walked by. He gave me a side-eye and smiled at me. It was subtle and crooked and just a little bit sexy. He sat in front of Peter.

"Diego Hurtado?" the official asked the last opponent.

I recognized him from when he'd greeted Salinger in the morning, when we waited to register.

"Yes," he said.

"Table one, seat two."

Diego took the seat across from mine. He glanced Salinger's way and nodded once in greeting. He turned toward me and smiled and nodded as well, but didn't say anything.

"Ladies and gentlemen, these are our final four!" an official addressed the crowd. "We ask you remain as quiet as possible." He turned toward the tournament officials standing near our boards. They each nodded at him. "Whenever you're ready, gentlemen." Salinger cleared his throat and the official glanced at me, his face turning pink. "And lady."

"Good luck," I told Diego.

"Good luck," he returned.

And thus we began. Diego was a good player, but I was better. I made short work of our game and by the end, he couldn't keep the look of shock off his face. When I took his queen, he smiled at me, a genuine smile, and stuck out his hand.

"Brilliant," he told me. "You're brilliant."

I took his hand as my face heated. "Good game," I

hushed his way.

He leaned over the board. "What's your name?" he whispered.

"Lily Hahn." I told him.

"Good game, Lily."

He stood up and walked from the hall with a small wave when he reached the exit. I waved back. Instead of following him out, I turned toward Peter and Salinger's game. I watched them battle it out for several minutes. I was impressed Salinger held his own, though Aurek had a higher rating. That's when I saw it, though, Salinger's fatal mistake. I didn't know if he'd seen it, but I knew Peter Aurek had.

In an additional twelve moves, Peter Aurek had defeated my poor Salinger. He sat back and looked up at Aurek when he stood.

"Good game," Salinger said, standing up as well and offering a hand.

"Good game," Peter returned, taking his hand.

The official who'd made the previous announcement raised his hands when the crowd began to titter. I could feel their stares on the back of my neck.

"Ladies and gentlemen, our final match between Lily Hahn and Peter Aurek will commence at six o'clock this evening. We hope to see you all there."

When he finished his announcement, Salinger ran over to me and picked me up.

"You did it, Little! You're in the final two!"

I hugged his neck then pulled back. "I wish it could have been the two of us, though, instead."

"Never would have happened," he said, setting me down. He screwed his face up. "Did you see

246

where I messed up?"

I smiled up at him and closed one eye. "A little."

He playfully balled a fist and hit an open palm. "Damn it!" He laughed. "I knew what I'd done almost as soon as I did it, but I am improving."

"I noticed that."

"It's because I've been practicing with you."

I lightly punched his shoulder in answer, a little embarrassed by his praise.

"Let's get something to eat and get ready for the final match. You hungry?"

"A little."

We grabbed our bags and headed toward one of the casual restaurants nestled amongst the walls of the convention hall floor. We found a table and settled in, glancing at the menus a waitress had handed us. Salinger tapped his foot on the side of my leg and I looked up. He threw his head to his left and I glanced that direction. It was Peter Aurek. He sat with another guy, older than me, mid-twenties, I thought.

"Peter Aurek," I said.

Salinger shook his head. "No, it's the guy he's sitting with."

"Who is that?" I asked behind my menu.

"That, Lily, is last year's National Chess Champion. Name's Tao Zhang. He has the highest rating of any person alive today."

I dropped my menu to study him.

"What is he doing here?"

"Not sure."

"Why isn't he competing?" I asked.

"Probably because he wouldn't gain anything

from it."

"I see."

"He's friends with Peter?" I asked.

"I guess so."

Salinger and I ordered a few sandwiches and a plate of fries between us then returned to the skittles room so I could relax, get out of my own head. I laid down and Salinger let me borrow his headphones. I closed my eyes and tried to calm my nerves. Before I knew it, they'd called for the final match.

I stood up and stretched.

"Watch my bag?" I asked Salinger.

"Sure," he said, hefting it onto his shoulder. "Ready?"

"Not really," I told him.

He smiled at me and shook his head. "Nah, you are ready. Tell your heart to catch up with your head." He turned toward the door. "Come on."

I followed him out and met his stride. When we reached the hall doors, Salinger kissed my cheek and whispered good luck to me. He went inside without looking back and I watched him climb the stairs to the observation decks. My fingertips went to the skin his lips had kissed. My whole body shivered. I brought my hands down and in front of my face. I studied them. They shook and I forgot everything around me.

I looked up at him, at his profile, at his stunning face, and it shone brighter than anyone's in that room. He resonated something in me and my eyes began to burn. I brought my trembling hands to my eyes and felt moisture. He was so beautiful inside and out.

Why do I want him so, so *much?*

"Miss Hahn?" an official asked me.

I shook my head. "Um, yes?"

"Are you okay?"

"Yes, sir."

"They're waiting for you," he said, gesturing to the table.

Peter Aurek already sat there, his gaze turned away from me.

"So sorry," I whispered and started to walk forward.

Time seemed to stand still as I entered the hall. I felt hundreds of eyes on me, flashes of bulbs, and small cheers from the crowd, but I could only feel them. My eyes went straight for Salinger and stayed there. He leaned on the railing behind my assigned chair, ran a hand through his hair, letting it settle on the back of his neck, and smiled at me.

A tight ball of tension rooted itself in my stomach and refused to budge. His small gesture, his small encouragement. His small kiss. It had done something to me, uprooted any feelings I'd desperately tried to bury. They were coming up with or without my permission to show me they were in control.

I'd never felt anything like that my entire life, that sort of incitement. It burned through every cell of my body. I fought the urge to crawl up the deck wall, jump the railing, and touch Salinger just to know what he felt like in that instant, as if every instant was a missed opportunity, as if every instant might prove something different, as if every instant my skin didn't know his was an instant to mourn.

My hands found my forehead and pushed my hair from my face.

What is happening to me?

I felt both profoundly sad and profoundly happy at once.

I looked up at him, my breaths coming fast. His brow furrowed in question.

He leaned over the railing. "Lily?" he whispered. My hands found my stomach and knotted the shirt there. "Are you okay?"

I couldn't answer him. I wanted to, but I was rooted there, unable to move.

"It's all right," he soothed. "Close your eyes. Forget the room," he coached. "Play for fun."

He didn't understand what was happening to me. He didn't know I couldn't care less for the room, couldn't care less about the game, how I understood in that moment I'd give up every single piece on that board just for him to touch my skin once more. He didn't understand how dangerous he was to me.

I shook my head as clear as I could get it and begged myself to remember why I was there, begged myself to remember my sisters. I fell into my chair and Peter Aurek finally glanced my direction. He slowly perused me from the top of my head to the tips of my toes before meeting my eyes. His eyes fell hooded, a slight smile on his face. He looked like he would either eat me for breakfast or offer to make it instead, but was torn between both. It was meant to intimidate me.

I looked up at the ceiling, sat up straight, cleared my head, then met his gaze again.

I'll be doing all the eating this evening, Aurek.

"Good luck," I told him over the board.

"I won't need it," he cleverly replied, and made the first move.

I moved my first piece and recorded it and he followed suit.

"You're very pretty," he whispered to me just low enough I wasn't sure the officials even took notice, unless they didn't care. I couldn't tell.

I didn't respond to him except to move my next piece. The room was quiet, but the spectators were so far away, I knew they couldn't hear him.

"Trying to join the club, are you?" he asked, moving his next piece and recording it.

I bristled in my chair but didn't respond. I moved again.

"I heard this is your first tournament?" he asked. I looked up at him and stared hard. This made him grin at me. "Interesting."

I cleared my throat.

"You really are a novelty, aren't you?" he asked, but I was certain he wasn't looking for an answer. "I take back what I said about your being pretty. I was wrong. You're quite beautiful, to be honest." He imperceptibly leaned forward. "Is that how you won all those other rounds? You distracted your opponents?"

I moved my next piece after his.

He smiled again, biting his bottom lip as he did so.

"I bet that's it," he needled. "Like lichen on rock, you're beautiful to look at but don't really belong."

I winced because that stung.

251

"Where do I belong then?" I whispered back as he made his next move.

He stared at the board but lifted his brow when I spoke to him. I'd shocked him by replying, I thought.

"Maybe you belong in my bed," he commented, still staring at the board. I felt my cheeks flush and he looked at me. "What do you say?" he asked, showing a snake's smile.

I ignored him and made my next move.

We volleyed back and forth *on* the board while he played his own game *above* the board. What he didn't realize, though, is I had already won. I knew his game, *all* his games. I knew the moment he'd grown silent he'd noticed his mistake.

"So quiet," I whispered his direction.

Cold, intense eyes met mine, but I smiled as kindly as I could at him. His face was wiped of all confidence.

He scrambled his pieces in a desperate attempt to salvage his game.

"Aww, wee lamb," I teased.

When I had him, he sat back in his chair, his hands going to his head in disbelief.

I stood, walked over to him, and leaned down at his ear. "Checkmate," I whispered.

When I stood back up, he stared at me. I winked at him and his mouth dropped open.

A small but substantial roar began from the crowd and built into a giant one. People jumped up and down and clapped. I turned when I remembered Salinger and saw him standing there, his arms crossed. He was shaking his head back and forth, fighting a giant smile.

I faced Aurek again, laid my arm across his shoulder, and whispered once more in his ear. "I can tell your lack of respect for me is a product of the power women hold over you, so let me let you in on a secret, pawn. Humility. Humility and kindness. Try it on and the good ones will come your way, I promise." I stood up and smiled at him. "Good game," I told him. I left him there in his chair with his mouth still agape.

I saw Salinger near the hall doors and started to sprint toward him but stopped short when someone blocked my way.

"Miss Hahn," Tao Zhang greeted. He was only an inch or so taller than I was, but he was a formidable figure.

"Mr. Zhang," I greeted in return.

"You know me," he more stated than asked.

"I do."

"You played well."

"Thank you," I told him.

"I hope to see you at Nationals."

"Sorry to disappoint, but I won't be at Nationals."

He looked shocked. He placed his hands in his pants pockets. "Just as well," he said, "you'd never win against me anyway."

I rolled my eyes. *Oh my God, what is up with these chess boys?*

"Yeah, okay, anyway, if you'll excuse me?"

He smiled and backed out of my way. I felt his eyes on my back as I walked away then ran straight into Salinger's arms.

"I won," I whispered into his neck.

"Told you," he said, hugging me tight.

He set me down.

"Excuse me, Miss Lily?" I heard behind me.

I turned to discover the two boys from earlier that morning, the ones who'd asked for Salinger's signature.

"Can I get your autograph?"

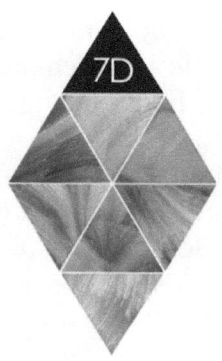

CHAPTER TWENTY-THREE

When we got back home, I was riding high from my win. I paid the roofer the following Monday the down payment and set up a payment plan with him, just in case I didn't win or even placed at the Richmond tournament, and they said they'd start work that Friday. Salinger helped me take pictures of what we'd done with the house to show the judge. I took extra pictures of the girls' room so they could see for themselves how different it looked since they'd last viewed the house's progress.

Salinger and I got back to our night shift at the market. I guess Salinger had told the night crew I'd won and when we'd shown up for work, they had a little cake there for me to celebrate.

Life went as smoothly as it could possibly go, considering my predicament, and I felt I made giant strides toward getting the girls back.

The next day, the day of my court hearing, I borrowed one of Katie's church outfits and a pair of heels, and curled my hair. I brought my phone out and texted Katie.

Off to my court hearing. Pray for me.

My phone immediately indicated a text.

Already done. Go see your sisters.

I smiled. I was *aching* to see my sisters. To show them how much better I was doing, to tell them about my new life's adventure, to prove to them I could take care of them.

I closed the front door and locked it before sprinting off to my Scout but panicked when I saw I had a flat. All four tires were flat. I bent over and inspected the one closest to the driver's seat. They weren't flat, they were *slashed*. Anger flared in my chest and I kicked one of the tires. I hefted the messenger bag carrying all my paperwork onto my shoulder and brought out my phone again. I dialed Ansen.

"Lily, what's up?"

"Trace slashed my tires. Can you give me a ride?"

"Son of a bitch. Of course," he said.

I would have called Salinger, but I was tired of relying on him all the time. To be perfectly honest, I wanted to distance myself from him. I was starting to more than like-like him and needed that to abate. That *had* to go away. Also, he was always coming to my rescue, and I knew he was sacrificing part of himself to do it. He never got enough sleep and he had to push through his school assignments. I didn't like being that kind of burden on him. I was grateful to him, though. Eternally grateful to him.

When Ansen showed up, he wanted to look at my tires, but I refused. Sylvia told me to be there an hour early and as it was, I'd only be there half an hour early.

"Do me a favor, though?" I asked him.

"Sure, kid."

"If I give you my card and keys, will you go buy four tires for me at Henry's?"

"Yeah, but how will we get the car there?"

"I'll have it towed. I'll let you know when the tow truck driver gets it. You just have to show up at Henry's."

"Done," he said. "Should I come pick you up when I'm done?"

I sighed. "No, I'll Uber it back to town and get my car."

"That'll cost a fortune."

I shook my head, exasperated. "Trace is such an asshole."

"No doubt."

I took my phone and sent a massive group text to all our friends.

Whoever is feeding Trace information about me and where I'm going better stop. You are causing a shit load of problems for me. He slashed my tires this morning when he knew I had that court date so just stop.

I threw my phone in my bag, done with that, then remembered I needed to have the Scout towed and took it back out. I searched tow truck companies and pulled one up. A woman answered but her greeting was unintelligible.

"Hi," I said, "do you have a flatbed tow?"

"Yes, ma'am," she said, thick southern accent drawing out "ma'am."

"I need my International Scout towed from my house to Henry's in Bottle County, can you do that?"

"Both in Bottle County?"

"Yes."

"Okay. It's seventy-five dollars, that okay?"

I cringed. "Sure, pay over the phone?"

"Yes," she said.

I gave her my card info.

"How long?" I asked.

"Within the hour."

"Within the hour," I repeated for Ansen's benefit and he nodded at me. "Thanks so much."

"Pleasure, ma'am. Thank you."

I hung up.

"How much?" he asked.

"Seventy-five freaking dollars!"

"God, Lily." He looked over at me. "Maybe you should report this one?" he hesitantly asked.

I looked at him. "Not yet," I whispered.

"Why not?"

"I'm just hoping he'll cool off and go away."

He shook his head. "He's obviously not, Lil."

I let out a deep breath. "I can't handle this."

He looked at me sympathetically. "It's not fair, but I think you should report him."

"I don't know."

I was reluctant because I knew if I reported him, he'd come after me even worse, and Trace was far down the list.

"Listen, when I get to Henry's, I'll take pictures of the tires."

"Not necess—"

"Just in case," he interrupted. "Just in case, Lily."

I nodded and we rode for a few minutes in silence.

"So you and Salinger?" he asked me.

I felt my face flame and tried to fight a smile. "Stop."

He playfully pushed my shoulder. "Dude, I really like him. He's good to you."

I shook my head. "Honesty time?"

"Go for it."

"I like him, Ansen. So much."

"Good."

"No, it's not good."

"Why?" he asked.

"Because he is *not* into me, dude."

"Bullshit." He looked at me like I was an idiot. "That's not how guys work. No guy would invest this much time in a girl if he wasn't into you."

I shook my head. "And when you help me out?" I asked him.

"That's different. We grew up together. We're like siblings."

"I know, but that's how Salinger is, or that's how he sees me." Ansen looked skeptical. "I'm serious, Ansen. He said something in New Orleans, like a sort of warning to me."

"What did he say?"

"Remember that girl Lyric from Ashleigh's party that night?"

"Yeah, kind of."

"That chick is in love with him."

"Damn, what does this guy have that I don't?" he

259

joshed.

"Shut up. Remember Katie much?"

The look he gave me made my mouth drop. "You don't have to remind me of Katie," he said in the most serious tone I'd ever heard Ansen talk. "Katie is all I think about."

Satisfied, I moved on. "That Lyric girl wouldn't stop sweating him. I guess she professed her undying love or some shit to him and he cut ties with her. He said, and I quote, *I don't understand how hard it is to take a hint. She just couldn't be cool.*"

"And you decided to take that as a warning?"

"Yes, Ansen! That was most definitely a hint."

Ansen rubbed the back of his neck. "I don't know, Lily, you might be reading too much into that."

"I don't think so, friendo."

He shivered. "Will you stop calling me that already?" I laughed. "He was too good in that role, you know? A little too convincing." He shivered once more and I laughed yet again.

Ansen smiled at me. "It's good to see you smiling again."

I sobered a little bit. "I'm starting to feel happy, Ansen, and I don't deserve it."

"Stop," he whispered.

Two tears slipped down my face. "Mama's not even cold in the ground yet, my sisters are in a stranger's home, and I have the audacity to feel happy? How dare I indulge that part of myself?"

"That's where you're wrong. It's not an indulgence. It's a right. Can't you see what kind of person you've become? You're transformed. You've quit drugs, got a job, revealed a pretty extraordinary talent, if I do say so myself, fixed up your house, and are fighting to get your sisters back. If you don't have the right to feel happy, then I don't know who does."

I shook my head and stared at my lap as the tears fell on my hands. "How can I feel happy when our mother is gone?"

"You're confusing the feelings, goofball. You're not happy *because* your mother is gone. The grief you feel for the loss of your mom and the happiness you experience because you're becoming a person worthy of happiness is mutually exclusive. You're allowed to know happiness and sadness all at once, Lily. It's a part of real life."

"Maybe," I whispered, but I wasn't entirely convinced.

"Anyway," he said as we pulled up to the courthouse, "tell your sisters Ansen says hi and that he loves them."

I smiled at him. "I will."

I handed him my card and my keys and squeezed his hand as I slid out of his car.

"Thanks, moron."

"You're welcome, dummy."

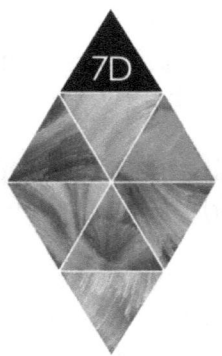

CHAPTER TWENTY-FOUR

"You're late," Sylvia whispered to me when I entered the courthouse.

"So sorry," I told her, without explaining why.

I knew telling her about the things Trace had done couldn't possibly help my case, nor would it endear her to me. I'm an ex-drug addict who had shifted her life, yes, but she'd probably seen hundreds of dysfunctional people make changes only to fall right back into dysfunction. Excuses probably weren't tolerated, and I wouldn't blame her. So I kept my mouth shut.

"Did you bring your paperwork?" she asked. "The pictures?"

"Yes, ma'am."

"Good." She took in my appearance. "You look nice. Great job."

"Thanks."

I clenched my hands together then tucked them into my sides.

"Nervous?" she asked.

"Yes."

"Don't worry. We have a very good chance of getting visitation today." She smiled at me. "Be hopeful."

I let out a nervous sigh and smiled.

"How is the house coming along?" she asked.

I opened my messenger bag and took out the photos. "See for yourself?"

She took them in her hand and started flipping through them. "Wow. Wow. *Wow!*" she said with every flip of a photo. "Lily, this is incredible."

I smiled at her. "Thank you."

She looked at me. "You have an eye for design."

"Thank you." I giggled. "Most of everything you see there we got in the clearance section of home improvement stores."

"We?"

I felt my face grow hot. "Yeah, my friend Salinger has helped me out a lot. I couldn't have done it without him."

"A good friend, methinks."

"Yes, ma'am."

"Well, you can't tell it's clearance stuff. Seriously, Lily. It's very pretty. Very, uh," she said, snapping her fingers and looking up at the ceiling, "boho modern."

"Thanks and I'm having the roof replaced this Friday."

"And the floors?" she asked. "Faye Briar will mention those at your eventual custody hearing."

"As soon as I'm done replacing the roof, I'll start on the floors. It's the last thing I need to improve."

She smiled at me. "Very good."

My phone indicated a text and I brought it out.

Good luck, Little. Let me know how it goes.

I smiled to myself.

Thank you. I will, I wrote back.

I put my phone on silent when they called our case. My heart beat in my throat. As soon as I walked into the courtroom, I saw Eloise and Callie. I burst out crying, unable to help myself, and ran to them. They started crying when they saw me too and ran up to me. I hugged them both around the neck and kissed their cheeks.

"I have missed you both so much," I whispered in their ears.

I let them go to get a better look at them. Their hair was shorter, well groomed, something I don't think they'd ever really had before. They both had headbands in their hair and sweet dresses on as well as new shoes. They looked healthier than I'd ever seen them.

"You look beautiful, girls." They smiled through their tears and I did the same. "How are you both feeling?"

Eloise looked at Callie. "We're okay," she said.

Callie smiled at me. "We miss Mama."

I burst into tears but stifled it. "I know, baby, so do I."

"But Hollie and Matt and are really sweet to us, Lily," Eloise said, pointing behind her.

Two admittedly sweet-looking people, people I'd not really gotten a good look at during my mother's funeral, stood behind them. They both waved at me.

"Come meet them!" Callie said. Both girls

dragged me by the hand over to their foster parents.

"Lily," Hollie greeted me and picked my hand up, holding it between her own, "I'm so happy to meet you. The girls have told me so much about you," she said, her eyes glassy, as if she was fighting back tears.

"Have they?" I whispered, barely able to talk.

"They have," the man added in. "It's nice to meet you. I'm Matthew and this is my wife, Hollie."

"Nice to meet you both," I could barely voice.

"We're so sorry for the loss of your mother," Hollie told me.

"Thank you," I told her, wiping an errant tear away.

"Your sisters are very sweet girls," she added, changing the subject. I thought for my benefit, but I wasn't sure.

"They're wonderful," I agreed.

I stared down at Callie's hand in Hollie's and felt a little overwhelmed. Callie swung their hands together like it was something she did all the time, like it was something with which she was familiar. I didn't know what to think of that. A feeling of sorrow is the only way I could describe it.

Hollie was dressed impeccably as was her husband. They were moneyed, that was apparent, which made me feel a little better just because I'd known so many foster kids whose foster parents were in it for the government check. These people obviously were not.

"Thank you for taking such good care of them," I told them. "They seem so happy and healthy." My bottom lip shook at my last statement. I was grateful to them, but it was hard to see them doing so well without me as selfish as that sounds.

"Happiness is their natural state," Matthew told me, making me laugh a little. *Ironic*.

"Yes," I agreed, unable to say anything else.

The bailiff entered the courtroom and we all turned their direction.

"Court is now in session, the Honorable Samuel McFadden presiding," he announced to the room.

I nodded to the girls and took my place next to Sylvia.

"Thank you," the judge said. He looked up from underneath his reading glasses. "If you'll be seated."

We all sat.

"Court calls number four on the docket, the city of Smithfield Child Protective Services vs. Lily Hahn," the bailiff announced.

"Good morning," the judge said.

"Good morning, Judge," we said.

"This court has been assigned as to the visitation rights of Miss Lily Hahn, sister of Eloise and Callie Bodine. This is a show cause hearing requested by plaintiff Lily Hahn as to an order entered by this court. The record should reflect that the previous ruling found Miss Hahn to be of unfit status and denied visitation. It is my understanding that Miss Hahn has entered a complaint and would like to revisit this previous ruling. Is that correct, Counselor Spears?"

"Yes, Your Honor," Sylvia replied.

"So at this time, I ask if you are ready to proceed on your show cause motion?"

"We are, Your Honor," Sylvia replied.

"Proceed."

Sylvia stood and gathered all the documents I'd brought with me. "At this time, I would like to present to the court weekly drug tests voluntarily taken by Miss Hahn proving she has remained sober since her mother's demise. We would also like to show that Miss Hahn has made drastic physical improvements to her property in order to make it fit for children to live."

"Bring these documents to me," the judge replied.

Sylvia approached the bench and handed the judge the documents.

He perused them for easily five minutes, paying close attention to the drug tests, then moved on to the photos of the property.

"And has the plaintiff kept employment?"

"Yes, sir," she said, approaching the bench once more. "Here is a letter from her employer, Casey Goodwin, showing the date she started work and her current employment status."

"Very good," he said, and Sylvia joined my side once more.

The judge addressed me directly. "And Miss Hahn, I understand it is your wish to regain full custody of your sisters? Is that correct?"

"Yes, sir."

He nodded.

"The court finds plaintiff Lily Hahn fit for supervised visitation once a week on a day to be worked out by the parties involved and only under the condition that Miss Hahn provides and passes weekly drug tests. Is this satisfactory for your

267

plaintiff, Counselor Spears?"

"Yes, Your Honor."

"Miss Briar?" he asked Faye from Child Protective Services.

"We agree."

"Good. Court is adjourned." Judge McFadden looked at me as he stood. "Miss Hahn, keep up the good work."

"Yes, sir," I replied, overwhelmed.

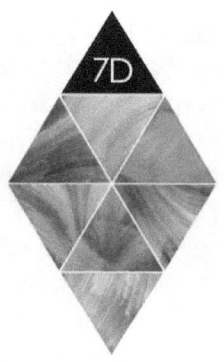

CHAPTER TWENTY-FIVE

I'd gained visitation rights with my sisters. I'd done it. I sat in the lobby outside the courtroom and waited for Sylvia. Hollie, Matthew, and my sisters came out of the courtroom and approached me.

"I did it, girls!"
"Yes!" Wheezy squealed.
Callie looked up at me, her eyes excited. "Does this mean you come to live with us and Matt and Hollie's house now?"

I furrowed my brows and swallowed nothing. "No, baby, it just means you can come visit me once a week."

"Cool!" Cal exclaimed, but instead of hugging me as I'd expected, she hugged Hollie, and my stomach sank to the ground.

Hollie, not realizing my turmoil, hugged her tightly back. Eloise hugged Matt around the waist. I watched them live out this intimate moment with people who were strangers to me.

"So what days work best for you for visitation?" I asked them. "I work nights, so my days are free."

Matt looked over at Hollie. "That's all you, babe."

Hollie smiled at me. "I think Sundays would be best. What do you think?"

"Sundays are great," I told her.

Hollie took her phone out of her purse. "Let me have your number," she said.

I recited it to her and she sent a text letting me know her own number.

"Whenever you need to get in touch with us, just call or text," she offered.

"I will, thank you."

"We should go," Matt said to Hollie, tapping his watch. "The girls have swim practice in an hour."

Hollie glanced at the time on her phone. "Whoa! Cutting it close." She looked at me. "If you'll excuse us, the girls have practice in an hour and a meet right after. We need to run home and get their stuff."

The girls squealed then bounced on their heels and spun the bells of their dresses excitedly.

"Oh, of course," I said, watching my sisters play.

"Girls," Hollie said, catching their attention. "Tell your sister goodbye and let's jet."

Callie and Eloise both hugged me hard and I kissed the tops of their heads. "I'll see you next week, girls."

"See you next week, Lily!" Eloise said, and started running toward the doors.

"Wait!" Matt called after her.

Callie chased after Eloise and Matt started after both. "Nice to meet you!" he called back.

"Nice to meet you," I said, but I don't think he heard me.

"Remember what I said," Hollie told me. "Call or text whenever you feel like contacting the girls or if you need anything."

"Yes, thank you," I whispered.

Hollie hugged me goodbye and ran off after her husband and my sisters.

I looked at the door, wondering what to think.

Tears started to fall; I felt so incredibly alone. It was weird to see my baby sisters living a life separate from mine. A life without me. A life they seemed happy in. Don't get me wrong, I knew they loved me. It wasn't that. It was just lonely. Really, unbelievably lonely. It was weird for me because they were all I had left.

I fell onto a nearby bench and waited for Sylvia, desperate for her to come out so I could go home and cry in peace.

But you don't get to do that, do you? You need to get your car, assess the financial damage, and try to make it to work tonight, don't you?

I took a deep breath. "One day at a time. No, one minute at a time," I told myself.

Sylvia met me in the lobby and shook my hand. "Congratulations, you're one step closer."

I smiled at her. "Thank you for all you've done."

"Please, baby, it's my job. Now," she said, handing me a stack of papers. "Keep these in a safe place. It's the terms of our court agreement today." She smiled at me. "Let's keep moving forward now."

I smiled at her and nodded. I turned to head outside but she stopped me.

"Before you go. I want you to know that you're one of those cases where I don't have to worry about my client. You're motivated and driven and I want to thank you for making my job easy."

"I don't know what to say other than if it wasn't for you, all that work would be for nothing. I'm grateful to you."

"As I of you. You should be proud of yourself."

"Sylvia!" a woman yelled our way and she looked back.

"I've got to go. Look out for my next email. Should have it in a couple days," she said walking backward. "Bye, Lily!"

"Bye, Sylvia! Thanks again!"

"No problem!" she yelled out.

I scheduled an Uber and it promised an arrival time of six minutes, so I went outside to absorb the warmth of the sun.

How'd it go, Little? Salinger texted.

It went well. I got weekly visitations. They're supervised, but I'll take what I can get.

That is freaking amazing!

Yeah

See you tonight at work? he asked.

Yeah, see you then.

I caught the expensive Uber back to Henry's Auto Shop near work and found out it cost me six hundred dollars to replace my tires. *That was all my money. I could kill Trace.* I drove home to change for work and dressed near the window in the living room just so I could watch my car to make sure he didn't try to do something again. I counted the ramen packets I had left in my pantry to see if I could make it to pay day. It was close, but I thought I could do it.

I drove my car up to work and parked her close to the entrance even though I knew Casey might get a little pissed. I'd just spent a fortune on the tires, though, and couldn't pay for it again if Trace chose to do it again.

I walked in and threw my keys at Danny. "Watch her, will you?"

He stuck them in his pockets. "Yeah, no prob."

I went to the back and clocked in. When I turned around, I came nose to chest with Salinger. He smelled so good I could barely take it and began to step back. He lifted his arm and offered his fist. "You must crush this," he said, smiling at me.

I bumped fists with him and yanked a pair of gloves from the bin nearby.

We started walking toward the dairy with the other guys.

"You happy?" he asked.

All the breath left my chest at once. He couldn't have known what that question would do to me. How could he? It was innocent. He was innocent.

I tried to steady my racing heart. "Yeah, glad to be making progress."

I went to the back of the dairy coolers and started piling in the new milk and tossing the old. I went there because everybody hated doing dairy. We usually had to flip a coin to see who'd be stuck with it that night. It was cold and it was hard work. I went hoping, no, wishing Salinger wouldn't follow me in. It didn't work.

He came through with one of the heavy jackets

Casey kept in the back for just this job. "What are you doing, crazy?" he asked, tossing the coat over my shoulders.

He brought the bin over to the racks and started fishing through each row of milk for the ones at or past their expiration date. *Why would he willingly endure this hellish part of the job?* I started organizing the racks, bringing the newer gallons toward the back of the shelves.

"Should we buy our tickets to Richmond?" he asked.

I squeezed my eyes shut and gulped down the fear I felt knowing I'd have to admit to him why I could no longer afford my ticket.

"I-I can't go now."

Salinger whipped his head my direction. "What? Why?"

I stopped what I was doing and looked at him. "I, well, something happened to my car today and I had to replace the tires."

"What, all of them?" he asked, a confused expression on my face.

"Yeah," I offered, hoping he'd drop it.

"All four tires? What, were they bad or something?"

"Yeah," I told a half-truth.

"Damn, well, that sucks, but that doesn't mean we have to skip out. We've already paid the registration fees. I'll spot you your ticket price and we'll get up there."

"Thanks," I said, trying for casual, but I didn't think I pulled it off, "but I'll try another tournament some other time."

He stopped working and stood tall. "Lily, what's going on?"

I tried to smile. "I'm just trying not to be such a burden on you. It's not fair to you."

"What the fuck are you talking about?" he asked, getting angry. The heat from his breath heated the air around him. "Will you stop saying shit like that? It's seriously pissing me off. You're not a gosh damn burden, Lily." He was cursing. I couldn't remember a time I'd ever heard Salinger curse. "You're my fucking friend, not a charity case, and I resent this attitude you have toward that friendship. Just fucking stop it already."

He turned back to the milk, working twice as fast and aggressively tossing it out. I started quietly bawling, the tears freezing on my lashes, only to melt with each new one.

"I'm lonely," I whispered.

"What?" he yelled, still peeved.

It startled me.

"Nothing," I said.

He tossed two gallons away and stared at his feet, his hands in fists. He heaved a sigh then marched over to me, landing inches from my face, forcing me to look up at him. Our frozen breath tangled with the other.

"What did you say, Lily." It wasn't a question. It was an order.

"I said I'm alone."

His face softened. "You're not."

I nodded my head in argument. "I am, though. I watched the girls today. They're living a life without me. I never realized how much I'd been holding on to them. I feel like they're the only ones tethering me to this earth, Salinger, and they're loosening the kite string. Every day they fall into the routine of their new family and I feel like I'm losing them."

"You'll get them back, Lily."

"What if I win them back but they don't want to come with me?"

"They will always want to be with you, Lily." He ran a hand through my hair. "Who wouldn't?"

"I'm fighting feelings I don't know how to process."

"That's understandable. That's normal."

"Grief for my mother is approaching and no matter how much I try to tamp it down, it won't stay there."

He nodded. "I can tell, Little."

"I'm weighed down by life, by responsibility, and I have a genuine fear I'm not capable of handling the load."

"We're going to compartmentalize," he said. "I'll help you. "We'll cross each bridge as we arrive to it, and we won't worry about the bridges ahead."

"That's the problem," I whispered. "I'm settled at the entrance of a thousand bridges already and I don't know which one to take."

"No. We'll build a new one. With tools we know are stable, and we'll cross it together."

I closed my eyes and let the heat of his words permeate throughout my cold chest. I opened my eyes to see him watching me. His eyes were kind and compassionate and full of something I couldn't peg, but I knew it was powerful, because I no longer felt cold.

"What can I do for you?" I asked him.

His eyes blew wide for a moment. "What?"

"What do you need?"

"Don't worry about me," he said, trying to turn away.

"No," I said, clutching his jacket, forcing him to face me again. "Tell me something I can do for you. Helping others is therapeutic. I want to be a better friend to you."

He looked a little shocked. His eyes searched my face, as if he could find what he wanted to say written there. He looked torn, like he was fighting with himself, as if he wanted to say something but was forcing himself to keep quiet.

"I-I can't think of anything," he lied.

I tried to read his face but he'd checked his expression and whatever he was torn about was no longer there to be read.

"I'll think of something," I whispered.

Pillows of warm breath billowed out of his mouth. "You let me know when you do then," he whispered back.

He had closed the remaining foot between us while we'd talked, landing inches from me yet again and forcing me to bend at the neck to see him. Heat pooled in my stomach.

"Tell me something," he said.

"Hmm?"

"What did you and Peter Aurek discuss during your match?"

I felt my face flame and it made Salinger smile.

"H-he told me I was pretty."

"Really?" he asked, a small tic in his jaw.

"He asked if I was trying to join their *club*," I said, emphasizing the word "club."

"Is that so?" he asked for his own benefit, another tic in his jaw.

"Then he told me he thought I was a novelty and that he took back that he thought I was pretty. That he found me beautiful but with that, he said I was like lichen on a rock. I was beautiful to look at but didn't really belong."

Salinger seemed to disappear altogether. He looked to the side, his jaw completely clenched.

"I didn't want to engage him, but I couldn't help myself. I took the bait. I asked him where he thought I belonged."

Salinger looked at me once more, fury in his eyes. "What did he say?"

"Maybe I shouldn't tell you," I whispered.

"Too late. I have to know."

"He said tha-that maybe I belonged in his bed."

Salinger closed his eyes. He was furious; I could see it in his choked jaw. He breathed heavily, as if he tried to control himself.

He looked at me. "I wish you'd told me what he'd said that day."

He'd turned once more, avoiding eye contact, so I took in his skin, the tension in his jaw.

"I would have if I'd known you wanted to know."

He met my gaze again. "Always tell me that kind of stuff." His voice was kind.

He swallowed nothing and I followed the movement. Something was building between us and not even I could explain it away. *Oh my God. I want him so much.*

Just then the cooler door opened and Danny came in. I thought Salinger would have pulled away from me, embarrassed at being caught that close to me, but he didn't. Instead, he slowly lifted his head, looking over my own but not meeting Danny's gaze.

"What's up, Danny?" he asked coolly.

"Just wanted to let Lily know that Trace is hanging around outside asking for her."

Salinger whipped his head Danny's direction; both of his hands met the bit of wall behind me, encircling me.

"*What?*"

"Trace is outside for Lily," Danny repeated.

Salinger looked at me. "What does he want from you?"

"I don't know," I told him.

Salinger's arms dropped and he headed straight for the cooler door, passing Danny and tossing his jacket near its hook. I chased after him, tossing my jacket as well, and yelled for him. Danny followed us out.

"Salinger, what are you gonna do?" I asked him.

"I'm just going to have a little talk with him, that's all."

I raced past him to see Trace pacing the sidewalk outside the doors.

"Trace, leave!" I demanded, checking to see how close Salinger was.

He was right behind me.

"What the hell are you doing here, Trace?" Salinger asked him.

"Lily, the cops came by my house today," Trace said, looking pissed. He was hopping around, full of energy. I thought he was on something. "You tell them about what I did to your tires?"

Salinger looked at me. "What did he do to your tires?"

My hands went to the top of my head. "He slashed my tires."

Salinger's eyes blew wide. "What!"

I turned toward Trace. "Why are you doing all this stuff, Trace? Huh? What's wrong with you?"

Trace started acting crazier. "You wanna know why? Because you're ruining my life!" he shouted.

Danny and a couple of the guys had come outside to see what was happening. Danny pushed forward and put a hand on Trace's chest. "Dude, calm the hell down."

Trace pushed against his hand, like he was going to come for me, but Danny and one of the crew guys stopped him. Salinger put his arms around me and tucked me against him.

"That bitch!" Trace pointed at me. "She fucking snitched on me and now the cops are hanging around my house. Can't have them doing that shit!" he rambled. *He's definitely on something.* "I'm going to catch you alone, bitch," he promised, his eyes full of insanity, "and I am going to take you the fuck out!"

"Whoa! Whoa! Trace, what the fuck! What the hell are you on?" Danny yelled at him, pushing him farther from us.

Trace turned to Danny. "She's a fucking bitch!"

Salinger held me tighter.

"Shut up!" Danny said.

"Everyone knows Lily is a whore." I flinched. "She would have done that shit sober; everyone knows that."

"Shut up, Trace!" Salinger yelled, bringing me even closer to him.

Trace pointed at me again. "Now the cops are crawling all over me and I can't fucking shake them." His tone had gone unhinged. "You better get them off me," he spoke directly to me. "Get them off me or so help me God, Lily!"

"Or so help you God, what, Trace?" Salinger asked him, inching forward.

He loosened his grip on me, and I knew he was getting ready to jump on him.

"Salinger, no!" I said, trying to hold him back.

Mark and Demetrius stepped forward and helped me hold him.

"I'm going to put you somewhere no one will be able to find you again." Trace stared at me, *scared* me. "They won't be able to find you!" Danny and the other night crew guys pushed Trace farther into the parking lot as Trace raged out.

Just then a squad car pulled up, as someone must have called the cops. Salinger found me again and wrapped his arms around me as we watched Trace break free from Danny's grip, racing straight for me. My breath hitched but before I could react, Salinger had already spun me around in his embrace and bent over me, his back to Trace in order to protect me. We braced for Trace to hit us, but it never came. I turned to see what was going on. One of the officers had Trace already on the ground, his knee in his back, and started cuffing him.

Salinger turned as well but kept me close to him.

"He threatened to kill her," Salinger told the cop,

who leaned over Trace.

"How many people heard that?" he asked Salinger.

Salinger gestured around us. "All of us."

The cop nodded. "Everyone stay where you are and we'll take statements from each of you."

Adrenaline started to leave my body as I shook. Salinger wrapped me from behind in his arms. "Just relax," he soothed.

"You were right," I whispered. "I should have turned him in."

Trace screamed at me through the back window of the squad car. He went nuts, screaming, banging his head against the glass and cage, trying to kick the door. Eventually one of the officers had to chain his feet to the floorboards.

They took everyone's statements. Luckily we'd been closed for more than an hour and there were no customers present. I think Casey would have fired me if there had been. After each statement, each boy went inside to get back to work, and I felt like such a freaking fool.

"I have to move," I whispered to myself after they took my statement. I turned back to the cop, remembering something. "Can he make bail tonight?"

"Probably," he answered, writing in his notebook.

I nodded. "Thanks."

I walked inside but pulled out my phone, ready to text Katie, but Salinger approached me before I could.

"You can't stay at your house tonight. It's not

safe."

I ran my hands down my face. "I know. I was about to text Katie."

"Don't bother. You can stay at my place again."

"Thanks," I said, feeling exhausted.

Because of Trace, we had to work twice as hard that night to get everything done before Casey came in. I apologized to the crew, but they shook it off. I knew it was annoying, but they were kind enough not to complain, though they had every right to. All the boys I worked with were really generous with me. At the end of our shift, I approached Casey and let him know what happened. He seemed sort of peeved, not at me, he assured me, though I wasn't sure. There wasn't much drama at the store, but I seemed to be the common denominator whenever there was. He said as long as all the work got done and it didn't cause a scandal, he didn't care. I thanked him and left his office.

Salinger was waiting for me in the back when I was done.

"Follow me to my house?" he asked.

"Yeah."

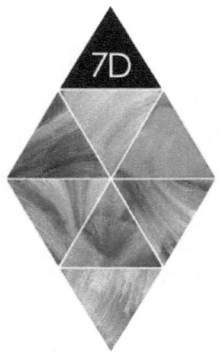

CHAPTER TWENTY-SIX

I stayed at Salinger's the next few days. I went home after my shift on Friday, though, since the roofers were supposed to show up that morning at eight. I was there to greet them and watched in amazement as they shed the sheets of old tin roofing. I saw pallet stacks of the new silver metal roofing and felt a little pressure to go to Richmond.

I swallowed my pride and asked Salinger to get our tickets.

"I already got them," he'd told me through a sneaky smile. He let his head fall back a little when he laughed, exposing the lines of his throat. I watched his Adam's apple move with each snigger.

I shook my head at him but laughed as well. "Thank you," I'd told him.

"No problem, Little."

I talked to the roof contractor and let him know I'd be back Sunday afternoon just in time to see my sisters. Salinger and I left that afternoon for the airport and caught a flight, slept on the plane, the first sleep we'd gotten in more than twenty-four hours, and arrived in Richmond at nine that evening.

The U.S. Open Invitational was at the Jefferson Hotel. We couldn't afford to stay there, so we picked a budget room in a hotel nearby.

When we arrived, though, we went straight to the Jefferson to check in. We stood in yet another registration line in the Grand Ballroom. It was stunning. I literally felt like I was immersed in a different time and place.

"Déjà vu, huh?" he asked.

"Yeah." I looked around me at all the people around us. "This is a much bigger tournament."

"Yeah, but this event is separated by ratings. We'll only be competing against other players in our class. There's only sixty-four and it has the fifty-thousand-dollar cash prize. It's fewer rounds."

I nodded. "That makes sense. Think Peter Aurek will be here?"

Salinger laughed. "Oh, he'll be here for sure, and probably talking the maddest crap about you."

I giggled. "Good."

Salinger elbowed me. "Look who it is." He threw his chin up.

I turned to where he was looking and saw Tao Zhang.

"Tao."

He furrowed his brows and stared at him.

"I heard he wasn't going to be at this one."

"Weird," I commented. I clicked my tongue and shook my head. "Damn, what's second prize?" I asked.

He laughed. "It's twelve thousand," he knocked his head back and looked down his lashes at me, "but why would you even worry about that, playa?"

I smiled and rolled my eyes. "Shut up."

He laughed.

We looked at Tao again and noticed he was talking to someone but was blocking our view. He shifted to his left as he laughed at whatever his conversation partner had said and we finally got a good look at who exactly he was talking to.

"Bernard," I whispered, shocked.

"What is that old fool doing here?" Salinger asked no one.

We were both quiet for a moment. I was unable to process what he was doing there, wondering why he'd break his disappearance streak for this one-off tournament.

We advanced in line.

"He's been talking to Tao a long time," Salinger observed.

"Yeah, it's making me a little jealous."

Salinger barked a laugh. "Me too."

We bumped fists.

Just off the ballroom was a large double staircase ascending to the hotel lobby. Every boy in that room, including Bernard, turned to see the pretty girl coming down them. I narrowed my eyes. *She looks familiar. Oh my God, it's Lyric.*

"Lyric," Salinger whispered, making me burn with jealousy, which felt so weird. It was a knee-jerk reaction. I didn't want to be a girl who grew jealous.

When she reached the bottom of the stairs, she meandered through the crowd saying hello to everyone she knew, and she knew a lot of people, flirting, and being charming. I watched her approach Tao. She disregarded Bernard, probably because she didn't know who he was, but it really pissed me off. Bernard was different, and I knew he probably couldn't care less, but it was rude, especially because Bernard had helped me so much. It made my eyes sting. I sat there and watched her dominate a conversation with Tao, slowly turning her back to Bernard and edging him out.

He looked lost. I could tell he was uncomfortable, and it made me feel sick to my stomach.

"Hold my bag," I told Salinger and handed it over without a second thought.

Within ten seconds, I was on Bernard.

"Bernard," I said as I approached him.

"Young lady, it is very good to see you." He looked around. He stuck his hands behind his back and looked at the crowd around us. "It's very different from when I used to compete. It's very loud."

"It is, but it'll calm down in a few, once the majority of everyone here registers and retires to the Player's Rooms."

"Ahh," he said. He glanced at Tao, who looked trapped himself, if I was honest. I was sure he was loath to pass up the opportunity to speak with Bernard. I could tell by his facial expression he knew exactly who he was.

Lyric glanced behind her at us. Her gaze followed my entire body. She was taking me in, sizing me up. She rolled her eyes and turned back to Tao.

"Would you like to join Salinger and me?" I asked

him.

"Yes, of course," he said, leaning forward, and throwing a hand in front of him. "Lead the way."

I brought him over to Salinger, who greeted him warmly.

"Awfully loud in here," he repeated.

I looked up at Salinger, wondering what we should do.

"We should go to the lobby bar, Bernard," Salinger offered.

"Yes. Let's do that. I don't like it here."

I nodded at Salinger when he handed me his registration papers.

"Let's catch that elevator," Salinger said.

He turned to me. "You'll be okay?"

"Yeah, just fine. Go."

He nodded at me and took poor Bernard away.

I waited another half hour before reaching the registration table. They tried to give me trouble with registering Salinger and I thought for a brief moment I'd have to call him back down but an official waved the registrar on and I got all the necessary entry lanyards and round information for both of us.

I started to make my way toward the elevators, but the line was atrocious. Fed up, I turned and made my way toward the enormous but elegant stairs.

"Lily!" I heard behind me and I turned to see who it was.

"Hello, Tao," I greeted.

"I heard you were here."

"Really? Who told you?"

"Bernard Calvin, of course. He's an old friend of mine."

"Cool. I like Bernard."

Tao laughed. "Yeah, if you like senile old morons."

I narrowed my eyes at him. "He is definitely not a moron, nor is he senile. I'm sorry, but did you say you were *friends* with him?"

He shrugged. "Yeah, but even you have to admit he's off his rocker."

I shook my head. "He's eccentric. Most bona fide geniuses usually are."

He smiled at me. "You don't like me."

"I don't know you. I don't care one way or another for you."

He laughed. "Yeah, but I can tell I annoy you."

"You were rude to me in Austin and you've insulted my friend. So far you're oh for two, Zhang."

His eyes bugged. "You pronounced my name correctly."

"Listen, is there a reason you stopped me? I've got to get back to Salinger and Bernard."

Tao looked behind me briefly and shifted and put his hands in his pockets. "Yeah, I've been meaning to ask you about that. Are you and Salinger, like, a thing or something?"

I shook my head. "No, we're just friends."

"Lily?" someone called for me. I recognized Salinger's voice.

I felt my stomach grow tight. *I wonder if he heard that?*

"Just checking on you," he said. "You coming?"

"Uh, yeah." I turned toward Tao. "If you'll excuse

me, we're gonna sit with Bernard in the bar upstairs."

"Oh, really? You don't mind if I join you, right?"

I looked at Salinger, unsure what to say.

"Uh, sure," I told him.

All three of us climbed the stairs to the main lobby and crossed the marble floor to the small bar there. Bernard sat at a table, sipping a drink.

"You were gone forever!" he said to Salinger.

"I was only gone two minutes, Bernard. Stop being dramatic."

Bernard leaned forward when I sat. He glanced at Tao but didn't greet him.

"Young lady," he said.

"Yes?"

"Do you know who this man is?" he asked me.

I coughed over a laugh. "Um, yes, I do."

"This is the boy you will play in the final round."

I turned to Tao. "I didn't know you were playing this tournament."

"When I found out you would be here and since you were explicit when you said you wouldn't be going to Nationals, I just knew I had to come see you for myself," Tao told me.

"Pish, posh!" Bernard interrupted. "She will be at Nationals. Why would you assume she wouldn't be at Nationals?"

"Because she told me so herself," Tao answered him.

Bernard stared at me like I had two heads.

"You are going to Nationals. Period."

I turned toward Bernard and chose to ignore his demand. "Bernard, you don't know if I will even make it to the final round."

Tao and Salinger looked at me, both boys with totally different expressions on their faces.

Bernard rapped his knuckle on the table. "Absolute horse hockey. You are the best player here."

Tao grinned at me.

"Well," I argued, "Tao's rating is so much higher than mine, Bernard. He's the better player."

"Wrong," he said. I felt my face and throat flame. "You are the best player here, probably the best player nationally, and even more likely to be the best player in the world."

He was giving me a panic attack. "Bernard!" I exclaimed. "You're overestimating me!"

He looked at me, actually met my eye line, something he'd rarely done. "That is an untruth. I have perfectly estimated you."

Tao watched me closely, very closely. He sat back in his chair, his head cocked to one side, tongued one of his eyeteeth, and smiled. He made me very uncomfortable.

"Excuse me, young man!" Bernard called out to the bartender. He stood and approached the bar, unaware of the tension at the table.

I looked toward Salinger, but he wasn't looking at me, he was looking at Tao.

"He's overestimating me," I said quietly, staring at my hands on the table.

"I guess we'll find out," Tao said, standing up. I looked up at him and he leaned over me, his hand resting on the table next to my own hands. "Don't you dare lose in the first few rounds." He stood upright again, stuck his hands in his pockets, and walked back through the lobby.

I watched him walk to the stairs then turned back toward Salinger. I was ready to say something to him but the expression on his face confused me. He almost looked angry at me. *He couldn't possibly be angry at* me, *right?*

"What's wrong?" I asked him.

He looked down at the table. "Nothing," he lied. "I'll be right back," he said, standing up and walking out.

"Wait! Salinger!" I called after him, but he ignored me.

I watched his back disappear under the stairs and wanted to chase after him, but I didn't want to leave Bernard either. He sat next to me again.

"This man didn't know what a sidecar was. Despicable. Calling himself a bartender." I turned his direction. He looked around the table. "Where are Salinger and Tao?"

"I think I scared them off."

"Unlikely," he commented. "You're not frightening."

"I just meant I must have said or done something to offend them both."

"You must remedy that then," he said, sipping his drink.

"I don't care so much to chase after Tao, but I do want to find Salinger."

"Check his room."

"We're not staying here."

"What? That is ridiculous. No, I'll have none of that. Come here, young lady," he demanded.

I followed him into the lobby.

"They had rooms available," I explained, not sure what he was so upset about and taking a shot in the dark. "We just can't afford them."

"That is such a stupid reason to not do anything."

I laughed. "Some would disagree with you, Bernard."

He studied me. "I suppose. I've never really had that problem, though. My family was rich and I made a lot of money in tournaments before I left the circuit. I invested well."

I stifled a giggle. "That's wonderful, Bernard."

We stood at the front desk until someone called us.

"What are you doing?" I asked him.

"I'm getting you two a room."

"No, seriously, Bernard, we don't have the cash for this."

"I know this, daft girl! I'm getting you two a pair of rooms."

"Bernard! That's too expensive. I can't let you do that."

He waved me off as he usually did.

"Mr. Calvin, a pleasure to see you again," the desk clerk said, but I could tell he most definitely did not actually feel that way. "How can I help you?"

"Yes, I need two rooms."

"Two *more* rooms?" he asked.

"Is there someone here who is not incompetent?" he responded.

"Bernard!" I kindly chided. "That's rude."

"It's fine," the clerk told me. "I'm sorry, Mr. Calvin. Yes, I can get two more rooms for you. Would

293

you like the same number of nights?"

"I am only staying one night. That is the minimum and maximum. Are you sure there isn't someone else here who might be able to help me? Not that inept bartender, though."

I'm sorry, I mouthed to the clerk.

"One night it is," the clerk replied.

He printed up a receipt and handed Bernard two plastic entry keys.

"Thank you, young man. You have performed satisfactorily."

"My pleasure, sir."

We walked off and Bernard handed me a key. "Here you are, young lady."

"Thank you, Bernard. It's really very nice of you."

"I am not nice. I am merely making it so you will be closer to the tournament. I want to make sure you are at your optimal tomorrow."

I smiled a knowing smile at him. "Sure, Bernard. Of course."

Bernard and I walked around for a few minutes trying to find Salinger but people kept approaching us wanting to talk to Bernard, and eventually he became overwhelmed, so I walked him back to his room. I went to the front desk to have them take my and Salinger's luggage out of storage and delivered to our rooms. We'd had them store it while we registered and had plans on taking it out before we left for our own hotel.

I made the rounds in the ballroom but didn't find him. Right when I was ready to give up and head for bed since it was getting late, I decided to try the skittles room once more.

That's where he was. Standing in a circle with Tao Zhang, Peter Aurek, Lyric, and a bunch of other people around our age. He laughed at something Lyric said and my stomach fell to my feet. I thought about going up to him and giving him his key to his new room but thought better of it. I decided, instead, I would text him my room number and he could pick it up himself whenever he was ready. The idea of approaching that group gave me so much anxiety I nearly felt sick.

I turned around near the door and started to exit the room.

"Lily!" someone called out to me. "Where are you going!"

I stopped where I stood and tried to compose myself before turning around.

It was Tao. He was waving me over to him.

Oh my God, should I just bail right here? I knew I couldn't do that or risked looking really stupid so I steeled my nerve and started walking their direction.

"Guys," Tao introduced, "this is Lily. She's the one who beat Aurek last week in Austin."

Everyone started teasing Peter, but he surprised me by blushing and waving at me.

"Hi, Lily, nice to see you again," he greeted.

"Hi, Peter," I spoke softly.

"So, Lily here is rumored to be trained by Bernard Calvin," Tao added, slapping even more unwanted attention on me.

Everyone standing had open, gaped mouths, as if they couldn't believe what he'd said.

"He's just a nice man who helped me with the

competition part of tournament. I'd only ever played online before Austin," I tried to explain away.

"Oooh," one guy I didn't know laughed and pushed his forearm into Peter's shoulder, "you got beat by a newbie?"

Peter blushed again. "Just you wait, Callahan. Pray you don't cross her path," he said, surprising me yet again.

The group got quiet and I stared at my feet, placed my nervous hands in the back pockets of my shorts.

"Good to have another girl around, huh, Lyric?" some guy asked her.

My heart started to race.

"Yeah," Lyric dodged. She smiled, but it didn't feel friendly and she avoided eye contact. Instead, she stared off to the side when she answered him.

"Lyric, I didn't see your name on the roster," Peter commented.

Lyric's face tinged pink. "Yeah, I, uh, didn't make the ratings minimum."

"Damn," Tao said, coughing around a laugh.

I actually felt sorry for her but knew anything I could say at that moment, regardless how kind I meant it, would be interpreted as anything but.

"She'll get them back up," Salinger said, coming to her rescue, and speaking for the first time since I'd joined the group. He smiled at her. "Won't you?" He pushed his shoulder into hers.

She smiled at him and he smiled back.

This is so selfish to admit, but I felt so betrayed for some reason. *Can't be betrayed by someone who doesn't belong to you, moron.* It felt more painful than I thought it would, though, because it was made worse in that Salinger hadn't looked at me, hadn't greeted me, hadn't met my eyes once since I'd joined the group.

Can inaction hurt your feelings? The answer to that was yes. He was idle in being my friend, I thought, and I deserved more respect than that. I stared up at the ceiling desperately trying to keep myself from crying. It wouldn't make sense to anyone around me, and I didn't know any of them well enough to explain it away. I didn't want a reputation.

I took a deep breath and let it out slowly while they kept up a conversation I wasn't following.

"What about you, Lily?" Tao asked me.

I looked at him. "What?"

He laughed at me. "Where have you been?

"Just thinking," I told him softly.

"You're kind of weird."

I felt my face heat up. I stood awkwardly, not sure what to say. I was a confident, quick-witted person around my friends but get me around strangers and I struggled fiercely.

"Isn't everybody?" Peter Aurek commented and everyone laughed.

It was apparent Peter's attempt to intimidate me at our game had embarrassed him and he was trying to make up for it. I liked that about him. I smiled at him in thanks, my cheeks growing hotter by the second. He smiled back.

That was the moment Salinger chose to look at me, or rather through me. His stare cold daggers.

"Can I talk to you for a second, Salinger?" I asked

him.

"Later," he told the floor, putting me on the spot.

Everyone stared between us, and it all felt a little heavy. Right when I was about to tell everyone good night, though, one of the guys I didn't know broke the tension by telling a funny story about how he lost his last tournament to a seven-year-old kid from Seattle. While everyone laughed, I noticed Lyric leaning into Salinger as she spoke into his ear. He laughed at whatever she said, and I decided I didn't want to be there anymore.

"Well, guys, it's getting late, I'm gonna head up to my room, catch a few winks."

I started to walk backward and waved. Everyone waved back and told me good night. I turned for the door and fought the urge to run.

When I turned into the hall, I remembered Bernard's room key for Salinger.

"Gosh damn it," I whispered to no one.

I decided to take the key to the front desk. They agreed to keep it in an envelope for him to pick up at his convenience, so I texted him what Bernard had done and headed toward my room. Most everyone had cleared out at that point as it approached midnight. The first match was just after lunch, though, so I knew I could sleep in, if I wanted, or even work on endgame strategies.

Keep it together, Lily. I got on the elevator and pressed for my floor, praying it wouldn't stop again.

Remember the list, Lily.

Focus on winning tomorrow, Lily.

298

It'll be okay, Lily.

Won't it, Lily?

Will it, Lily?

Your sisters seemed happy, didn't they, Lily?

They don't need you anymore, Lily.

Salinger's grown tired of you, Lily.

So who are you doing all this for, Lily?

You don't know anymore, do you, Lily?

Oh my God, you're not worth it, Lily.

Worthless Lily.

Stupid Lily.

Lost Lily.

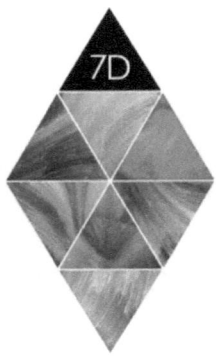

CHAPTER TWENTY-SEVEN

The hectic had caught up to me and I was teetering on a knife's edge. It was all proving a lot for one person to take.

I'd lost my mom.

Lost my sisters.

I was assaulted and tormented by Trace.

I'd had to avoid eye contact with everyone in a town I knew had seen pictures of my naked body and whose antiquated ideas probably led them to believe I was some kind of whore.

I endured the emotional turmoil of fighting for my sisters.

And the physical toll of making our house livable so I could get them back.

I quit a drug I'd always used to help me cope.

I'd held in the enormous, unbelievable grief I felt for Mama.

And struggled to come to terms with my role in her death.

And the guilt I felt for the girls losing their mother.

I tried my hardest not to let all of the above send me over the edge.

I did all that while striving not to fall in love with someone I didn't deserve.

I was proving idle, worthless, ineffective. I was losing. I *knew* I was losing. I *felt* it.

I'd relied too heavily on Salinger and I just had this feeling he was *done* being my friend. I knew boys. They were simple. Not dumb, just, you know, uncomplicated. They either liked you or they didn't. Something had happened, something had clicked for him, I thought. He wasn't acting angry or pissed. He was usually blunt enough to tell me when something bothered him. He acted exactly like a boy who'd had a change of heart. I was familiar with that behavior. I was privy to its inner workings.

And I didn't think there was a cure for a change of heart.

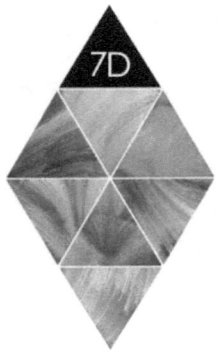

CHAPTER TWENTY-EIGHT

I fell asleep immediately. I knew life always looked different in the light of day, at least that's what I'd hoped. Around three in the morning, though, I was woken up by a few loud partiers across the hall. I tried everything I could to get back to sleep to no avail. They were getting louder and louder and louder until finally I couldn't take any more.

I threw the covers off me and opened my room door to see Lyric, of all people, in T-shirt and wind shorts, her hair sticking up at all angles.

"You're waking up the whole damn floor!" She was yelling at four obviously inebriated men.

They all turned toward me when I opened my door.

"Lyric?" I asked, my voice scratchy from sleep.

She ignored me and turned back toward the men. They had the decency to appear appropriately checked.

"So sorry," one of them said. The others fought a giggle but kept quiet. "We'll keep it down."

They went back into their room and shut their door. As Lyric turned around, she glanced at me but didn't acknowledge me. She went straight into *Salinger's* room, closing the door behind her.

I stood there, my heart racing, my stomach queasy.

Why is she in Salinger's room?
What is Lyric doing in Salinger's room?
Oh my God, I'm so stupid.

I stood there, my mouth opening and closing like a fish out of water.

Well, if that isn't a giant bucket of ice water...

Confirmed.

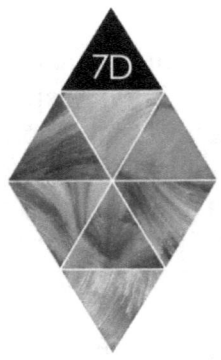

CHAPTER TWENTY-NINE

"Get up," I quieted to myself for the hundredth time that morning.

I fought the urge to stay where I was, to forget everything, and just let the world swallow me up how it saw fit. I'd cried for hours, cried myself back to sleep, only to wake up at eleven in the morning and cry again. I had an hour before my first round was to begin.

I didn't know what to do. I honestly didn't know what to do.

"I miss Mom," I told the ceiling, tears streaming down the sides of my face.

I imagined her sitting on the edge of the other bed in the room.

"What should I do, Mom?" I asked her.

She didn't answer me, though.

I imagined she smiled at me, and that made me miss her more than I could possibly explain. I wanted to roll over and hug her as tight as I could to keep her from leaving me again.

"Mama, I miss you," I told the imaginary figure sitting there. "So much. I wish you could have seen me make something of myself. I wish you could have seen all the work I should have done while you were here. I wish you could have seen that in person. I regret not doing that for you. I know you were only capable of so much, and I should have shown you what it meant to be strong. I'm sorry I didn't pick you up that night." I sobbed into my hands then wiped my face on my sleeve. "So sorry for that. More sorry than you could comprehend.

"I feel awfully alone without you. I know I have Ansen and Katie, but they're their own entity, aren't they? They'd do anything for me, I know it, but it's not the same.

"The girls seem to be doing so well it's actually scaring me. I'm scared they don't need me anymore. That frightens me because I love them more than I love myself. And I want to be someone's most important person. Know what I mean? I feel if I was someone's most important person I would have reason, value."

I stared at her beautiful face, forever stuck in that state, never to grow old, never to see me marry or my sisters marry, never to know grandchildren.

I rolled onto my side and curled into a ball.

"I feel like I stole a lot of things away from you and the girls, Mama. I'm desperate for forgiveness, but you can't forgive me, can you? That's why I feel stuck. So stuck."

I pulled the covers over my head, unable to look

at her anymore, regardless that she was only there because I'd put her there. I laid there for countless minutes, counting the breaths I took that didn't really belong to me.

My phone began to ring and it startled me. I tossed the cover once more to stop the grating sound but when I sat up, my mother was gone. I stared at the perfectly unrumpled bedding where I'd imagined her.

The phone rang once more and I picked it up.

"Hello?" I asked.

"Young lady, where in the Sam Hill are you?" Bernard asked me.

"I'm still in my room."

"What in heavens—" he began but stopped short. "It's no matter. Get up. Come down here. You have half an hour before your first round. I expect to see you in ten."

I sighed. "Yes, sir."

I hung up and decided I'd obey him. He'd come looking for me if I didn't anyway. And for some reason, I didn't want to disappoint Bernard. He'd been so kind to me, despite his rough demeanor. I was starting to learn that Bernard had his own way of caring for others. It was unconventional, but it was kindness.

So I stood up, stripped my clothes off, and headed for the shower, brushed my teeth, and dressed in clean clothing, placing my lanyard around my neck. I'd barely towel dried my hair when I decided I no longer cared. I forewent makeup, didn't bother to dry, let alone brush my hair, and wore an old pair of slippers I'd brought from home on a whim instead of my nicer shoes.

I left the room, the key in my back pocket, and headed for the elevators. My saturated hair dripped down the back of my T-shirt. When the doors opened, there was a group of women standing, waiting to get on. They looked at me strangely as I passed them.

The skittles room was *packed*, but I found Bernard at a table in the far back. The stares I got walking from the front of the room to him made my skin crawl. Bernard's eyes bugged when he saw me. He stood.

"There's something wrong with you," he told me.

"I'm fine," I could barely say.

He looked worried. "Let me get Salinger," he said.

"No," I said a little too forcefully. "No," I said again, softer.

He leaned toward me. "Are you sure?"

"I'm certain. Shall we discuss strategies?" I asked him, desperate to change the subject.

"Only if you are capable," he stated.

"I'm more than," I assured him.

He eyed me as if he didn't believe me but gestured to the nearest table. "Sit then."

We discussed strategy vigorously, but I found without a cluttered head I remembered everything as if I was recalling my own name. And my head was just that. Uncluttered or unable to cope with anything, however you wanted to look at it. Either way, I was starting to feel okay with it.

It was the most peace I'd felt in a long time.

Someone blew open the skittles room door and announced the first round. Bernard stood when I did.

"The best of luck to you, young lady."

"Thank you, Bernard."

I turned and made for the double doors that led into the corridor. Halfway through the room, I noticed a group of people. Among them were Salinger and Lyric. They stood next to one another. I searched my chest and stomach and wondered where my earlier feelings were, but they weren't there. *Just as well.*

"Is that *Lily*?" Peter Aurek asked the group.

I felt everyone's eyes when they turned to see who Peter was referring to. My dripping hair stuck to the sides of my face. I was certain my eyes looked red and swollen. I knew what I looked like.

Salinger's eyes popped wide. "Lily?" he whispered.

I closed my eyes when he did it. A sliver of pain blasted through my entire body when he said my name but dissipated just as quickly. I was broken.

I ignored him.

"She's fucking crazy," Lyric said, probably delighting in my current state.

I didn't blame her. If I was an opportunist as she was, I'd exploit me for everything it was worth too.

I'd just passed them when I heard her laugh. "Something is seriously wrong with her."

I felt their eyes on the back of my head but kept going.

"Lily!" Salinger called out again, but I didn't respond.

Instead, I passed through the doorway and straight for the tournament hall. When I reached it, the official stared at me, confused.

"Are you... competing?" he asked.

"Yes. Lily Hahn."

He stuttered out an okay and flipped through his list. "Uh, uh, table twelve, seat three."

I nodded and found my spot.

I sat.

I waited.

And waited.

A boy, maybe sixteen or seventeen, sat across from me.

I stared at the tall, heavy-looking velvet curtains encasing the small stage the room possessed.

When all the seats were filled, they allowed spectators to fill in along the walls. Lyric came in and meandered her way through people until she reached Salinger's table. I saw Bernard as well. He was stuck somewhere near Salinger as well, but he'd voiced his displeasure, I'd heard him, about how he wanted to stand on the stage. He kept asking why he couldn't get on the stage.

They told him he couldn't several times and he finally agreed to stay where he was.

"Young lady!" Bernard yelled into the room.

Everyone quieted, a few giggled. I looked over at Bernard. I noticed Salinger staring at me as well as Lyric.

"Good luck, my girl!"

I nodded and stared at my board.

The official made a big to-do emphasizing the importance of staying quiet that I thought was for Bernard's benefit only then called the time.

"Good luck," the boy told me.

"Same," I was able to mutter back.

I defeated him. Easily. So easily he was speechless. I was the first to finish. When the official was done marking our results I shook the boy's hand and started for the doors.

"Already?" Bernard practically shouted, calling for the official to shush him.

The whole room turned toward me as I left.

"Wherever you are going, young lady, be back within the hour," he shouted after me.

Everyone started laughing, but I just raised two fingers, my index and middle, together in acknowledgment.

"Mr. Calvin, do you need to leave?" I heard an official ask him as I left, his tone pissed.

Bernard shook his head. Tao watched me, followed every step I made until I was out of view. So did Aurek.

So did Salinger.

I decided I'd go back to my room. My hair had dried, but my shirt was still soaked through and it made me cold, so I changed. I laid down and as I did so, I thought about my sisters. I decided to text Hollie.

Hi, Hollie, it's Lily. I wanted to know if it would be okay to talk to the girls.

I immediately received a reply.

Of course! Let's facetime. Are you free now?

Yes, I texted.

She called and our phones connected. I saw the girls' faces and I nearly burst out crying. They crowded into the camera, jumping up and down, and waving at me. I could see Hollie in the background giggling at their excitement.

"Lily!" they both screamed, smiling. "Lily, we miss you!"

The tears I'd been fighting came anyway. "Aww, I miss you too, girls! I can't wait to see you tomorrow evening for dinner."

Callie left the screen, but I could hear her chant "I'm excited" over and over, which made me feel more human again.

"Where are you at?" Hollie asked. "It looks like a hotel?"

I nodded. "Yes, I'm at a chess tournament in Richmond, Virginia," I explained.

Hollie looked surprised but happy. "Wow! Are you competing?"

"Yes, ma'am," I said.

"Are you any good?" she asked me.

"I try," I told her.

"Well, that's awesome!"

"Thank you."

"Lily," Eloise began, "I lost a tooth!"

"What! Crazy! That's so cool," I told her.

"I know! And the tooth fairy gave me five dollars! Can you believe it!"

"Wheezy, that is so neat. What are you gonna do with it?"

She looked up in thought then back at me. "I don't know yet, Lily, I have so many ideas."

I choked back tears. "Well, you let me know as soon as you've decided."

"I will!" she promised.

Callie came back, but I could only see part of her face at the corner of my screen.

"I wanna lose a tooth, too, Lily. I check every day for a loose one."

"Hang in there, ladybug, it'll happen."

"Just don't force it," Hollie contributed, laughing.

"Yeah," I agreed with her. "Where's Matt?" I asked them.

"Dad went golfing," Callie explained.

My heart slowed to a complete stop before picking up at a feverish pace. *She said* dad.

"Th-that's cool," I stuttered.

I saw Eloise step down from a stool or chair. "We gotta go," she said. "Cal and I were playing Barbies, Lily. "

"Oh, yes, I get it, baby. Go play. I love you both so much."

"I love you," Eloise told me and ran off.

"I love you!" Callie called out and presumably ran with Eloise.

"Sorry it was so short," Hollie added.

"No, I get it. I love they're so happy. I-I wouldn't have it any other way," I barely got out. I meant it. I actually meant it, but it was hard to say, all the same. "Thank you so much for letting me talk to them."

She smiled. "Call me any time, Lily. Any time."

I smiled back. "See you tomorrow then."

"See you then."

I hung up.

"I wish I knew what I was doing," I told no one.

I went downstairs twenty minutes before my second round. I decided against the skittles room. Instead, I waited by the tournament room doors. When a group of officials opened the door, I had to step aside for a few of them to pass. They headed straight for the Player's Room, so I approached the official by the door.

"Can I come in?" I asked him quietly.

"Sure," he said. "Name?"

"Lily Hahn."

"Table seven, seat two."

"Thank you."

I went in and sat down. The room was empty but for me, of course, and it felt so weird. I looked across the tabletops at all the beautiful boards, at all their beautiful pieces. The beautiful queen that sat before each one us. We were all desperate for her. She was our endgame. To capture her, we were forced to navigate around the unexpected, around strategy, around tactics. In the end, though, it was how well you anticipated, wasn't it? It was about your ability to play defensively as well as offensively.

That's your problem in life, isn't it, Lily? I played defensively. Always defensively.

I coped with my own laziness by convincing myself one day I would make something of myself, just not right then. I coped with not figuring out my dreams by telling myself I wasn't worthy of them anyway. I coped with my mom's desperation by ignoring her. I coped with a diminished life because I wasn't alone in it. I coped with Sterling's abuse by smoking weed.

I'd coped with life by avoiding it.

I can't do that anymore.

People started trickling in and I felt more than saw Bernard standing beside me. I looked up at him.

"I have been calling your room," he said. "I was worried."

I looked up at him, his eyes frantically searching my own. "I'm sorry, Bernard. I'm," I took a deep breath, "I miss my ,mom very badly today and I'm having some trouble."

His face softened. "I'm very sorry, L-Lily," he said, finally using my name.

"It will be okay," I told him. "I will figure it all out."

"I'm not very good at talking," he told me, wringing his hands and looking away from me, "I-I-I have difficulties understanding and processing emotion, but I'm not blind to them. I am very human and seeing other people suffer makes me feel strange inside. I hate it."

"Don't worry about me, Bernard."

"It's too late, young lady."

I tried to smile at him. "Bottle up your worry, Bernard, and I will tell you when to release it again."

He looked at the tops of his shoes then into my face. "I believe I can do that if you can promise to keeping moving forward."

"I promise," I whispered.

"We've struck a deal then," he said. "You are not allowed to renege."

"I promise," I assured him again.

"Win this game then."

"I will."

I won.

I won the third round as well.

And the fourth.

I noted that Peter Aurek lost that round.

I won my game in the fifth as well, guaranteeing a place in the final round.

Salinger lost to Tao. Guaranteeing myself at least twelve thousand dollars to fix the rest of my roof and flooring as long as I sat at the board to play. Salinger had won eight thousand and that made me feel happy for him.

Despite what might come to be, I felt a small weight lift from my shoulders.

It was Tao Zhang versus Lily Hahn in the finals, just as he desired.

I laid down in the lobby on a large leather couch waiting for the final round.

Boys kept passing by me, whispering, but I kept my eyes closed. I felt someone sit near my feet so I peeled one eyelid open to see it was Tao. I began to sit up, but he pushed my shoulder back down. He gathered my feet in his hands, sat, and laid them on top of his lap, resting his arms on the back of the sofa.

"Just you and me, Lily," he said.

"As I see," I told him and closed my eyes again.

"Just what I wanted."

"I remember. You told me."

"I'm going to win," he promised.

"Probably," I told him.

He laughed.

"Why don't you ever fight back?" he asked me.

"Because my hands are busy with another war at the moment."

He was quiet for a moment. "What could you possibly be fighting?" he asked me.

I lazily opened my eyes and stared at him. "We're all fighting something," I sidestepped.

"What?" he teased with a smile. "Boy won't pay attention to you?" he poked. "Hair turned out the wrong color purple? Lip kit sold out?"

I watched him but didn't say anything.

His smile faded. "You got a broken heart or something?" he correctly guessed, but I was certain he was wrong about its cause.

"Something like that," I told him.

"Easy fix," he told me.

"No, it's not."

"Yes, it is. Just go up to Salinger and tell him how you feel."

I shook my head.

"Tao, Salinger Park is not the root of my heartbreak. He's a contributor to its agony, but that is all."

"What is the root then?" he asked.

"I'd rather not say."

"Is it bad?" he asked.

Two tears slipped past and ran down the sides of my face.

"I did something terrible and I won't ever be able to amend for it."

Tao's brows furrowed in confusion, but he didn't

316

press me for answers.

"Let me let you in on a secret," he told me. "Pasts cannot be fixed. Ever. They are permanent, but you get to choose how they alter the future. Take whatever is affecting you, Lily, and make something with it. Make something you can be proud of."

He stood up, swinging my feet to the floor as he did, and pulled me up with him.

"Let's go play a game," he said. I nodded, still absorbing what he'd said to me. "If you lose because of this crazy state of mind, I'll never forgive you."

I laughed, wiping my face with my hands.

"If I lose," I told him, "it will not be because of that."

"Promise?"

"I promise."

We approached the tournament hall doors and walked in side by side. The place was packed and everyone went crazy loud cheering and clapping, whistling and calling out our names. We sat down at the board. He offered his fist and I bumped it with mine.

Tao was the best player I'd ever encountered, even better than Bernard, I thought, but it didn't matter.

Because I was better.

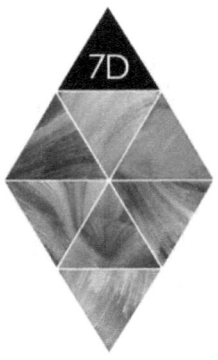

CHAPTER THIRTY

I got home very early Sunday morning and took a taxi home. It cost a fortune, but I didn't have much to worry about in that respect anymore. I wasn't rich by any means, but I had enough to fix my floor, enough to make some real plans for myself. Tao was gracious in his loss. He actually laughed so hard he teared up when I felled his queen.

"You're my arch nemesis, Lily Hahn," he told me, handing me a piece of paper with his email on it as he shook my hand and laughed all the way out the door.

I'd turned around to find Bernard. He'd greeted me with glassy eyes.

"Good job, young lady," he'd said.

Though I was tired, I agreed to meet Hollie and Matt with the girls for dinner that night. They were dressed so prettily it made my heart ache. We met at an old lobster house near the shore where I lived. It was a nice place. I'd never been there. Whenever I passed it as a kid, even as a teen, I always thought it was the kind of place only rich people went to.

I looked down at my phone when we sat at our table. I didn't know what I was looking to find. Salinger hadn't been on my flight on the way home. I'd planned on talking to him there, but he'd purposely avoided me. I ignored the pit in my stomach it caused. When my check cleared the bank, I had plans to pay him back, not just for the flight but for all the help he'd given me while I fought to improve my old house.

"What looks good?" Matt asked the table, perusing the menu.

"I want chicken fingers," Callie said, propping a small Lego set on the table.

"I don't know if they have chicken fingers, Cal," Hollie absently answered her. Her finger scrolled down the menu and landed at the bottom. "Good news for you, Cal, they have chicken fingers."

Eloise looked at Matt. "Who doesn't have chicken fingers?" she joshed.

He made a goofy face at her. "I know, she's silly."

My heart started to break all over again. Their easy banter, easy manner amongst them hurt so deep.

"What are you getting?" Matt asked me.

I startled aware. "Oh," I cleared my throat, "haven't really looked."

"Well, pick whatever you want," he said, "our treat."

"Th-thank you," I whispered.

"Oh!" Hollie exclaimed. "How did your chess tournament go?" she asked me.

Matt smiled at me. "Hollie told me all about it," he said. "We looked it up and everything. How'd you do?"

I swallowed nothing. "Yeah," I blushed, "well, I won."

The table got quiet, including Eloise and Callie, but they were looking up at Matt and Hollie trying to figure out why they looked so shocked.

"What's going on?" Eloise asked.

"You won?" Matt asked for confirmation.

My face grew hotter. "Yes, sir. I won the whole tournament."

Hollie squealed in excitement and clapped her hands. "Oh my gosh, Lily, that is so wonderful. Congratulations!"

"Congratulations indeed," Matt said. "I'm so impressed. I think this is a celebratory dinner then."

"Someone tell me what's going on?" Eloise insisted again.

"Your sister Lily has won a very difficult chess tournament, Ellie," Hollie explained, striking a dagger through my stomach with her new nickname for my sister.

Eloise looked at me, her eyes wide. "Wow, Lily! That's so cool!"

"Thank you, baby."

Callie nodded at me and smiled like she had any idea what we were talking about. I winked at her.

"Hey, we've got some good news, too," Eloise told me.

"Oh yeah?" I asked her.

"Yeah!" she said. "We want Matt and Hollie to be our mommy and daddy now. Isn't that cool?"

My heart beat a million miles an hour. I scooted out of my chair a little and stared at Hollie and Matt, who looked surprised by Eloise's outburst.

"What is she talking about?" I asked them.

Matt crouched, trying to decide whether to stand. He decided against it and sat back down.

"We didn't want to spring this on you," Matt explained.

"*Spring* this on me? What are you *talking* about? You can't have them. You can't have them!"

"Now, Lily," Hollie tried to soothe.

"Don't," I bit. "Stop. They're mine."

"Lily," Matt quieted.

"No!" I practically yelled. The restaurant grew silent. "You have no right!"

Eloise looked up at me confused. "Don't yell at them!" she defended.

I looked at her. "Wheeze," I desperately pled, "you don't mean that. Don't you want to come back home with me? You and Callie?"

Eloise looked like she didn't know how to answer.

"Baby, I'm your sister. Don't you want to come back home with me?"

"Could Mom and Dad come live with us too?" she asked. She reached for Hollie's hand. She was reaching for reassurance. She was reaching for security.

I felt sick to my stomach.

Callie stood up and went over to Matt, sitting in his lap. She was doing the same. They were scared.

Scared I'd take them away from Matt and Hollie.

I stood up, my napkin falling to the floor. "Oh my God," I repeated over and over.

"Lily, sit, please," Matt offered. "Let's just have a discussion. That's all."

"Oh my God," I said. "I can't lose them," I whispered.

"We don't want that either," Hollie assured me.

"But you *do* want to keep for yourselves."

Hollie looked at Matt and that was all the confirmation I needed.

"You can't have them," I told them. The girls looked scared and both clung to Matt and Hollie. "No," I pointed at them, "you can't have them, do you understand me? They're mine. They're mine and you can't have them."

I ran away from the table, straight for my car, and hopped inside. With shaking hands, I called Sylvia up.

"Sylvia," I greeted, my voice trembling. "It's Lily Hahn. I have to talk to you."

"What's wrong, baby?" she asked. "Are you safe?"

"Yes," I said. "I met the girls for dinner and something happened."

"What?"

"They told me they asked Hollie and Matt to be their mom and dad." I didn't hear a response. "Did you hear me?"

"I'm sorry. Yes, I did. I-I'm just not sure what to say."

I felt my stomach sink. "You're not making me feel better, Sylvia."

She sighed. "I know. Listen, I know this is

difficult. Let me assure you that you have not lost your sisters. You can fight for them."

"I will fight for them."

"But listen to me," she hushed, "really think about what's all at stake here."

"What are you trying to say?" I demanded.

I had pulled out of the restaurant parking lot, not really knowing where I was going to go. My first instinct was to go to Salinger's, but I couldn't go there. I drove toward Ansen's instead, knowing Katie would probably be there too.

"I'm just encouraging you to consider every option. Try to imagine what is truly best for your sisters. Try to comprehend a life where you are their sister and that is all."

"No," I demanded, through gritted teeth.

"Just—" she sighed again, "just mull it over, baby. Ask yourself the hard questions. Ask if their being with you is the absolute best thing for them. If you can answer yes, then we'll *both* fight tooth and nail. B-but promise me you'll rationally think it all through first."

I was bawling at that point.

"Fine," I said and hung up.

I turned onto Ansen's street stopping short in front of his house. I got out, slammed my door behind me, and ran toward his door. When I reached it, I banged on it with a fist until my hand went numb.

A tired-looking Ansen threw the door open, looking pissed. "What the hell, Lily!" he said.

I threw myself into his arms. He didn't question it, just held me while I cried into his T-shirt.

"What happened?" he asked eventually.

"Callie and Eloise want to stay with their foster family, Ansen."

Ansen's arms stilled around me. "What?"

I pulled away. "They asked them to be their mom and dad."

Ansen walked backward until he met the arm of his dad's chair and sat. "They actually asked them this themselves?"

I tried not to hyperventilate, so I steadied my breathing. "Yes," I answered him.

"Why would they do that?" he asked me.

This wasn't want I thought he would ask. It surprised me, shocked me, really.

"I don't know. They're confused. Brainwashed, maybe?"

Ansen cocked his head to the side, thinking. He didn't look convinced by my theories.

"Stop it, Ansen. Tell me what you're thinking."

He sighed. "I don't know, Lily."

"Bullshit. Tell me what you're thinking."

He shook his head. "I can't tell you, Lil. Only you would be able to know how they're actually doing, how they're getting on with these people. What are their names?"

I sucked in a breath. "Hollie and Matt."

"Are they nice people?" he asked me.

"I don't know. I don't know them."

"From the little you've interacted with them, what are your impressions?"

I scrunched up my face, desperate to keep in control. "They're nice."

He nodded.

"But no one can love them as I love them," I whispered.

He nodded again. "I don't think anyone would doubt that, Lily."

"I can't lose them, Ansen."

"I have a question for you. You're not going to like it, but just bear with me."

I steeled myself. "What?"

"Why can't you lose them?"

I was dumbfounded. "What kind of question is that?"

"Is it because if you lost them, you feel as if you failed your mom?"

I started crying. "Stop."

"Is it because if they stayed with Matt and Hollie you fear they'll forget all about you?"

I cried harder. "Stop it, Ansen."

"Is it because they're your only link to your mom and you think if you aren't their caretaker that you'll lose that link?"

"Stop!" I demanded. "Stop!"

"Lily."

I bawled into my hands. "Yes. Okay? Yes."

"That's okay."

"No, it's not, though, is it? That makes me just about the most selfish person in this world."

"No," he said with authority. "It absolutely does not. You love them. You love them with every fiber of your being. I can see that. Hell, everyone can see that. You quit drugs for them, Lily. You build your house up for them. You became a better person for *them*. You love them so much you think you're the only one who can take care of them. They're a part of the life you had before your mom died, and that life can't be severed or you fear you'll lose them too."

"Yes. I'll lose them."

"Will you, though? Really think about that."

"I don't want to," I cried into my hands and sank to the floor.

"Do Matt and Hollie seem like the type of people who would sever all ties with you? If that's the truth, they must not love your sisters very much and then they'd be deemed unfit in all our eyes. So figure that out, kid. Figure out what the dynamic would be if they stayed with this family. Figure out what role you'd play in all of it. Make your decision from there."

I slumped forward, my cheek on the carpet, then sat up. "This isn't the life I thought I'd have," I cried. "What kind of life did you think you were going to have, Lily?"

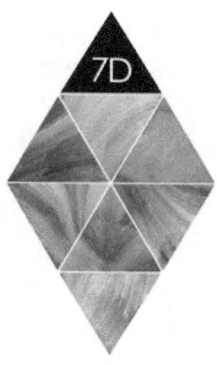

CHAPTER THIRTY-ONE

The next day I cashed my cashier's check, got another to pay off the roofer, another to pay the floor guy who'd come out to assess the damage, and one more to pay Salinger back for all the work he'd done for me. The rest I put in the bank, save for two thousand to pay for a few pieces of furniture, including a new living set. One that didn't smell like smoke, was covered in stains, or had duct tape holding it together.

I called Casey up and told him I needed the week off. He told me it wouldn't be a problem, so I stayed home and did exactly as Sylvia asked me. I pondered a life where my sisters were in a family with proper parents. I imagined what it would mean for me, for them.

I called Hollie several times. She was grateful I called her. She explained to me how much she and Matt had fallen in love with my sisters, how they wanted me to know this, how important it was to them that I knew that, despite my being of age, that I was welcome in their family as well, to come and go as I pleased, to visit, to spend holidays with, to rely on implicitly.

I thanked her and told her I'd think about it.

The floor guys came and went, replaced all the rotten wood, which was plenty, and replaced them with new subfloor and planks.

On Friday night, I sat in my quiet home contemplating what all I'd accomplished, with the unreal help from a certain boy who I'd thought of as much as my sisters and the greatest game I'd ever played.

I missed playing with him. I *missed* him.

The next Sunday, I had the girls and Hollie and Matt over. I'd made dinner for them and wanted them to see what I'd accomplished for them, even if they wouldn't be living there with me.

"What do you think?" I asked the girls.

They ran around the house, screaming, and pointing at all the new furniture and plants, the painted walls, the new tile and updated kitchen, the new fence and mowed lawn. They couldn't believe what I'd done. Even Hollie and Matt, who never really saw what the old house had looked like, told me they were impressed with what I was able to accomplish when I explained all the work I'd done.

I encouraged everyone to sit while I served the salad. I sat with them.

"I've been thinking," I told them. Everyone laid their forks down. "I'm going to give the girls to you."

Hollie broke down crying, as did Matt. She stood

up and Matt held her, the girls ran to their sides and they tucked them into their embrace.

I struggled.

I hurt.

I was grateful to them.

I loved them for loving the girls.

How can I feel so happy yet so heartbroken all at once?

That's when Hollie and Matt turned toward me. Matt held his hand out to me. I stood and gave my own to him. They brought me next to the girls, surrounding me with their arms.

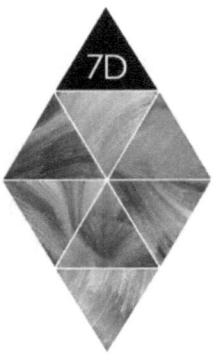

CHAPTER THIRTY-TWO

The following Saturday, Sylvia and Hollie and Matt's attorney worked together to begin the uncontested adoption process and we all signed the necessary documents. I spent most of the day with them, touring their home, and the girls showed me their rooms.

When I left that evening, I felt peace about it all. I didn't think I'd ever seen the girls happier, healthier, or better adjusted. No more dysfunction for them, and I was relieved because I think even my mom would have been pleased with how much they were loved.

When I made it home, I locked my doors and made sure all the windows were still shut, checking all the rooms to make sure they were as I'd left them. I stood by the back door, looking over the top of my fence at Trace's house. All his lights were on and there were people inside, I could see.

Good, he's not alone, I thought. *Maybe he'll leave me be again tonight.*

To take my mind off him, I turned the TV on but it didn't work. I took my phone out.

Salinger, I texted, not worried for the time since I knew he'd be at work.

He didn't reply so I continued on.

I don't know what happened at the tournament. Just confused. I tried to talk to you but you blew me off. If I've done something, please know it wasn't intentional and I'm sorry. I miss you. I have so much I want to talk to you about. So much. There's things that need to be said but would be better in person, you know? Anyway, please consider meeting up with me later.

I dropped my phone on my new coffee table and laid back on the new sofa, staring out the window. I didn't expect a reply, but I wanted him to know regardless.

I'd come a pretty far way from what I'd used to be. I looked down at my body.

"No bruises," I told myself.

It'd been a long time since my body had remained unmarked for any period of time. A wave of guilt washed over me when I thought how I was glad Sterling was dead because it also meant Mama was as well.

I was coming to terms with her death, though, coming to terms with my role in it. Avoiding those who needed me didn't rid me of the eventual blame, as I said before. Yes, I *was* still left holding the gun and didn't notice until after the trigger had been pulled. But as Tao had encouraged, I was deciding how that past would shape my future. I had decided it would mean I would dedicate my life to helping those who had suffered from domestic violence. I was letting my past predict a better future, not just for myself but for others.

I had decided I needed to go to school.

I had also decided I wasn't going to stay in Bottle County much longer.

I had no future there because the past was no longer an anchor.

I stood up and headed for the kitchen. It was growing close to one in the morning and I thought I'd get a bottle of water and head to bed. I'd just wrapped my hand around the fridge handle when I noticed something weird happening at Trace's.

"What the hell?" I asked no one.

I ran over to the sliding glass door and noticed there was small fire in his kitchen.

"What a dumb ass."

There was a lot of movement. I slid the door open and heard them yelling. A girl I didn't recognize rushed down the back deck and grabbed the hose. She attempted to bring it up to the house, but it didn't reach, so she ran back inside. I watched, hoping they would get it under control, but when it seemed there was no hope of that, I turned, ready to get my phone to call the fire department.

But I never made it. The loudest sound I'd ever heard in my life blasted through my chest and ears before I was thrown forward, sharp slices slit across my skin, a shower of glass tinkled all around me. I landed on my stomach, the breath knocked out of me. A second, roaring blast rumbled through my house, and I flinched where I laid.

I groaned and slid onto my back, a silent scream of pain when my skin met the glass there. I gasped in air, but it wouldn't come. I felt myself losing consciousness there on the kitchen tile.

It's funny the things you think about when you think you're dying. First instinct is to save yourself, your body naturally fights to stay alive, but when your heart catches up with the fact that your body is failing you, you turn to reflection. My first thought was Salinger Park. Not Mama. Not my sisters. Not Ansen. Not Katie. I thought of Salinger and how I wish he could have known I loved him.

How I wish I would have properly thanked him for showing me a better way. The crumpled wallpaper, the thin walls, the shallow ceilings, the confined, empty rooms. The hurt, the hatred, the rage, the resentment, the heartsick. The guilt. He'd erased it all. He fixed it all.

When Mom died, I felt like I had nothing to lose and when you've got nothing left to lose, you tended to get reckless. I had been reckless personified and since I'd made my bed, I'd chosen to lay in it, sinking deeper and deeper into sheets of nothing; the fabric of apathy enveloped me over and over.

And I'd done nothing for a long time.

He'd discovered me, grabbed me, and held me against him, shook the petrified flint from my bones. He was the first shift I'd chosen to make. My hands had wrapped around his waist, no longer idle.

I regretted not telling him.

I love you, Salinger Park.

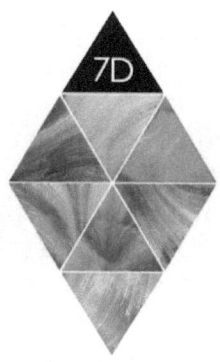

CHAPTER THIRTY-THREE

Salinger

Tao looked at me briefly, shifted, and put his hands in his pockets. He looked back at Lily, her back to me. "Yeah, I've been meaning to ask you about that. Are you and Salinger, like, a thing or something?" He knew I was standing right behind him. He knew *exactly* what he was doing.

She shook her head. "No, we're just friends."

"Lily?" I called out to her.

I felt my stomach grow tight. *I am nothing to her.*

"Just checking on you," I said. "You coming?"

"Uh, yeah." She turned toward Tao. "If you'll excuse me, we're gonna sit with Bernard in the bar upstairs."

"Oh, really? You don't mind if I join you, right?" Tao asked.

She looked at me. I opened my mouth to tell him

to go bother someone else, but Lily answered for me instead.

"Uh, sure," she told him.

All three of us climbed the stairs to the main lobby and crossed the marble floor to the small bar there. Bernard sat at a table, sipping a drink.

"You were gone forever!" he said to me.

"I was only gone two minutes, Bernard. Stop being dramatic."

Bernard leaned forward when Lily sat. He glanced at Tao but didn't greet him.

"Young lady," he said to Lily.

"Yes?" Lily answered.

"Do you know who this man is?" he asked her, referring to Tao.

She coughed over a laugh. "Um, yes, I do."

"This is the boy you will play in the final round."

She turned to Tao. "I didn't know you were playing this tournament."

"When I found out you would be here and since you were explicit when you said you wouldn't be going to Nationals, I just knew I had to come see you for myself," Tao told her.

"Pish, posh!" Bernard interrupted. "She will be at Nationals. Why would you assume she wouldn't be at Nationals?"

"Because she told me so herself," Tao answered him.

Bernard stared at Lily. He thought she was crazy, I could tell. I didn't necessarily disagree with him.

"You are going to Nationals. Period," Bernard answered.

She turned to him. "Bernard, you don't know if I

will even make it to the final round."

Tao and I stared at her. Everyone there at that table knew she would make it. Everyone knew but her.

Bernard rapped his knuckle on the table. "Absolute horse hockey. You are the best player here."

Tao grinned at her, sending me into a jealous internal rage.

"Well," she argued, "Tao's rating is so much higher than mine, Bernard. He's the better player."

"Wrong," he said. I saw her face and throat flame. "You are the best player here, probably the best player nationally, and even more likely to be the best player in the world."

"Bernard!" she said. "You're overestimating me!"

"That is an untruth. I have perfectly estimated you."

Tao watched her closely, very closely. He sat back in his chair, his head cocked to one side, tongued one of his eyeeth, and *smiled* at her. I wanted to hit him so bad.

"Excuse me, young man!" Bernard called out to the bartender. He stood and approached the bar, unaware of the tension at the table.

I stared at Tao. He was flirting with her. I didn't think she realized, and that made it all the more frustrating. The very idea of another person in her life beside me made me crazy inside. Imagining it as Tao nearly knocked me over, because he probably would have been good to her, they were closer in talent regarding the game. He obviously liked her and that seethed inside me.

"He's overestimating me," she said quietly, staring at her small hands on the table.

"I guess we'll find out," Tao said, standing up. She looked up at him, her big round green eyes staring straight into his and he leaned over her. *Too close. He's too close to her.* His hand rested on the table next hers. "Don't you dare lose in the first few rounds," he flirted with her. He stood upright again, stuck his hands in his pockets, and walked back through the lobby.

She watched him, actually *watched* him, walk to the stairs, then turned back to me. *She's never going to be in to me.* I gritted my jaw, pissed at myself for letting myself fall in love with her. She was emotionally tied. She was suffering and she needed a friend. It was my duty not to let those lines cross. I shouldn't have let myself fall so easily.

And it was easy.

Too easy. *So* easy.

She was sweet and quiet but unbelievably strong, though she didn't know that about herself. She was kind and gentle and wished the best for everyone. She was too hard on herself. She felt as if she was culpable for everything that had happened to her mom and stepdad. She wasn't, and I knew I was willing to spend every second of my life making sure she understood that.

She was targeted, and often because she was too tolerant and beautiful. Sterling had targeted her. She'd never admitted it to me, but I could tell he was gearing up to something worse than physical abuse. The very thought sent me reeling in anger. And then there was that asshole Trace, that disgusting piece of shit who *drugged* her and *assaulted* her. Then a thought struck me.

Wait, am I targeting her? I felt sick to my stomach. I wanted her. I wanted to help her, but my intentions had turned to love. I'd promised her I had integrity. *But you don't, do you? Because you would sell everything you own to kiss her, wouldn't you?*

"What's wrong?" she asked me.

I looked down at the table, unable to face her, too ashamed of myself. "Nothing," I lied. "I'll be right back," I said, standing up. I practically sprinted out of there.

"Wait! Salinger!" she called after me, but I ignored her.

I wanted to run back to her, but I didn't. Instead, I headed for the skittles room so I could think. Inside, I ran into Peter Aurek. He looked slightly embarrassed when he saw me.

"Aurek," I greeted him coldly.

"Hey, dude," he said, his hand going to the back of his neck.

"Heard about what you said to Lily in Austin last week."

He had the decency to turn bright red. "Yeah, about that."

"That's pretty shitty of you."

"Yeah," he agreed, "I know. In fact, I'm looking for Lily. I wanted to apologize to her."

"I saw her in the bar upstairs with Bernard Calvin last."

"Thanks, I'll go up there later and tell her I was being a dick."

"Good."

He studied me. "You look like you've been rode hard and put away wet."

I ran my hands through my hair. "Yeah, I'm fucked in the head."

Peter laughed. "You just described every motherfucker in here."

I nodded in agreement.

"I think I lo—" I cleared my throat, "love Lily Hahn." I'd stuttered over the word like a fool. I didn't know why I was confiding in the jackass.

He laughed. "Never fall in love with the queen, Salinger, or you won't be able to tumble her." I sighed. "Besides, been there, done that," he added.

"Who?" I asked.

"You know, Lyric?" he asked me.

I choked on nothing. "Yeah, uh, she's cool. A little bit psycho, but if she could settle down, she'd be a lot cooler."

"Yeah," he agreed.

I gotta get control of myself before I talk to her again.

Eventually a couple of other people joined us, including Lyric and Tao. More time passed and I noticed Lily before anyone else did. Oh my God, she was beautiful. She was foreign to that room, otherworldly. She didn't belong. Everyone knew it; everyone saw it. She was better than all of us, and I wanted her.

I noticed the moment she saw me, and my heart began to beat a crazy rhythm.

Don't look at her. Don't look at her. Whatever you do, do not look at her. All your careful planning will be for nothing if you look at her.

340

"Is it me or is Tao kind of a douche?" Lyric said under her breath.

I laughed mostly as a distraction from Lily.

Then she did something odd, made like she was going to leave. Tao noticed her.

"Lily! Where are you going!" he yelled.

She walked over to us and I felt my skin heat up.

"Guys," Tao introduced, "this is Lily. She's the one who beat Aurek last week in Austin."

Everyone started teasing Peter. He waved at her, obviously still embarrassed.

I mostly ignored the conversation until some random asked Lyric if she thought it was nice to have another girl around. I knew Lyric hadn't made the ratings minimum, so I tried to help her dodge that line of questioning.

"Yeah," Lyric answered him.

"Lyric, I didn't see your name on the roster," Peter commented.

Yikes, Peter, read the room.

Lyric looked mortified. "Yeah, I, uh, didn't make the ratings minimum."

"Damn," Tao said, coughing around a laugh.

I felt sorry for her. I didn't want to have to come to her rescue, but I didn't think anyone else would.

"She'll get them back up," I said. "Won't you?" I pushed my shoulder into hers, hoping to convey something friendly.

"What about you, Lily?" Tao asked her.

She looked at him. "What?"

He laughed at her, incensing me. "Where have you been?

"Just thinking," she explained.

341

"You're kind of weird."

I balled up a fist, ready to sock Tao right in the eye.

"Isn't everybody?" Peter Aurek said, though, coming to her rescue. I felt like that had been my job. I felt like a failure.

She *smiled* at him. *Smiled*. I felt like my heart shattered.

She looked at me.

"Can I talk to you for a second, Salinger?" she asked.

My skin grew heavy. "Later," I told the floor, hoping she would drop it. I needed time to decide how I was going to handle my feelings for her.

Lily left the group soon after that. I watched her leave, wishing I could chase after her. Soon after that, I got a text from her, stating Bernard had gotten us each a room. I went to the front desk to get the key she'd left and thought about just saying screw it and going up to her room to talk.

When I headed for the elevators, Lyric happened to be approaching at the same time.

"Going up?" she asked.

"Yeah, what floor?" I asked her.

"Five," she answered.

"Same," I said.

"Cool. What room?"

I looked at the key they'd given me. "Five-thirty-two."

"I'm down the hall, the other end."

"Cool," I said.

Whenever we reached our floor, we heard loud partying near my room.

"Just my freaking luck." I sighed.

"Listen, if you want, we can switch rooms. I'm not competing or anything, so rest isn't at the top of my list or whatever."

I studied her. "Are you sure?"

"Yes, Salinger. Get your stuff, we'll switch."

I did as she said and met her at her room. We switched keys and I went to bed, my every thought consumed by Lily.

***

I missed my damn flight. Taxi driver got into a small accident with someone else and we were forced to stop.

***

When I finally got home, I had to work that night, which sucked. It helped I'd made eight grand at tournament, though. When I got in, Casey told me Lily had taken off the following week. *Maybe she's trying to get the house done,* I thought. I dug my phone out of my back pocket. My finger hovered over her number.

I sighed. I'd made things awkward. I waited too long to contact her and was confused on what to say.

Just say anything. *Apologize for being weird. Congratulate her on her win, you douche.* I opened a text window, then closed it, opened it, then closed it one more time.

I'll wait until she comes back, figure out what I'm gonna say to her.

***

The following Saturday night, I was missing Lily like crazy. I wondered how she was doing, wanted so bad to talk to her. I'd picked up my phone at least a thousand times to call or text but couldn't do it. I was in love with her. I'd struggled with it. I didn't want her think to my intentions weren't good, but I loved her. So much. My phone indicated a text.

Salinger, Lily texted. My heart in my throat.

Without thinking, I threw my gloves to our friend Pablo.

"Gotta go," I told him. "Something's come up. Clock me out, will ya?"

"Yeah, no prob," he said.

I hauled ass to the lot and sprinted to my Jeep, hopping inside and starting her engine. I passed by Chuck's, where we'd eaten our first meal together. I passed by Court's street, where we'd sat and talked on her front porch steps. I passed by Ashleigh's, where I'd first met her.

I don't know what happened at the tournament. She texted again, my throat going dry as I read her message. Just confused. I tried to talk to but you blew me off. If I've done something, please know it wasn't intentional and I'm sorry. I miss you. I have so much I want to talk to you about. So much. There's things that need to be said but would be better in person, you know? Anyway, please consider meeting up with me later.

I wanted so badly to text her back but thought better of it while driving. *Just another minute or two,*

I promised myself. I threw my phone on my seat and confess I sped a little to get to her as fast as I could.

As I approached the light right before her street, my stomach filled with anticipation. My knuckles gripped the steering wheel until they turned white. The light had turned red and I impatiently had to sit there. I briefly contemplated abandoning my car where it was just to run to her. I was a moron.

My blinker clicked in the dead silence of my car. The only other sound was my shaky breath.

"Come on, come on, come on," I whispered.

That's when I heard it. The most powerful, thundering boom. I thought lightning had struck until I'd heard a second explosion, a second ear-piercing rumble. My whole body tucked into itself in instinct. When I sat up again, I saw orange flames licking up into the sky.

"What the actual fuck?" I asked no one.

I ran the red light and raced through Lily's run-down neighborhood, passing Trace's house, which was blazing. Without a second thought, I whipped around his block and hung a left on to Lily's street, stopping at her house. It was pitch black, as were all the houses next to Lily's, realizing whatever explosion had happened had also tripped the electricity.

I pulled my Jeep into the gravel drive and slammed it into park, tossing my body out of my seat as quickly as I could, rushing up the deck to Lily's door. I tried the knob, but it was locked.

I started banging my hand on the door. "Lily! Lily! Can you hear me?"

I looked at the front windows of her house. Every

single one of them was blasted out. *Oh my God.* I jumped the deck fencing and scaled the front living room window, using a nearby rock to break off any glass still attached to the frame. I jumped in and scaled around the furniture. I hit my knee on something I wasn't familiar with.

"Lily!" I yelled into the dark but didn't hear a response.

My heart beat so hard in my veins I could hear it.

"Lily!"

I took out my phone and scrolled up, looking for the flashlight and turned it on. I held it out in front of me and started wading through the glass, my boots crunching with every step I took.

"Lily, are you here?" I called out.

When I raised the light slightly I caught a glimpse of a still form on her kitchen floor.

"Jesus! Lily!" I shouted and ran to her, kneeling down beside her.

There was blood everywhere. I used my phone to try to find the root cause, but it seemed to be everywhere on her. "Oh, Jesus, Lily." I checked she was breathing and found she was, beyond relieved. I scrolled to my phone and dialed 911.

"911, what's your emergency?" an operator answered.

"Yes, my friend is badly injured. There was some sort of explosion at the house next door. It's blown out her windows and cut her."

"Is she breathing?" the operator asked.

"Yes," I told her.

"Your address, sir."

"Um, uh, 2314 Salem."

I heard beeps and reverb.

"Dispatch, this is four-three-seven. I've got a reported explosion at or near 2314 Salem. One confirmed injured. Victim is breathing but bleeding," I heard the operator tell the dispatcher.

"Your name, son?"

"Salinger."

"A callback number."

I rattled off my phone number to her. I could hear her typing.

"When did this happen?"

"Not five minutes ago. The house behind hers is up in flames."

"Is it safe for you to remain at this location?"

"For now? Yes," I answered, desperate to remain as calm as possible.

I heard more beeps and reverb.

"Dispatch, this is four-three-seven. Reported large fire at or near 2314 Salem," I heard her relay. "Can you locate the source of her cuts?" she then asked me.

"They're all over. Literally hundreds." My hands found her face and held her. "Lily, wake up for me, baby," I begged. "There's blood and glass everywhere and the electricity is out. I can't even really see how badly she's injured."

"Sir, try to get her clear of the glass," she said.

"Yes, okay."

I stood up, my chest panting air, and ran through the hall, straight for her bathroom, collecting six or seven towels from her cabinet, and ran back. I laid the phone on the ground, trying to prop it up so the flashlight could guide me, and put the operator on speaker.

I went to her broom closet and grabbed her broom, sweeping all the glass around her away. I threw down the broom and bent over her. I slid her onto her side. An involuntary groan slipped between her lips; I felt my eyes burn.

"I'm, uh, I'm trying to brush the glass off her skin," I explained to the operator as bloody glass came tumbling to the tile, and I brushed it clear before laying her back down and doing the same for her chest, abdomen, neck, face, and legs.

"She's—. Oh God, there's so much blood," I panicked.

"Just stop the bleeding," she encouraged. "Press a towel or something similar against the wounds to stop it."

I did as she asked, finding all the places Lily seemed to be bleeding from the worst and applying pressure. One area near her left leg seemed to be particularly bad, so I wrapped a hand towel around her thigh, took my belt off and wrapped it around her, like a tourniquet.

"Lily!" a man I recognized as one of her neighbors shouted through her house.

"She's here!" I yelled back. "I've got her!"

"Is she okay?" he asked.

"Sh-she's breathing."

"Good!" he bellowed. "There's two more houses affected. I'll be back! Checking on them."

I heard him run off and looked down at Lily.

"When are they gonna be here?" I asked, examining her closer.

"Estimated three minutes," she said. "Is she still

breathing?"

"Yes, still breathing." I felt her pulse. "Her pulse is shallow. Really shallow. Please, God!" I shouted. I leaned over her. "Lily, can you hear me? Lily, wake up, baby."

"Sir, keep applying pressure. When the paramedics get there, we'll disconnect. They should be there soon."

I took a deep breath and let it out slowly. My hands kept pressing wherever I found fresh blood but I couldn't keep up with it and I knew she was bleeding out.

"Lily!" I screamed at her. "Wake! Up!"

Her face never reacted, not once.

I sat up when I heard the sirens down the street. Not able to wait a second longer, I gingerly scooted my hands under her knees and back and lifted her up. She weighed practically nothing. I sprinted out the door, down the deck, just as the ambulance pulled up.

Two men hopped out and immediately began working around us; one took a gurney out from the back of the ambulance while the other approached me.

"What happened?" he asked, laying down a duffel bag.

A large fire truck and several police cruisers came barreling down the street.

"Other side!" the paramedic at the gurney yelled at the truck, swinging his arm around toward Trace's house.

The truck sped off, along with one of the cruisers. The other stayed; one officer gathered all the neighbors who'd come out of their houses when the explosion set off, I can only assume, to keep them away from the scene, and the other ran from house to house to check for more injured.

"All clear!" he shouted and ran up to the ambulance. "Couple of minor cuts. They're coming this way."

I helped them lay Lily on the gurney then stepped aside for them to work.

"Sir, can you tell me what happened?" he asked once again.

I shook my head clear.

"I was sitting at the red light waiting to visit her, actually, when I heard this incredible explosion, so I just sped here. I have no idea what happened next door, but it must have blown out all her windows and knocked her out. I found her on the floor like this."

They leaned over her, checking vitals, treating any obvious wounds. Within thirty seconds, they'd strapped her in and had loaded her in the ambulance.

"Can I ride with her?" I asked.

"Not that kind of vehicle, son."

"Where are you taking her?" I asked.

One jumped in with her while the other closed and secured the doors.

"She's got a bleed that will probably need a surgeon. We'll medevac her to Smithfield Methodist."

He ran to the front and drove off.

I hauled ass up the deck again and saw my phone, its flashlight still on. I picked it up and used it to find Lily's phone. When I found it, I ran back out and jumped in my Jeep. My phone was almost dead, so I plugged it in and searched directions to Smithfield Methodist. I opened Lily's phone and dialed Ansen, putting it on speaker, and backed out.

I noticed the firefighters were still fighting the fire at Trace's house.

"What's up, goof," Ansen answered.

"Ansen, it's Salinger."

"Oh, hey, Salinger, what's up?" he asked.

"Lily's been hurt—" I began, but he interrupted me.

"What the hell! What happened?"

"What's going on?" I heard Katie ask him in the background.

"Some kind of explosion at Trace's. It blew out all her windows, tossed her to the ground. Sh-she's been cut up. They're flying her over to Smithfield Methodist right now."

"I'll meet you there," he said.

I hung up and raced through the streets to the main intersection down the country road where her neighborhood sat. The light turned red right as I got there. My hands straining against the leather of my steering wheel, I turned to Lily's phone.

Would she want me to call Hollie and Matt?

Without thinking, I picked up her phone and searched her contacts for Hollie's name. It rang three times before she picked it up.

"Hello? Lily?" she asked as the light turned green.

"Miss Hollie, we don't know one another, but I'm a friend of Lily's. Unfortunately, the house behind hers caught fire and there was some sort of explosion, and Lily was wounded."

I heard rustling and a snap, like she was turning on a light. "Is she all right?"

"I-I think so. I don't know," I told her truthfully. "They've medevacked her to Smithfield Methodist. I just thought I'd let you know, if you, well, if you wanted to inform her sisters."

"I'll wait to tell the girls until we have more information. I'll be sending my husband down to meet you. Does she need anything?" Her voice broke. "Do you need anything?"

"Not at this time. Thank you."

"I'll be in touch through Lily's phone then. Please let me know as soon as you have anything?"

"Yes, of course."

I hung up the phone and stuck it in the back pocket of my jeans. With adrenaline pumping, I sped through the small bits of traffic caught up on the highway into Smithfield and landed at the hospital in record time. I parked, ran through the ER sliding doors, and landed at the nurse's desk, severely out of breath.

"Lily Hahn," I said, gulping in air. "Is she here?"

"Oh," the woman said. I could tell she recognized Lily's name immediately. "She's in surgery. Are you a friend or relative?"

"Relative," I lied.

She smiled kindly at me. "No worries, sweetheart, they've gotten her stable, and she's had a transfusion. Surgery should be less than an hour. They're just fixing a nicked artery and cleaning anything up that requires attention."

"So, she's fine?" I asked. I wanted to hear it again.

"Yes, sir. Just fine. I'll come get you when she's out."

All the adrenaline that had been pumping through my veins surged in relief. Suddenly more tired than I'd ever felt, I plopped myself down and took out Lily's phone. I texted Hollie what the nurse had said then called Ansen.

"Salinger," Katie answered.

"Yeah, it's me. She's in surgery now—"

"She's in surgery," Katie relayed to, I assumed, Ansen.

"She's stable and will be out in less than an hour," I explained.

"Stable and will be out soon," she told him.

My hands shook as the adrenaline left.

"What happened?" she asked me.

"I was going over to her house when I heard this incredible noise, like a bomb had gone off. I sped to her house and found her lying there."

"Jesus," she whispered then sighed. "I'm so glad she's stable."

I ran a hand down my face. "I've lost ten years off my life."

"I'm sorry," she said. "The thought of something happening to her makes me break out into a cold sweat." She paused. "Lily is too easy to love, isn't she?"

I thought about what she'd said.
"So easy to love it frightens me."

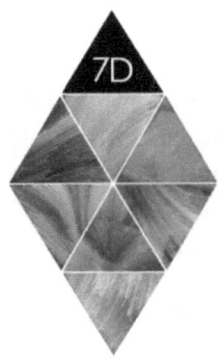

CHAPTER THIRTY-FOUR

Lily

"Miss Hahn," someone whispered. "Miss Hahn, it's time to wake up. Can you hear me?" they asked.

I peeled my eyes open to see the face of someone who looked like a nurse.

"Hi, darlin'." She smiled. "Know where you are?"

"No," I scratched out.

"Well, there's been an accident, although I'm not too clear on the details, but you were caught up in it, child. You had a little surgery and now you're out and will be right as rain pretty soon here."

"Okay," I said, unsure what she was talking about.

"Do you have any family, baby? Anyone who would be here?"

My eyes began to water. "No, ma'am."

"Oh, well, that's okay, baby. I'll be here. See this little button?" she asked, handing me a remote. "Just press that button if you need anything."

"Okay." I nodded, thoroughly confused as to how I'd gotten there.

We both turned toward the door when we heard some light rapping.

"Come in," she said.

Katie pushed through, running to my side, bawling her eyes out. Ansen quickly followed, as did Matt.

"*Matt?*" I asked, confused.

"Salinger called us," he explained, standing next to my bed.

"Salinger?"

Everyone looked toward the door, so I did the same.

There stood Salinger. He was beautiful; it made my heart ache to see him.

"Hey, Little," his deep voice soothed, making two tears slip through.

"How did you know I was here?" I asked him.

"He's the one who found you, knucklehead," Ansen answered for him.

Katie grabbed my hand. "I guess Trace was trying to build a meth lab in his kitchen and it blew up."

My mouth gaped wide. "What? D-did they make it out?"

Katie looked at Ansen, so I did the same.

"No, Lily, they didn't."

"Oh my gosh," I quieted.

We were all silent a moment.

"What about the neighbors?" I asked them.

"Fine," Salinger answered, making my heart race.

"Everyone seemed to be in bed and not affected badly."

I nodded at him, wishing I could just stare at him. "Good," I whispered.

I turned toward Matt. "Do the girls know?" I asked.

"We didn't want to wake them until we knew what the status was."

I nodded again. "That's great. Good. Let's just keep this to ourselves then."

"You don't want them to visit?" he asked.

"No," I insisted, "let's not scare them. I'll just see them on Sunday."

Matt looked uncertain. "Are you sure?"

"Yes," I answered and smiled at him. "If there's one thing I want for them, it's that they never know fear again."

He smiled at me. "They won't," he promised. "I'll make sure of it."

"I know," I told him.

Matt sighed. "What a night!" Everyone laughed. "Does anyone want a drink or a cup of coffee?" he asked.

Everyone shook their heads. "Well, if I don't have some caffeine soon, I'm going to drop. I'll be right back."

I smiled at him as he left. He had to slide past Salinger to leave, as he just stood there, afraid to come in, I thought.

Katie looked behind her, then at me. "Ansen, come with me. You know, now that he mentions it, I could use a Dr Pepper or something."

"Okay," Ansen told her, grabbing her hand as

they left the room.

It was just Salinger and me at that point.

"You saved me." I heard him audibly swallow. "Thank you."

His body was tense, like he wasn't sure what to do with himself.

"How do you feel?" he asked me.

"Just a little sore, to be honest. The pain meds have already worn off."

He looked alarmed. "Should I get the nurse?" he asked, panicked.

I smiled at him. "No, come here, Salinger."

Hesitantly he came into the room and pulled up a chair to the side of my bed then sat down, scooting as close as he could get.

"I got your texts," he said.

I didn't know how to respond to him so I only nodded.

"What happened?" I asked him.

He stared at the floor. "I need some advice," he said, ignoring my question.

"Go on," I encouraged.

"I—" He shook his head, fighting a smile. "I'm in love with this girl." He looked at me. "You don't know her," he said, a crooked smile on his face. "She's the best friend I've ever had; we get along like chocolate and peanut butter. She's, well, she's beautiful," he explained, his face burning bright red and turning back to the floor briefly before meeting my gaze again. My heart started to race when he looked at me. "She dazzles me, actually."

Then a thought sobered me.

"Are you talking about Lyric?" I asked him.

He looked shocked. "What are you on about?"

My face flamed hot. "I saw her."

"Saw who?"

He looked perplexed.

"At the tournament, Salinger. She was in your room."

He went from confused to amused within two seconds. "We traded rooms. There were these really obnoxious morons partying next door and I wanted to get some sleep, so we switched."

I nodded. "I see and so this girl?" I encouraged.

"Yeah, so this girl, she's talented. Never met anyone who could challenge me like she does." He looked at me; his face turned sad for a moment. "She's been through a lot, you know? And, you see, this is where I've been struggling, because I told her I was someone who had integrity. I'd promised I would help her without her feeling vulnerable to me. I wanted her to know she could rely on me."

I began crying. "I think she knows, Salinger."

He studied me. "Does she, though?" he asked.

"I know she does."

"I think I have to tell her how I feel then."

"I think you should."

He leaned back in his chair, looking more relaxed than I'd seen him in a very long time. He exhaled hard. "I'm going to," he said, smiling at the ceiling.

"When?" I asked him.

He looked at me and bit his lip to keep from smiling. "I'll let you know, Little."

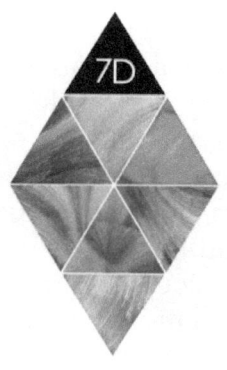

EPILOGUE

It'd been three months since the meth lab accident and I'd had the windows replaced, fixed the damaged fence, and repainted the back of the house. It had only taken me a couple short days to get everything back to par.

Trace had died that night. I would never condone what he'd done to me, but I wouldn't have wished death on him either. He'd made national headlines due to the nature of his death and the sensationalism of the story. His house had literally burnt to a crisp. Not even the grass remained in an even circle around what used to be that home. There'd been two other victims, but they weren't local and so none of us recognized them when they were finally identified.

I'd put my house up for sale for a mere hundred grand and it'd sold in two days. Ironically, to one of my nearby neighbors.

I'd been visiting the girls regularly and they were thriving, and when I was in town to see them once a week, I'd also stop by a counselor's office to work out the issues I had about Mama's death. I'd been searching for places to rent around my sisters so I could be near them, but had yet to find any.

Salinger left Bottle County as well as the market, as did I. I'd joined a couple online classes and was sort of bumming around random cities, exploring them, trying to find a good fit.

Salinger came with me.

Right in that moment, that very second, I was taking my Scout up to Banner Elk, North Carolina, to a cabin called Big Bear Lodge because it was an hour away from this year's National Open, a million-dollar cash prize, and I was joining twelve other master chess players, including one Mr. Salinger Park.

As I'd been recovering, selling my house, and visiting a therapist, Salinger hadn't made one single move on me. I knew he'd been talking about *me* as I'd laid there that night. I knew he was in love with me. He was biding his time and I tried to respect that, as I'm certain, he tried to do with me.

I'd given Salinger the reins and he was aware of it. He was careful around me, respectful. He took care of me before he took care of himself. I'd never been around a guy like that before. Most of the time I'd had to peel them off to set them aside, it was annoying.

I didn't dare touch him; though I'd wanted to, really wanted to. When he smiled, it sent me over myself. That's what the tension did for me. I'd given him the reins and I was letting him determine the course and I'd discovered that boundaries could be unbelievably sexy. There is nothing like the feeling of earning something you actually want, and I wanted Salinger Park.

I pulled into the lodge and parked between four others, lifting out my bag, and scaling the winding shallow stone walk to the front door. I walked in and saw seven of the guys we were meeting up there sitting in the large, expansive living area, including Peter Aurek and Tao Zhang.

"Lily!" they all shouted.

I threw my bag in the foyer and started walking toward one of the couches. I squealed when someone sideswiped me, surprising me, and lifted me off my feet.

The guys started taunting Salinger, ordering him to put me down, but he ignored them. Instead, he swept me through a pair of open doors between the kitchen and the living area in the back of the house.

I started giggling.

"Where are you taking me?" I asked as we bounced down the expansive deck stairs.

"Shh, Little," he whispered, tossing me on his back. He ran for a few minutes, his chest pumping harder and harder.

"You've got some endurance, punk," I whispered in his ear.

He looked back at me, his eyes bright. "Adrenaline," he explained, making my heart race.

He slowed down when we reached a small deck next to a sweet-smelling lake with the moon's reflection big and bright, veered slightly left, and stopped when we reached rocky shore, setting me down near his feet.

His chest panted air. He was quiet, but he watched me. I smiled at him. He slowly smiled back, tilting his head back slightly, exposing his neck. As the quiet surrounded us, his breaths began to slow.

"Lily," he finally said. "I have to ask you something."

"What is it?"

"Are you happy?"

I thought about it a moment and decided I was, indeed, very happy.

"Yes," I told him.

"Why?" he asked, confusing me.

"What does—"

"Just answer."

"Because I like my life."

"But why?"

"Because Wheezy and Cal are safe and healthy and loved. Because Ansen and Katie are happy." I stared up at him. "Because *you're* happy."

He shook his head.

"I'm not entirely happy."

I furrowed my brows at him. "You're not?"

"No, Lily, I'm not. Not entirely."

"Why not?" I whispered.

"What would you say," he began, staring hard into my eyes, "if I told you that my happiness depends on one thing."

He inched his way across the gravel shore and landed mere inches from my face. I looked up at him.

"What's that then? I'll get it for you," I told him.

He smiled at me. "It can't be gotten, Little. It can only be given."

362

He looked down at my left hand and ran his fingers up the back of my arm, sending shivers down my spine. He followed the skin there until it met shoulder, and stopped at the back of my neck.

He smiled. "I love you, Lily." I closed my eyes when his lips found the side of my neck. "Lots," he whispered. "It's immeasurable, actually," he breathed against the skin there.

I let out a shaky breath. "I have something to tell you in return," I secreted.

I felt him smile against my neck. "What's that then?"

"I love you too."

His hands wrapped around my waist and he lifted me off the ground, closer to his face. His mouth found my ear.

"Say it again."

I brought my hands from his shoulders up around his neck. "What do you want me to say?" I teased.

He laughed against my hair. "Don't, Lily, tell me. Come on."

I fought a giggle, happier than I'd been in a very long time. "I love you, Mr. Park."

His lips found the base of my neck and softly bit my collarbone. "That drives me crazy," he breathed, giving me goosebumps.

With his left arm still around my waist, his right hand found the top of my head. His fingers threaded through my hair there, sliding all the way down. He playfully pulled the ends.

His eyes met mine and things went from flirtatious to serious.

"I can't believe I'm touching you right now," he told me.

My eyes burned with unshed tears. "I know. Finally. I feel like we have fought really hard to get here."

"We did, Lily."

"Thank you, Salinger."

"For what?" he asked.

"For picking me. You could have picked a million other girls, but you picked me."

"You're the only one I've ever seen, the only one that ever stood out."

"I know that feeling well," I told him.

"I would do anything for you, Little."

I looked up. "Would you fetch that star right there?"

"Let me get my lasso."

I smiled at him.

"Would you climb a mountain?"

"Barefoot, Little. I'd do it barefoot."

"Would you cross the Sahara?"

"With only the memory of your smile to sustain me, I would go."

"Would you build a house with me?" I asked him, a small tear escaping.

He stared at me a long while. "I would again."

"Would you love me when I couldn't love myself?"

"I would again."

"Would you hold my hand when I was lost?"

"I would again."

More tears escaped. "Would you kiss me?"

"I thought you'd never ask."

When his lips found mine, I felt it all, every single sacrifice, every single emotion, every single ounce of passion we'd built up since the day we'd met.

He tasted like devotion.

Like respect.

Like admiration.

Like worship.

He tasted like forever.

IDLE

AS WITH ALL MY BOOKS, I LIKE TO ENCOURAGE DONATION TO A PARTICULAR CHARITY. USUALLY, I'D SUGGEST ONE RIGHT ABOUT HERE, BUT THIS TIME I WANTED US ALL TO RALLY BY GIVING TO A LOCAL BATTERED WOMEN'S SHELTER. SOMEWHERE LILY COULD HAVE BENEFITED IF SHE'D LIVED NEAR YOU.

LOVE YOU ALL TO THE MOON AND BACK.

PEACE AND LOVE,

FISHER AMELIE

IDLE

PLAYLIST

FISHERAMELIE.COM/IDLEHANDS

CONNECT WITH FISHER AMELIE
FISHERAMELIE.COM

OR FIND ME ON ALL SOCIAL
PLATFORMS
@FISHERAMELIE

SIGNUP

FOR FISHER'S NEWSLETTER
FISHERAMELIE.COM/NEWSLETTER

FISHER AMELIE

MORE
OF FISHER'S
WORK

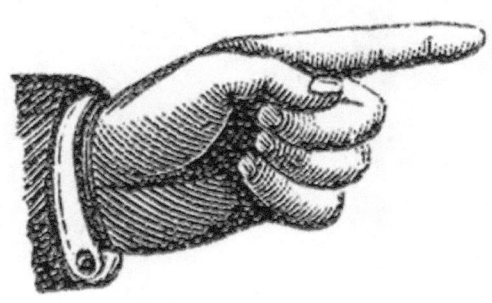

THE TRUE STORY OF

Atticus and Hazel

FISHER AMELIE

BOOK ONE OF THE SEVEN DEADLY SERIES
FISHER AMELIE

7D

VAIN

BOOK TWO OF THE SEVEN DEADLY SERIES
FISHER AMELIE

7D

GREED

BOOK THREE OF THE SEVEN DEADLY SERIES
FISHER AMELIE

FURY